A
WORLD OF
HURT

Also by Mindy Mejia

The Dragon Keeper
Everything You Want Me to Be
Leave No Trace
Strike Me Down
To Catch a Storm

A WORLD OF HURT

A NOVEL

MINDY MEJIA

Atlantic Monthly Press
New York

FIRST EDITION

Printed in the United States of America

First Grove Atlantic hardcover edition: August 2024

This book is set in 11.5-pt. Scala Pro
by Alpha Design & Composition of Pittsfield, NH.

Library of Congress Cataloging-in-Publication data is available for this title.

ISBN 978-0-8021-6311-0
eISBN 978-0-8021-6312-7

Atlantic Monthly Press
an imprint of Grove Atlantic
154 West 14th Street
New York, NY 10011

Distributed by Publishers Group West

groveatlantic.com

24 25 26 27   10 9 8 7 6 5 4 3 2 1

For Nick and Melonie, artists, friends,
and all-around amazing humans.

You'll never know how much that room meant.

December 2019

Kara

I always knew I would die young, a firework exploding and leaving nothing but an ugly smell in the night. There and gone. I knew it would be violent and, no matter when or how it came, that I'd deserve it. But, more than anything else, I knew when I reached my last moment on this garbage planet, when death finally rolled out the red carpet, I wouldn't feel a thing.

I jerked awake.

Gloved hands lifted away from my body as I thrashed. A voice somewhere to my left told me to calm down.

"Where am I?" But my eyes answered the question before the voice could. A fluorescent light glared overhead, reflecting off the portable exam table I was lying on. It was set up in the middle of a storage room lined with boxes and equipment on one side and a desk and couch on the other.

"You don't remember?" Dr. Jillian Ostrander's face appeared above me, and that's when I did.

I was at the clinic—the Des Moines emergency overnight veterinary clinic housed between a tutoring service and a tax office

3

in a strip mall east of downtown. I remembered driving across the state as the road wavered in and out of focus, wrapping a blanket around my shoulder as the clothes underneath it became clotted and sticky, staggering to the back door of the building as the weak December sun finally started to rise. Knocking. And then a heavy, sucking blackness. That was it.

"How . . ."

She shoved my head back down to the table with an elbow, which in Jillian-speak covered all the pleasantries.

I first came to the clinic years ago, for a sliced-open bicep. Normally I would've sewn it up myself, but it was on my right arm and I was right-handed. Jillian had been on duty that night, manning the desk while her tech was in the alley on a smoke break. The veterinarian had glanced from my arm to the doorway, like she expected more bleeding humans to invade her space.

"Gangs?" she asked, arching an eyebrow. It wasn't an unreasonable question. I'd cycled through gangs in high school until Sam recruited me into his operation, which felt about as far from a gang as a hospital was from this clinic.

"Fluffy had an accident." I rewrapped the arm. "But she's super shy about paperwork."

"Look, I can't—"

"A grand." I said, shrugging my arm back in the jacket and stopping whatever ethical terms and conditions she was getting ready to regurgitate. "Fluffy can pay you a thousand dollars for a few stitches and some antibiotics. I'm sure this place could use a new"—I glanced around at the aging Ikea furniture and dusty animal art on the walls—"whatever."

"No painkillers?" Her gaze narrowed.

"No."

She didn't believe me, didn't want to get involved. Later, I would learn Jillian rarely got involved with any type of human, bleeding or no, but that first night I assumed the problem was me. I was only twenty-one at the time, but it'd always been true in the past.

The back door opened, and I heard the tech coming back from his smoke break.

"Forget it." I turned to leave.

"Come here. Now." She stood up and led me to the secure storage room.

The room hadn't changed much in the last five years. Shelves of meticulously labeled supplies and medicine ran from floor to ceiling, the same mysterious, astronaut-looking dome sat on a counter, and the same yellowed cartoon was taped to the wall next to the desk. But there were improvements beyond the locked door: more advanced equipment, machines, and tools to treat the catastrophes that came in night after night. I'd financed a lot of those purchases.

Dr. Jillian Ostrander hadn't changed either. She still had the same long blond hair tied up in a ponytail. Her surgical glasses framed large blue eyes, her nose was straight and skinny, and she had a full, frowning mouth that gleamed with ChapStick. I hated blondes as a rule. The only good thing about them was watching how quickly age shredded their looks, but the doctor's beauty was annoyingly untouched. She must've been pushing forty and she looked like Veterinarian Barbie, if Veterinarian Barbie had chucked her eye shadow, grown a decent ass, and kept creature-of-the-night hours.

"Welcome back." Jillian kept her bloodstained gloves in the air, elbow planted on my forehead, and waited for me to calm down. "And stop moving."

I rolled away from the light and tried to check my shoulder, but the effort of fighting the pressure of her elbow felt enormous. I was covered from neck to waist with a surgical sheet, and a tray of bloody instruments sat next to her.

"Did it . . ." I closed my eyes, trying to bring the thought together. "Did it go all the way through?"

"Clean shot. Missed your major arteries, which you should know already, because you made it here. And you're doubly lucky because my technician today is Todd. He's stoned out of his mind and didn't even hear me dragging you inside."

Satisfied I was going to remain still, she lifted her elbow and continued working. I couldn't feel a thing. My entire shoulder felt like a black hole.

"Did you give me anesthetic?" I kept my voice low, beneath the notes of the new Taylor Swift album drifting from the computer.

"I didn't want you flinching or moving around while you were unconscious. There's a lot of damage here."

I watched the instruments flash as she pulled a cobweb-thin string in and out of the wound. Sewing me up. All the king's horses and all the king's men. I closed my eyes and fought to remain awake. "I feel dizzy."

"So I gathered when you fainted at the back door." There was a snip and the click of an instrument hitting the tray. "A common side effect of blood loss."

I made a casually interested noise and wondered how much blood a person could lose without dying. It was probably something

I should know, like I knew how to stitch myself up—when I could use my right hand—or recognize the smell of singed body hair before my skin started to burn. They were the little things that had gotten me to the ripe old age of twenty-six. My own personal survival encyclopedia, a manual no one else in the world would ever need.

An IV bag was hooked up to my other arm, the red tube winding into my vein. "Are you putting dog blood in me?"

"Only pig blood has a chance of not being rejected, and, no, that's not animal. It's human. A positive, your blood type."

"How did you . . ."

"I've stocked it for a little while. You need all of that"—she nodded to the IV—"and more, but that's all I have. Take iron supplements as soon as you can and keep them going for a while. And you'll need antibiotics. If you get a fever, you're going to have to bite the bullet and go to the hospital. The infection'll be what kills you."

The infection could get in line.

"Any casualties besides Fluffy?" Jillian asked after a while.

"No animals were harmed in the making of this film."

"Good." She sounded satisfied. Anyone else would've been worried if a gunshot victim rolled up at their back door, but one of my favorite things about Jillian was her general disregard for the human race. She was a vegan and an animal rights activist living in America's pork capital. The funds she didn't use for the clinic went to a farm sanctuary near the Amana colonies where three-legged cows became best friends with chickens, or something like that.

Years ago, I'd had a weird infatuation with Jillian. I couldn't call it a mommy thing, though that's what you'd think with the age difference. She was the least maternal person I'd ever met. I didn't even know if she was gay. Asexual, as near as I could tell, but that hadn't stopped me from fantasizing. Then I met Celina.

It was a tale as old as time. Drug trafficker meets diner server. Falls in love. Server convinces trafficker to go straight—get out of the business and become a DEA informant. Just when they're about to roll off into the sunset together, trafficker's boss finds out about the betrayal. Server claims she was the informant and sacrifices herself to save the trafficker. Trafficker plots against boss. Helps kill a ton of assholes to bring him down. Gets shot in the process and still can't manage to die.

Where's a fucking curtain when you need one?

"I don't have any cash on me," I mumbled. Jillian didn't say anything, and I couldn't tell if she was mad or just concentrating on the mess I'd made of her supply room. "I can send it."

"Don't send it here." She snipped another stitch. "I'll give you the address for the sanctuary. We need a new goat barn."

A movement caught my eye. On top of one of the shelves, a cat peered down at us, wearing a cone around its head. One of its legs had been shaved, and a neat scar lined the front of its shin.

Jillian noticed my gaze. "Fluffy, meet Maleficent."

The cat twitched its tail and I tried not to think about fur floating into my open wound. "Hi, Maleficent. What did you do to get locked in here?"

"She murdered a rooster, but he didn't go down without a fight."

"Some roosters have it coming."

A bell chimed from the reception area and muffled voices brought the technician knocking.

"Dr. Ostrander? I'm sorry to bug you while you're sleeping. There's some cops here and, um . . ." Even through the metal door,

Todd was clearly high and not doing well with the unexpected visitors.

Jillian's hands stilled. "Are they with Animal Control?"

"No . . . uh, I don't know. They have some questions."

Jillian looked back at me, her expression closed. "Tell them I'll be right out."

His footsteps shuffled away.

My pulse thunked. No one knew I was here; that's why I came to the emergency veterinary clinic in east Des Moines. Here I was invisible. Here I didn't even have a name. If I died on this table, I had full confidence Jillian would use my clothes for animal beds and shove my body into some crematory to burn. I'd never even told Celina about Jillian. So how could anyone . . .

I sat bolt upright, knocking the surgical sheet off and making the IV pole sway.

Fuck me: the truck . . .

I'd stolen it from Sam's farm. I should've ditched the thing blocks away and walked, but I hadn't trusted myself on the ice, especially not with the chance of leaving a blood trail. I'd assumed Jillian could stitch me up and I'd be gone before anyone noticed the truck.

Sitting up almost made me pitch forward off the table, the room still turning. My head lolled and I realized I was naked from the waist up. Great. I breathed deep, inhaling stale blood and antiseptic, the faint earthy smell of cat.

"Lie down." Jillian pushed me back to the table. "You're going to rip all your stitches."

"I have to get out of here." My boss was dead, along with several other people. I'd left an entire pile of bodies behind me this morning and a few more that were hardly moving. I wished I could say it was all justice for what they'd done to Celina, but the truth felt a lot darker.

Jillian held me down until I stopped fighting. Her face was so close I could see flecks of silver in her eyes, and she held my gaze until the world around those flecks came into focus again.

"You wouldn't make it a block."

Releasing me, she adjusted the IV and wiped my shoulder down with antiseptic. Her stitches had made a ragged cross four inches above my heart. The vine tattoo that climbed up my arm and over my shoulder puckered into the scar, mangling the leaves in that spot. On my bicep, a bright white bird nestled in the vine, staring back at me.

"You can turn me in." I swallowed. It was what Celina would say. I knew it, even through the noise in my head. She'd died for me. I had no choice but to live for her. "Say whatever you need to and I'll go along with it. No hard feelings."

Jillian covered me with a new sheet and stripped off her surgical scrubs before punching in the combination to unlock the door. "What I need is a new goat barn. Stay quiet."

Max

Everything hurt.

I sat in the back of an ambulance at a weigh station that looked like a parking lot for emergency vehicles. State troopers, city police, tow trucks, even a fire truck with a crane—all surrounding a tipped-over semi, a pickup, and a bright blue sedan with a shattered windshield. Medics had cut my jacket off and were busy treating me for my second gunshot wound of the year. With only a few weeks left in 2019 and a leave of absence from the Iowa City Police Department staring me down, I hoped to hold the number of unintended holes in my body at an even two.

The adrenaline had worn off long ago and the cold seeped into my skin, making the pain sharper. My whole body wanted to seize. I tried not to think about it.

What a weekend.

The weigh station was on the interstate less than forty miles from Iowa City, but an ice storm had paralyzed the state, covering every road and flat surface with an impenetrable layer of ice. Even after calling in two bodies and a semitruck full of drugs, it had taken first responders over an hour to get here. Now the place was swimming in blue.

As medics wrapped my arm, Jon Larsen, the field operations division captain, appeared at the ambulance door. He had the same pale redheaded complexion as me, but where I'd bit the bullet and shaved off my receding hairline years ago, he still sported a full, military-neat crew cut. A server once asked, at a department holiday lunch, if he was my cranky older brother. Larsen was out of earshot or the server wouldn't have gotten a tip that day.

He glanced from my discarded jacket sleeve soaked in blood to the chaos behind him, where crime scene photographers crawled over the semi, taking pictures of the two bodies slumped inside.

"Give us a minute."

The EMT objected. "He's still losing blood."

The captain ignored her, which was his standard move anytime someone outside his chain of command told him things he didn't want to hear. "Can you walk?"

"Yeah."

I climbed out of the ambulance, light-headed, but the slap of wind brought me back to the scene, chapping my face raw. The EMT secured the bandage around my arm and I followed Larsen on a slippery path through the cars.

"I put you on leave, Summerlin."

"I know." There'd be a full report later, probably more than one. I wasn't planning on wasting my breath trying to explain myself here, but I also hadn't planned on seeing my direct superior, who'd ordered me off the job less than twenty-four hours ago.

"You going rogue on us?"

"No, sir. I went to help a friend off duty." I didn't need to say the name. Jonah Kendrick, my best friend since our freshman year in college, was the reason I'd been put on leave. He was a PI who'd gotten tangled up in the investigation of a drug trafficking ring, and—as usual when it came to Jonah—he'd tangled me right up along with him. "I identified Russell Ash on the road while I was on my way back to Iowa City and followed him and the semi into the weigh station. They boxed me in and I started taking fire."

Ash was responsible for both of my gunshot wounds this year. He wouldn't be handing out any more.

"Russell Ash? He the one handcuffed to the door?"

We passed the cab of the semi. I couldn't see inside and didn't need to. The dead men were etched in my brain. "Yes, sir. He's the one with the stab wound to the neck."

Larsen gave me a sharp look.

"Self-inflicted."

He didn't comment on that. We reached the back of the semi, where another team of investigators swarmed the cargo hold. Boxes, hundreds of them, lay everywhere, some still wrapped in plastic, others mangled and exploded open. The writing on the side said CAUTION: DE-ICING AGENT. On the surface, it appeared to be exactly the kind of shipment this storm needed.

An investigator picked his way through the boxes. "Sir?"

Larsen looked up, but the investigator waited for another man walking over from an unmarked car, a big Latino guy with a jaw like a full moon. Larsen introduced him as Agent Santiago Morales of the DEA.

"Mixed in?" Morales asked. He was finishing what looked like an Egg McMuffin.

The investigator dragged a box over. "Separate bags." He pulled out a plastic bladder that had been buried among the de-icing pellets. "Medical-grade plastic, two layers. They were careful."

"What is it?" I stepped closer, peering through the bladder at the amorphous white contents. I'd already found one of these before I called in the situation, but I'd been off duty and driving a civilian car. I didn't have any test kits on me.

"Opioids." The investigator surveyed the number of boxes. "Based on what we've found so far, we've probably got a twenty-million-dollar street value right here."

Morales whistled and balled up the sandwich wrapper. "This the guy who got 'em?"

He pumped my good hand, which still sent pain ricocheting through my body like a Ping-Pong ball, and slapped me on the shoulder for good measure. "You ever think about applying for the DEA?"

"Easy there." Larsen had been on the verge of suspending me twenty-four hours ago. Now he held up a hand to ward Morales off. The federal agent chuckled.

"ICPD will be happy to assist with whatever you need."

"We'll be in touch." Morales slapped me again before hauling himself into the truck. Investigators surrounded him, cracking jokes and smiling. The scene in the back of the truck could've been Christmas morning, and I breathed easier seeing it. My job was safe. Hell, I might even get out of this with a commendation when all was said and done. It was easily the biggest bust of my career, the biggest I could remember in the whole department.

Compared to how things looked yesterday, it was nothing short of a miracle.

But I had so many questions. That was always the problem. I needed answers long after everyone else stopped caring. There were two dead men in the front of this truck: drug traffickers, people no one gave two shits about. One of them had died in the crash and shootout. The other had taken his own life. Russell Ash chose death over facing the fallout of getting arrested. Was he afraid of the law or was it something else? The image of him plunging a shard of glass into his own neck ate at me. The wondering, the not knowing why, was the only thing keeping the pain at bay.

"I want on this investigation," I told Larsen when we got back to the ambulance.

"You're on leave."

I started to fire back, but he cut over my objections. "Compulsory. Officer discharge of a weapon."

I nodded as the EMT started working on my shoulder again. "As soon as I'm back, then."

"We'll talk."

"I'll talk to the DEA. Sounds like they've got openings."

Larsen grunted and shook his head, which was the closest he ever came to outright agreement. "We'll talk."

Shelley appeared behind him, crowding into the open door.

"What are you doing here?"

"Jon brought me." My wife was on a first-name basis with everyone from the mail carrier to my direct superior. She climbed into the ambulance wearing pajamas underneath her winter coat, the fuzzy purple ones with a coffee stain on one sleeve. Her hair was going in every direction and the shadows under her eyes looked like bruises, but her gaze was full and fierce with love. In fifteen years of marriage, she'd never looked more beautiful.

"Your wife started calling the station at 5:00 a.m."

"Where's Garrett?"

"At the neighbor's. I needed to know you were all right." She wanted to say more than that, I could tell. I would have a lot of explaining and apologizing to do when we got home. Probably months' worth. But she was here now. For me.

I found her hand and squeezed. "Jonah's alive. He's okay."

Her expression darkened for a second. Her hand didn't return the squeeze. "That's good."

"We just got confirmation that all of them arrived at the hospital in Des Moines." Larsen tapped something on his phone.

"What about the caller?" It was another question, less visceral than Russell Ash's suicide but one that kept nagging at me, turning over and over in the back of my head. Someone had called in my best friend's location and brought emergency services out to a barn in the middle of frozen farm country. Whoever it was clearly knew a lot more than what they'd said to the 911 operator. And the call came in hours ago. We needed to find the caller before they slipped through the cracks of this storm and disappeared forever.

"We've got officers mobilized across the state." Larsen stood back as the EMT loaded everything, preparing to transport me back to Iowa City. "Trust me, Summerlin. Anyone with any connection to that farm is going to be in a world of hurt."

Kara

I was trapped in a locked room. The single air vent in the ceiling was out of reach and the door was solid metal. I was still shirtless, barely stitched up, and my head spun, probably fighting my other organs for oxygen. There was nothing I could do except wait and see if Jillian told the police I was here. To breathe and try to channel Celina. I bandaged my shoulder and wondered how much goat barns cost.

It was an hour, maybe more, before I heard someone punching in the keypad from the other side. Jillian walked in alone, eyes clocking the amount of blood left in the IV bag. It was close to empty now.

"You look better," she said without looking at me.

"Everything okay?"

"It is now." The cat, which I'd completely forgotten about, jumped off the highest shelf and started making figure eights around Jillian's legs. "They towed a stolen truck that was parked in the alley. We're the only business in the place that's open today, so they came here first. Said there's a white female suspect in the area. Brown hair, petite, possibly injured."

"And?" We were both keeping our voices down, but I felt ready to scream.

The cat jumped on the desk, demanding to be petted while it glared at me.

"And humans are occasionally helpful. Todd swore he saw someone getting picked up on the corner a few hours ago. Too far away to give a description, but he said it looked like a girl."

"They bought that?"

"They circled and sat on the other side of the block for a while. I took one of the dogs for a walk and saw them hit the lights and peel out. They're gone now."

"Thank you." I exhaled pure relief.

She handed me a bag. Inside were clothes, fresh gauze, the address for the animal sanctuary, and a bottle of pills. "Don't use that arm for anything for at least a week. Take the antibiotics three times a day and watch the incision for streaks of redness." She pulled out the IV and began bagging the garbage and bloody clothes. I didn't have to ask if she would make them disappear.

She peeled back the bandage to check her handiwork one last time and her hand paused on my arm. For the first time since coming back in the room, her eyes found mine and there was an earthquake underneath that unblinking blue gaze. She was angry, and at first I thought she was upset about lying to the police, but something else welled inside the anger, a sorrow that caught me like a punch in the ribs.

"Get out of here." Her voice was barely more than a whisper. "This is what people do to each other. The damage they cause. Get away from this while you still can."

An answering ache rose up in me, the grief I carried every minute of every day. Before I could say anything her eyes slid over me and away, blinking back whatever had fought its way to the surface. And what could I tell her anyway? What could I say to Dr. Jillian Ostrander? I was the person she was talking about. I caused the kind of damage that couldn't be sewn up. But maybe she already knew that. Maybe this was how good people told you to leave them the fuck alone.

She turned, giving me privacy. I pulled the shirt on—a little big, but soft and smelling like lemons—and a hoodie over the top of that, being careful not to move my arm. To pretend it was hurt. It always felt stupid when nothing in my body felt wrong, but I knew better than to listen to my body. Nothing it ever told me could be trusted.

"Malley, stop." The cat was busy trying to claw the cone off its head. Jillian clucked and cinched the thing so tight, I figured the cat's eyes would bulge out of its head, but it just jumped back to the high perch and ate a few bites from the dish up there.

"I didn't know which one of them was going to make it. The cat or the rooster. Usually roosters can spread their wings and intimidate smaller mammals, but that didn't work with Maleficent. She stalked the coop for a week before pouncing on a hen. Peck marks up and down her back, and that rake opening her leg. She swatted and hissed like mad, both of them chasing each other around and around, like a dance I couldn't stop. In the end, it's who finds the neck first."

Jillian looked at the black face peering at her from above.

"That's what I love about animals. They win, they lose, they live, they die, and no matter what they never complain." She moved to the door. "That's why I let you come back, Fluffy. You don't complain, either."

"And you want a goat barn." I dry swallowed one of the antibiotics.

I could hear the smile in her voice as she led me out the back exit of the building. "That too."

Love's Travel Stop was a truck stop perched on a hill above criss-crossing freeways. It looked like they'd been swamped over the last few days of the ice storm. A clusterfuck of tractor trailers lined up to file back on the freeway, where hundreds of their kind had ended up jackknifed and upside down in ditches and exit ramps across the state. The ones who'd made it to the truck stop had probably been stranded here for days and were anxious to finish their hauls for whatever the loads were still worth. They wanted out of this place. We had that in common.

Behind the truck stop, the dark edge of the world met the dark edge of the sky. North, south, east, and west. The roads stretched out in four directions, four choices. I didn't have the first clue which one to make. At least the blood Jillian had given me seemed to be working. My head was clearer and I didn't sway as I crossed the lines of pumps toward the travel plaza building.

Inside, the place smelled like ammonia and old coffee. I paced the aisles and grabbed what I needed: scissors, clippers, clothes, snacks—iron-rich, according to Jillian's orders—ibuprofen, a back-pack, plastic wrap. I paused at the row of hair dyes before choosing Touch of Gray from the men's selections and taking everything to the register.

"Are the showers coin-operated?"

The cashier looked me over. I kept my head down, scanning the lottery tickets. "No, honey. You pay up front."

"Okay, I'll take one, please."

The shower room was actually nice. It had been days since I stood under a stream of hot water, and after binding my shoulder with enough plastic wrap to keep it dry, I braced myself against the wall and scrubbed off blood and grime until my skin was raw.

Afterward, I stood at the mirror and cut my hair, throwing section by section into another sheet of plastic wrap. Celina had woven her fingers through the ends of this hair, had nuzzled into the back of my neck and breathed deep, inhaling it like a refuge. It was a tiny, trivial connection and I didn't deserve to keep it.

I switched to the clippers, buzzing it short around my ears and neck and longer on top, ending up with sort of a 2012 non-binary Bieber look. The kind of kid you want to punch and wipe from your brain as soon as possible. Then I mixed up the dye and went to work turning what was left from dark brown to a streaky gray.

While waiting for the dye to set, I looked at the U.S. map I'd grabbed out of the gas station turnstile. There were two main ways out of Iowa: I-80 took you to the East or West Coast, and I-35 led practically all the way to Canada or Mexico.

Get out of here, Jillian had said.

There was no reason to stay. Sam was dead. The drug empire he'd killed Celina to protect was finished. I should have been celebrating or downing a bottle of whiskey or spitting on Sam's grave. I should have felt something, but the truth was I hadn't expected to live through it.

I'd stopped at a storage facility on my way here and emptied the safe inside. Sam paid most of his people in crypto and I had my share of that, but I'd collected more over the past seven years. Cash, an ID, a passport, an unlocked Nokia phone, and a stack of prepaid Visa cards purchased across the Midwest. Sam had taught me to be prepared.

When I left the shower room—wiping down everything behind me and packing every hair and scrap of garbage into the backpack—the hall was empty. I looked at the map again, trying to imagine anything beyond the horizon. That was always the problem. For seven years Sam had made the plans and I followed them. I never had any dreams or vision boards mapping my future. I never expected to have a future.

"Howdy."

A guy walked into the laundry alcove and popped open a dryer, shoving clothes into a drawstring bag. He was scruffy and bleary-eyed, wearing a ball cap that looked permanently fixed to his head. "Time to get the hell out of Dodge."

"Which way you headed?" I asked.

"South."

"Me too." I put the map away. "Got any spare room?"

"Sure, I can give you a lift." He stuck out a hand. "Buck."

I shook it. "Betty."

He grinned, flashing teeth that edged between yellow and brown, and waved me ahead of him toward the parking lot. "Pleased to meet you, Betty."

His semi was one of the last parked in the overnight lot. I climbed in and was shrugging the backpack off, taking in the maroon upholstery flecked with crumbs and the scuffed and dirty carpet, when a shove to my back sent me flying into the cabin behind the seats. I fell on top of a pile of shit on the floor, cans and bottles and rags all rolling underneath me, and tried to grab for anything stationary.

"How much?" The door slammed and I heard a belt buckle being unstrapped. "Haven't seen you at this stop before. You a friend of Stacy's?"

I twisted, getting a flash of a giant American flag hanging above the bed before sitting upright on top of the pile of junk. Buck stood between the seats of the cab, one hand already down his pants.

"Wrong idea, Buck." The sudden movement made me dizzy. I braced a hand against my head, willing the blood Jillian had pumped into me to circulate faster.

He grinned again and his teeth looked even dirtier in the dim cab light. "Tell you the truth, I was losing hope one of you would show up. Guess you girls don't like being out in the cold. But don't worry, Big Buck'll warm you up."

He moved in, his pants shoved low on his hips. I grabbed one of the metal cans on the floor and punched it into his boxers. He cried out and fell against the seats.

"I said"—I drew myself to my feet and hitched the backpack over my bad shoulder—"you've got the wrong idea. I just wanted a ride."

"I'll give you one hell of a ride."

His fist arced, a swift hook I couldn't block in time. My head snapped around. My whole body hit the shelves on one side of the bed and bounced onto the mattress. He landed on top of me, pinning me down by the bad shoulder.

"That hurts, don't it?"

He squeezed the shoulder harder. He must've seen my bandage inside the gas station. He knew exactly how much pain this kind of pressure should cause and it probably would've worked. On someone else.

"If you settle down, I won't have to hurt you more," he grunted, trying to pull my sweatpants down with his free hand.

"Hey, Buck?"

He glanced up and I shoved the heel of my hand into his nose. Blood spurted around my palm, warm and sticky. Buck howled and grabbed for his face. It always fascinated me how people turned toward their pain. They cradled it like a baby, like they knew it was something precious, this voice of destruction.

I rolled up and my hand brushed the metal canister. Gripping it, I swung the can into the side of his head. Not once or twice, but ramming the cylinder through the air as fast as I could, hitting him in the jaw, the temple, the ear.

I wasn't big, only five foot two and a hundred and twenty pounds, max. I didn't have the brute strength to knock someone out in one blow, but my blows kept coming like rain. Each drop by itself was insignificant, but put them together, fast and relentless, and they would drown you.

I kept hitting him, scissoring my arm quicker and harder, past the point where anyone else would get tired or feel their own joints and muscles screaming in protest. I'd never heard that scream. My body didn't have a voice of destruction, nothing to cradle tight, to clench around. The doctors called it CIP Disorder. I only knew pain by what it looked like on other people.

Buck finally fell off me. He caught my arm on the way down, pulling the whole thing out of its socket. The canister dropped out of my hand, and I smacked into the side of the driver's seat and landed on top of him. I pressed one knee into his breastbone and the other foot on top of a wrist.

His breath rasped wet and heaving beneath my knee and his eyes bulged white over the top of the hand braced against his head. "What the fuck are you?"

"I was a girl looking for a lift, Buck."

The arm he'd yanked dangled uselessly at my side and I used the other one—the bad one, the one Jillian told me not to use—to position the ball of the shoulder joint and snap it back into its socket.

I could've robbed him, but I didn't need the money. I could've locked him in the back of his truck and driven myself all the way to the border, but I didn't need the trouble. Buck stared at me, silent and suddenly small, like he knew all the ways I could make him pay. Streaks of blood coursed down his cheeks and matted his beard. This was what humans did to each other. This was the damage we caused.

I shoved my knee into his chest one last time, making him grunt before getting up and slinging the backpack over my shoulder again. The new gauze felt wet under my shirt. Great.

"Time for you to hit the road."

I waited outside the station, watching as his truck fired up and slowly pulled to the exit. I should've gone back to the shower and stripped, checked my body for signs of damage. Redness. Contortion. A seeping wound or two. In the CIP Disorder universe—the people who couldn't feel pain—the disease killed us young. We went out big and quick, dying before we ever figured out how to live. But I couldn't afford to stay at this truck stop any longer, not after that little encounter. Another driver came outside and lit a cigarette.

"Which way you headed?"

He puffed out a cloud of smoke. "North."

"Me too."

Max

Jonah's hospital room didn't have much going for it. No plants or flowers broke up the sterile gray of the walls or medical equipment. There was no TV and the only window in the room had a view of a brick wall. The bed was empty when I walked into the room for the third time in the last week and a half. Jonah sat in a chair by the window reading a book. A brace held his left leg stiff and immobile in front of him. Chin-length black hair fell in a greasy mess around his face. He needed a shave.

I dropped a duffel bag on the bed and bent to check out the book's cover, which showcased a half-naked couple embracing on a hill.

"Any good?" I grinned.

"The sex scenes are hot, but otherwise they're just trying to figure out each other's feelings."

"Lucky fucks."

"They don't know how good they have it." Jonah didn't have the luxury of not knowing people's feelings. He was a psychic, the only actual psychic I'd ever known, which meant he was forced to feel whatever anyone around him felt whether he wanted to or not.

It made living in a world lousy with people and their never-ending emotions a daunting if not impossible task. It was also why I made sure he got a private room at the hospital.

He tossed the book onto the table next to him. "One of the nurses lent it to me. She felt bad that I didn't have anything to do."

"I can get you something better than that."

"A message?" He glanced at the duffel bag, a spark of life flashing across his face.

The last time I'd visited, he'd given me a note for Dr. Eve Roth, the physicist who helped him track down two people who'd gone missing from Iowa City in the last few months: Jonah's niece, followed by Eve's husband. I hadn't seen a connection between their cases at first, and Eve had been my best suspect for her husband's sudden disappearance, but the two of them had gone rogue and become surprisingly close in the process.

"She didn't write a note back, but I'll ask again after gym class."

"How is she?"

"That's all you two ask me. If the nurse supplied you with porn, I'm sure she could get you a phone."

"It's not porn. It's romance."

"What's the difference?"

"Foreplay. And feelings." He shook his head. "Christ, I feel bad for Shelley now."

"Shelley's fine." I lied, and we both knew it.

Shelley had tolerated my friendship with Jonah for years. She'd smiled politely as he gave the world's most awkward best man speech at our wedding and let him hold Garrett once or twice after he was born, but my wife had always kept my best friend at a cautious distance. Waiting for the other shoe to drop. And it had. A few months ago, an off-the-books investigation into the disappearance of Jonah's niece had left me shot, riddled with chronic nerve pain, and nearly ended my career. She never came out and said I had to choose between them, but you don't spend fifteen years married to a woman without learning the language of what she wasn't saying.

Things changed after Jonah was admitted to the hospital. I refused to abandon him again. If I'd been there for him in the first place, he might not have ended up nearly murdered in a barn. When I told Shelley I was visiting him, she turned away to fill her coffee cup and stalked silently out of the kitchen. We hadn't spoken about it since.

"So which is it with you and Eve. Feelings? Or foreplay?"

"It's not like that." He glanced at the book and away. "She's married."

"To a drug trafficker—and not for long from what it looked like. She and her father-in-law were wasting no time packing their things."

His eyes flashed with something I hadn't seen in Jonah in a long time. His niece's disappearance had almost driven him mad, and there was a while when I didn't know if I'd ever again see the friend I'd met in college. Maybe there was a chance now for him to recover, a reason to look forward, to hope. And because of a scientist. Who would've thought?

"She seemed good." I let my head fill up with an image of the last time I visited her, holding a baseball bat, weak but ready to beat me to a pulp if I happened to be someone who tried messing with her. I concentrated on details: the shine off her dark red cap of hair, the UI sweatshirt, the mountain of cardboard boxes filling her living room, and her father-in-law in his wheelchair, unwaveringly by her side. Jonah exhaled as the image reflected in his mind. He closed his eyes, like he wanted to block everything else out.

"Thank you."

"No problem." I pointed to the duffel bag. "There's some clothes in there, and shower stuff. You might want to wash before we head out."

Jonah was getting discharged today and I'd offered to drive him back to his house halfway across the state, but I didn't necessarily want to smell him the whole way.

He grabbed a crutch and stood up. "Read the book while you're waiting. Get some pointers."

"Thanks, but I've got a soon-to-be ex-husband I'd like to chat with again." I turned to the door. "Back in twenty."

I took the elevator upstairs and paced through a few corridors, passing enough people in scrubs and hospital gowns that I started feeling overdressed. I didn't have my badge—that was sitting on Larsen's desk along with my gun while they investigated the weigh station incident—but the sling on my left arm afforded me a similar level of clearance. A few nurses gave me a once-over as they reviewed charts and handed out orders. An orderly balled up a green surgical mask and gloves and made a two-point shot behind my back into a hazardous waste bin, and another one buzzed past me so fast while balancing a tower of donuts, I thought he was wearing Rollerblades.

Matthew Moore's room was the only one in the ward being guarded. This was my third visit and the officer knew me by now. We also both knew I was out of my jurisdiction. Even though Matthew

Moore's missing person case had been assigned to me, that case was long closed and I was on leave. I should've been doing physical therapy and meeting with the department shrink, driving my friend home from the hospital and helping Shelley put up Christmas decorations. Normal, civilian things. But as much as I wanted it to, that wasn't how my head worked.

"Summerlin." The officer looked nervous, like he'd been told not to let me in.

"Last time I'll be stopping by. Just a few follow-up questions."

In the last two interviews Matthew Moore had given, he'd admitted to developing formulas and cooking opiates for the drug lord who'd been his childhood neighbor. He connected that operation to the truckload of drugs at the weigh station and to Celina Kendrick as well. Jonah's niece had been killed because of these people, a twenty-year-old woman with her entire life ahead of her. And in his interviews, Matthew Moore had the nerve to say he was sorry.

"Ten minutes."

"Five." I countered.

The officer smiled, nodded, and let me inside.

Matthew Moore's hospital room made Jonah's look homey. It was dark, windowless, and the ring of machines, tubes, and wires around the single bed looked like some techno horror movie.

Blankets covered him to the chest and his arms lay on top— long, pale, and ending in stark white balls of tightly wrapped bandages. They'd amputated both his hands a few days ago, unable to save them from gangrene. I stared at the white wraps, imagining the rot of dead skin seeping up his fingers and palms, killing tissue as it spread, and almost felt bad for the guy. Almost.

Moving to the side of the bed, I cleared my throat. He didn't stir. I tapped him on the arm, gently at first, then a little harder. He finally roused.

"I don't know, I said."

"You don't know what?"

He gradually focused on me, then looked around the room like he was expecting more people. The last two times I'd been here was with a contingent of local PD and the DEA. "Where . . ." He trailed off, blinking in confusion.

"Remember me?"

If he did, he didn't acknowledge it.

"Investigator Summerlin with the Iowa City police."

He made a noise and tried to sit up, banging his bandages on the bed rails like he'd forgotten he didn't have hands to grip them.

"Hey, easy. I only have a few questions." I touched his shoulder until he settled back to the pillow.

"I don't know where he kept it."

"Who?"

"Sam." The next-door-neighbor drug lord. His boss.

"You don't know where Sam kept what?"

He muttered something that didn't make sense and his head lolled away. Maybe he'd been dreaming. Maybe he still was.

"Look, Matthew. I know you're going through hell right now. I know this isn't easy. But there's one thing we still need to know, something you can help us with, and trust me when I say your cooperation will not go unrecognized in court." *I* would recognize it, anyway. I couldn't speak for anyone else.

"Matthew?"

I waited for him to look at me, for his pupils to contract and focus.

"Where was that truckload of drugs going?"

It was the one piece of the puzzle I couldn't find. Everything else had slotted into place with the information Matthew Moore, Eve Roth, and Jonah had provided. I even figured out who'd made the anonymous 911 call to alert authorities as to where the three of them could be found that day. Kara Johnson, the drug trafficker who'd allegedly been in love with Jonah's niece. She'd flipped on Sam and the rest of the traffickers to help Jonah and Eve escape. The call had come from a burner phone, pinging off a cell tower outside Des Moines, before she disappeared. A lot of people had probably followed Kara's example and crawled into the shadows in the last week and a half, but right now I was only interested in one—the person or group who was supposed to receive twenty-two million dollars' worth of opioids before I stopped their delivery from happening.

I'd busted plenty of dealers before, but they were all low-level, feeding on the college kids and campus life that kept Iowa City thriving. I had no idea who could traffic the amount of drugs we'd found in the back of that semi. But if they could handle a shipment like that, it wasn't their first. Or last.

Matthew didn't answer. He didn't even seem to hear the question. His eyes rolled back in his head, exposing the undersides of his eyeballs, glossy white and popping with tiny veins, and something about this felt very, very wrong.

"Hey." I snapped next to his ear, trying to bring him back. "Can you hear me?"

I glanced at the wall of machines, looking for some indication of what was going on. Patients in hospitals didn't have regular day/night schedules and I understood that this guy was recovering from some traumatic surgery, but he'd been a hundred times more responsive the last two times I was here. Then I saw it: the heart monitor, the blips drawing further and further apart until they stopped altogether.

Oh, fuck.

I ran to the door, but the nurses' station was already alerted. Two women in scrubs burst into the room and swarmed the bed. I stood near the wall while the officer assigned to the door hovered next to me, looking like he wanted to slap some cuffs on, but he wasn't sure who or for what.

"His eyes were dilated. He was talking, but he got more and more disoriented. And then he just passed out," I offered. One of the nurses looked at his IV while another brought out paddles and tried to shock Matthew Moore's heart back to life.

"What the . . . ?" The nurse pulled a mostly full IV bag down. "I was coming to change this. It should be empty."

She looked at the other nurse, who was too busy trying to restart Matthew's heart, and then turned on the two of us.

The officer shook his head. "That other nurse came in and changed it."

"What nurse?" She took a step toward us.

"I d-don't know—" the officer stuttered, looking to me as if for help. "Another one."

"He's not responding," the first nurse said as more people in scrubs rushed into the room.

I pulled the officer into the hallway. "Who was in there before me? Who was the other nurse?"

"Some guy. Brown hair, scrubs. He had an IV bag and was wearing green gloves."

Green gloves. The orderly I'd passed on my way here; the guy who'd met my eyes as he balled up and threw away his surgical mask.

"Lock it down!" I started running, the officer right on my heels.

"What?"

"The hospital. Call Security and put the building on lockdown. Now!"

The guy had walked right past me, heading for the main elevator bank. I crowded my way into the next one going down and punched the button for the ground floor, the fastest way to the exit from this ward. By the time I made it to the locked entrance and the few people milling in front of it, murmuring in confusion and worry, it was too late.

The guy in scrubs was gone and Matthew Moore was dead.

August 2020

Kara

One year.

I gave up on sleep and rolled off the cot in the corner of the laundry room, stuffed my feet into some Docs, grabbed a notebook, and headed down to the beach. No one was up in the main building or dorms. My flashlight beam bounced off broken concrete steps going down, down, down. Jagged stone cliffs hugged either side of the staircase until it opened at the bottom to a rocky shoreline with a firepit and a couple of chained-down picnic tables. I threw the notebook on a table and stared in the direction of water I could hear but not see. Superior was calm this morning—this night? whatever the hell it was—the waves lapping at the shore like a heartbeat. Not even the biggest lake in the world was going to give me a distraction today.

It was August 13, 2020. Exactly one year since Sam murdered Celina.

We'd been together for ten months before she died, which meant she'd been dead longer than I'd known her. And every relentless trip around the sun would take her further away. I hated all the anniversaries to come, the sleepless markers I would dread for however long I was stuck on this Celina-less planet. I flipped open the notebook and started drawing. Lines turned into shapes. The form grew in the slash of the flashlight's beam while the lake whispered in the darkness.

One year.

I was achingly aware of every breath that filled my chest, this gift I hadn't asked for and could never return. I had to live because she decided to take the fall for me, to steal my violent end, and I couldn't even scream at her for her fucking presumption, for thinking my life would ever be worth more than hers, for making the biggest mistake of her stupid, blindingly hopeful life. I hated her sometimes. I really fucking did.

One year.

I drew until the world lightened from black to gray, until red streaks bled over the sky into the water and daybreak made the flashlight pointless. Celina loved sunrises. She said she saw them upside down after punching out of her overnight shifts. She liked ending her day at the beginning of things.

A boy walked down the concrete steps, fast and trying to be quiet. I rubbed a sleeve over my eyes and kept drawing. He stopped a few feet away, shifting from foot to foot.

"Morning."

Terrance was from Milwaukee, a nervous rabbit of a kid and even smaller than me. He'd been one of the first people who tried to befriend me when I'd arrived at this camp on the Canadian shores of Lake Superior. The place was a haven for runaway boys, which is what someone in a Thunder Bay gas station thought I was when they directed me here last January.

The owner didn't want to let me stay—they'd established a breast-free zone—but my queer card managed to bend the rules.

That and five hundred dollars. Not much cash flowed through the place. The buildings were old, the porches crooked, the shingles continuously ripped off by the lake. The furniture looked like Goodwill couldn't move the stuff and didn't want to waste the lighter fluid to torch it. The owner set me up on a moldy cot in the laundry room and told me any trouble would land me a one-way trip back to Thunder Bay. I agreed. For the first time in my life, trouble was the last thing I wanted.

Most of the kids postured or ignored me, putting in their laundry and going out to the adjoining mess hall, where everyone ate, played cards, and took turns on the Xbox that hummed day and night. Terrance was the only one who stuck around, sitting on the washing machine and staring at the bird drawings taped to the wall above my cot. Eventually he showed me a couple of his sketches—heavy on the skulls—and I gave him a few tips on his shading. That's all it would have been, a passing nod between strangers before I figured out my next move, but then March 2020 happened.

It started with travel advisories. China, Italy, nowhere any of these runaways dreamed of running. Then it was everywhere. Canada's borders closed to all nonessential travel, locking the door behind me only a few months after I had walked through it. They told everyone to isolate, and the camp became an island.

Some of the place's sponsors dried up as the stock market tanked, and the owner relied more and more on the cash I supplied. Breasts weren't so bad compared to coronavirus. Terrance's drawings changed, too. Some of the skulls started wearing masks. Others had long beaks, like plague doctors had mutated and died. He was entering a new period: Covid-era art.

He looked over my shoulder now as I finished the page and dated it, 20200813.

"Jordan."

"I know." This drawing was different than my usual subjects, the exploded birds that lived at the edges of my eyes no matter where I looked. Yesterday it had been a crow, its feathers peeled back to expose a maze of tendon, bone, and organ. But I didn't have a choice today. This drawing had been decided a year ago.

"There's someone here. Looking for you."

For me? A ping of adrenaline cleared out the fog of the sleepless night. The social worker who used to come around stopped visiting because of lockdown, and her Zoom chats were a lot easier to avoid. The local cops had stopped out a few times, always for something runaway related, and it was a simple thing to disappear into the forest until they left again.

"Who is it?"

"I don't know. An American." Terrance shifted from foot to foot, and his eyes reflected the same burn of wariness and nerves lighting up inside me.

An American. Not Russell. I'd read about that asshat's death before I even hit Canada. Someone else had taken out Matthew Moore, though, and while he was under police protection. That kind of skill set could easily track a person across the border to a broken-down collection of cabins outside Thunder Bay.

I glanced up the concrete steps. Unless I hit the water or got real good at rock climbing in the next two minutes, stairs were the only way in or out of this narrow, secluded cove. I was trapped down here.

"What does he look like?" I knew it was a he. It was always a he.

Terrance jerked his chin at a man who appeared at the top of the stairs, his silhouette shaded by the trees.

"Like that."

I couldn't make him out. I had no weapons on me, but I scooped up a jagged rock underneath the picnic table and waited.

The man eased his way down the stairs, his squat calves taking their time on every step. He wore a nylon windbreaker, shorts, and a ball cap. His hands clutched the railing, and when he looked up at the halfway point, his wide, tan face broke into a smile I recognized.

"You know him?"

"He thinks he knows me."

Terrance shifted closer, looking at the notebook, and made a *hmm* noise.

"You don't like it."

"No, I do. It's just—" He fumbled for the right word. "It's alive."

The bird was all curves and feathers, perched high in a tree with the entire sky stretching open behind it. It was staring at the ground, even as its wings unfurled, ready to fly. If I had colored pencils, I would have made it bright white. Blinding, lit up like fresh snow.

Terrance looked confused, glancing between the notebook, the man, and me. I shifted the rock into a better hold.

"What kind of bird is it?"

"An extinct one." The man reached the bottom of the stairs and I flipped the notebook closed. "Get out of here."

"Jordan, is it?"

"Agent Morales."

My gut didn't unclench when I ID'd the DEA agent. It wound tighter because I couldn't fight this off. A U.S. government operative meant there were a dozen more just out of sight. I stuffed the notebook in one pocket and the rock in the other and paced to the shore.

"Nice place you got here."

"It's not mine."

"I'm surprised you didn't try to get farther away. You can spit on the U.S. from here."

"How'd you find me?"

He waved the question away like some magnanimous prick of an uncle rejecting a thank-you. "We would've been here a lot sooner if it wasn't for this damn virus. You should be grateful to corona for buying you this lovely vacation."

"And now?"

Two more people appeared at the top of the stairs. Now that I was cornered, they were closing in. I wondered the same thing I always did, the knee-jerk reflex that happened twenty times a day, every time I faced a decision: If Celina were here, what would she do? It didn't matter how big or small the thing was. Crunchy or creamy peanut butter. White or wheat. Hang up the bird drawing or burn it in the fire. Celina was the reason I stayed at this island of misfit boys, the reason I tried to help Terrance and handed over more cash than I needed to, to put food on their cracked and tagged tables. Because Celina would have. She would have given everything without a thought. She would have felt their pain so deeply, it would cut her into a thousand pieces.

The agents at the top of the cliff waited. They were patient. They knew I wasn't going anywhere. My fingers tightened on the rock in my pocket.

"We have a situation."

Morales toed the mounds of pebbles beneath his feet like a tourist looking for agates. He didn't even bother watching his back—there were already enough eyes doing it for him. "We've spent the last nine months tracking down strays like you. Like the one who took out Matthew Moore."

"Did you find who did it?"

He didn't answer. "We thought the bulk of Sam Olson's operation imploded with that barn—that everything would fizzle out in paybacks and hits."

Anger flooded my vision, pooling like saliva in my mouth. Paybacks and hits. That's all he thought Celina was, the reason he'd done nothing when I came to him a year ago and told him that Sam murdered Celina over a tip I'd passed to the DEA. I was their goddamn informant—me, not Celina—but she'd taken the fall when Sam figured out there was a leak. And when I told them what happened and demanded justice, this grinning shit stain of an agent told me there wasn't enough evidence. I hadn't seen it happen and couldn't point the finger at Sam when it could've been Russell. It could've been anyone Sam ordered to pull the trigger. And if they couldn't pin a drug empire on him, it would be impossible to convince a jury that some old white Iowa farmer had executed a young woman in cold blood.

That's what Morales said, to my face. He told me to wait. To look at the big picture. To be a good fucking girl and go get some more intel. And I'd tried, for Celina. I'd worked with Matthew Moore—another Sam Olson University drop-out—to gather as much information as we could. Feed the DEA until they grew enough balls to finally arrest Sam. But Sam knew something was up. He always did. He dismantled his entire operation like it was a going-out-of-business sale.

"What do you want?"

That's what this came down to, the reason Morales was here at all. If he wanted to arrest me, he could've sent the Canadian authorities. He wouldn't take the time and trouble to get across a closed border to slap cuffs on me.

"We've had some troubling developments in the last few months. We need someone on the inside."

"I'm not inside anything anymore."

"Maybe. You're going to have to find out."

"Or?"

He pushed a mound of pebbles with a New Balance sneaker, fanning the rocks out in a swirl. "You don't really need me to read the charges, do you?"

There it was. I could either become a DEA informant again or go to prison. Even if I did the informant gig, I had no guarantees. This might be a trip to jail no matter what, the only difference in whether I was allowed to pass go or collect two hundred dollars.

As far as I knew, the operation died with Sam. Russell was dead, I was gone, and the rest of the grunts I knew would've scattered, taking their money and whatever product had fallen through the cracks. There was the hit on Matthew. I had no idea who was behind that, but it had happened months ago, almost before Sam's body was cold. What kind of developments was Morales talking about?

The DEA agent kept pushing rocks around with his dumb shoe, smiling that shit-eating grin like he thought he had some kind of leverage here. Like he could scare me with consequences when I'd already lost everything I cared about. Then the question came again, sneaking into my head.

What would Celina do?

I nodded and looked over the water. "Fine."

Morales made a noise and turned toward the guys on top of the cliff, ready to carry out phase two of whatever bullshit he thought was coming next, until I added, "Arrest me."

"What?"

"Book me. I don't care. Prison sounds nice."

"You don't know what you're talking about. A little thing like you? They'd eat you."

I grinned now. "Let's hope."

"Coronavirus is everywhere. It's running rampant in prisons."

"We all gotta go sometime."

He kept talking, and the more he tried to scare me, the more I knew how much he had riding on this. Men. They were always giving themselves away.

"Trust me, you're not going to get another offer like this. You're looking at twenty to thirty years if you turn this down."

I sat on top of one of the picnic tables and pretended to think. "And if I do it?"

"We'll get it down to five. Maybe even nothing."

"What about Celina Kendrick?"

"What about her?"

In the search of Sam's property, they'd found Celina's body. I'd held my breath for a week, obsessively tracking any hint of coverage, waiting for the story of her sacrifice to surface, for people to know what she'd done. But there was nothing. Days went by, then weeks. A local paper mentioned that her body had been returned to her family in New Orleans. Two sentences buried underneath a page of 4H announcements and they didn't even bother saying her name. *Local restaurant worker's body returned to family.* That was it.

"I want Sam Olson charged with her death. I want the world to know what happened to her and why she died."

Morales crossed to the opposite side of the picnic table. "DAs hate posthumous trials. They won't go near 'em."

A movement caught my eye in the woods at the cliff's edge overlooking the water. I thought it was an animal until it moved again. Terrance. He crouched behind a tree, watching me even as he seemed poised for flight, like the drawing this morning. The white bird.

"An affidavit, then. A public record of everything that happened."

"You willing to provide one?"

I nodded and took the jagged rock out of my pocket, laying it on the table between us. Morales stared at the rock for a beat, digesting it, before offering his hand.

"Deal."

Max

"I don't see why it has to be you."

Shelley paced the kitchen, jerking cupboard doors open and closed, a whirlwind of pent-up frustration.

"Why not me?"

I sat at the table drinking coffee and scrolling the headlines, which seemed to get worse every day. For the last six months, Covid-19 had shut down the world and every new day brought a fresh horror waiting to pounce from the top stories banner. I went to work in a mask and sat at a desk six feet apart from everyone around me. One-way arrows marked the routes I had to walk to the bathroom, interview rooms, and evidence rooms. Offenders got their temperatures checked during booking. It was a whole new world.

Shelley mixed something in a bowl at the counter, watching me without watching me. She'd lived another kind of nightmare for the past six months. While I had no choice but to be in public, risking exposure to the virus every day, she'd been furloughed from her job at the school and had spent the rest of the spring as an unpaid teacher for Garrett. Seventh-grade science experiments and half-completed algebra papers littered the house. She caught him spending most of his Zoom class time playing a Game Boy underneath his desk, and had resorted to ordering a locking steel cabinet from Amazon that she called screen jail.

By the time summer came, she'd given up and I couldn't blame her. I came home most days to find Garrett on his Xbox, talking to a friend through headphones while Shelley read a book or watched Netflix in the same pajamas I'd seen her in that morning. I didn't know if either of them were showering. The house had a rank, overused odor, like a squatter's den. We took walks as a family, wandering through streets in the neighborhood we'd never been down before, because *before* there were too many other things to do. Activities, appointments, tournaments, parties. The drone of suburban family life. All of that vanished, leaving an incredible silence behind.

In June, everything changed again. The death of George Floyd at the hands of the Minneapolis police sparked social justice protests around the world. Signs sprung up on every other lawn in the neighborhood. BLACK LIVES MATTER. BLUE LIVES MATTER. THANK YOU, FIRST RESPONDERS. DEFUND THE POLICE. The ICPD cruiser in our driveway became a lightning rod of outrage and emotion. The movements swelled and pitted everyone against each other. It felt like a poised battlefield, violence waiting to happen.

Our yard stood blank, filled with only the same overgrown grass and tired mulch I should've changed this spring. They'd passed out ALL LIVES MATTER signs in the department but mine was stuffed behind a stack of rakes in the garage. I couldn't make myself put it up. I saw the profiling, the videos of police violence, and I couldn't endorse any of that. But I'd also lived the hundreds of encounters those officers had experienced before the videos, the daily assault of dealing with people at their worst moments, and I knew what those incidents had done to them. So our yard remained silent, choking with weeds, and we stopped taking our neighborhood walks.

We drove to new places instead. Quarries, lakes, reserves. Trips to the Devonian Fossil Gorge were the highlight of our weeks now, and we'd gone so many times I could identify the *Hexagonaria* from the horn coral.

"Can you imagine?" Shelley had picked her way from rock face to rock face last night. "This was all a shallow, tropical sea two hundred million years before dinosaurs were even here."

Garrett made a dismissive, intrinsically thirteen-year-old noise before catching my look and amending it to a bored "Wow."

Trees ringed the exposed rock that spilled down the side of a hill like petrified rapids. Groups of people, mostly families, gathered in clusters over the expanse, carefully keeping their distance from each other. Shelley pulled Garrett to another spot to show him something else he wasn't interested in. I moved to the edge of an outcropping and stared at the impression of a brachiopod, a crescent-shaped creature with shells that spread out in butterfly-like wings, smooth and perfect almost four hundred million years later. It was such a tiny thing, inconsequential to the world even when it was alive, yet it looked whole, complete, in a way that jabbed right into the widening cracks of my composure.

I kept it together for Shelley and Garrett, acting like everything was fine even when a neighbor accused me of covering up police brutality. I told them we would be okay even as the governor lifted all restrictions on mass gatherings, spouting sound bites on freedom and liberty, and our case counts rose higher every day. I pretended

I was sleeping at night despite my lifelong dance with insomnia, making me pace the house at 2:00 a.m. as the damaged nerves in my arm sent erratic pain signals to my brain, my nervous system screaming warnings about all the wrong things. Every day it got a fraction harder, wore me down a little more. I felt like I was splitting apart, and this year was barely half over.

I'd gotten a few chunks of sleep last night and thought it would be a good day. A *new* day. Something I hadn't had in six months. But I couldn't just walk out of the house and not tell Shelley why this day was different. She was still stuck here, riding the same pandemic loop that oscillated between brain fogging tedium and shocks of fight-or-flight apocalyptic news. So I told her my news.

Last week, Agent Santiago Morales from the DEA called and offered me a position on a multiagency task force. He was putting together a team to shut down the last of the Belgrave drug trafficking operation and he wanted me on it.

"You already have a job," Shelley said, ladling batter onto a griddle.

"It's all cleared with Larsen." He'd approved my participation before Morales even approached me. With our current unofficial scale down in policing and arrests, the investigations department had been slow all summer and the mood around the station was tense, everyone braced for the next law enforcement scandal and wave of protests, hoping it wouldn't hit too close to us even as we absorbed fallout from across the country. When I got the call from Morales, I felt a chug of adrenaline—of anticipation—for the first time in months. I'd almost forgotten what it felt like to look forward to something, to have a brand-new investigation in front of me like a feast of questions and possibilities.

What I hadn't forgotten was Matthew Moore's murder. I'd unknowingly watched the steady drip of fentanyl seeping into his veins, arresting his heart and any more answers he could provide. The killer—the fake orderly I'd spotted in the hospital that day—had never been caught. Then the pandemic hit, and the world turned upside down.

The DEA was back now, which meant something had shifted in the case—a new player maybe or another bust—and they wanted my help. I said yes almost before Morales finished talking.

"What are you going to do on this task force?"

"Whatever they tell me to."

Shelley's jaw started working, which happened when she was deciding between staying quiet or telling me what she really thought. Her hair was tied up on top of her head, a brown, curly mess with pieces falling around her face. She'd gotten some gray hair over the years and a few wrinkles that she fussed over in the mirror at night, but she was still beautiful, prettier than any wife on the block. Those dark doe eyes that drew me across a crowded bar almost twenty years ago could still break me with a look. She kept them down now, refusing to look at me as she flipped the pancakes.

The bathroom door slammed down the hall, which meant Garrett was up. Our time to have this conversation was running short.

"Say it."

But she didn't. I got up and refilled both our coffee cups, emptying the carafe and rinsing it out one-handed in the sink. We stood a foot apart and the only noises in the kitchen were the clunk of aging water pipes and the slap of a spatula against a plate.

"That," she finally said, pointing to the sink.

I followed her gaze, trying to figure out what she meant.

"You still don't use your left hand if you can help it."

I put the carafe upside down in the drying rack and turned to her.

"I can see the pain on your face, even when you try to hide it. Every time I wake up in the night and you're not there—"

"Shelley—"

In the bathroom the toilet flushed. The sink turned on and off for less than two seconds. A teenage handwashing.

"You've been shot twice in the last year. Twice, Max."

"Third time's a charm."

She pushed me until I bumped into the counter. "That's not funny."

I took her by the shoulders, deliberately using both hands, and bent my head to hers. "I promise you I will not get shot again."

"You don't know what's going to happen. No one knows. The schools are reopening even though the case counts keep going up. I have to go back to work or I'll lose my job, and it's not like I can just quit. We need the money. Garrett's going to be in classes all day with kids who may or may not be wearing masks depending on their idiot parents. And you're going off to hunt drug traffickers. God."

"Come here." I pulled her in and wrapped my arms around her, ignoring the pain that shot like sparks of low-grade electricity up my arm into my shoulder. She buried her face in my chest, smashing her hair against my mouth. I could feel her body shaking, could feel the big gasping breaths she took against my shirt, which made me feel like an even bigger jerk.

Because I was excited for this.

Because I needed it.

Garrett walked into the room with a screen in hand, glancing up as he slouched toward the table. "Gross."

Shelley turned away and wiped her eyes.

"Shelley—"

"We'll talk later."

"No, it's—the pancakes are burning." Smoke started billowing from the griddle, where the batter had gone from bubbling to black. I tossed the pancakes into the trash and stared at the scorched outlines left on the pan, the impression of things ruined and gone. And for a moment—with another sleepless pandemic night behind me and the task force looming ahead—it felt like I was back in the fossil gorge with the brachiopod, a tiny life caught between forces infinitely larger than itself.

Kara

Iowa City had changed. The town should've been bursting with college students swarming the dorms, coffee shops, and clubs. Traffic should've been a nightmare. Townies bitching, campus buildings coming to life, cards swiping in every store, summer midriffs on full display. It should've been chaos, a full-on starting line mood.

We drove through the empty streets of downtown. The stores were dark. The ped mall, with its cobblestone streets where I'd laundered Sam a fortune through a thrift shop called Find and Consign, had trash blowing through it. Two kids played on benches while a woman sat nearby, scrolling her phone.

"Is the university closed?"

"Mostly online, I heard."

Morales sat next to me in the back seat of an unmarked car. He'd barely let me out of his sight for the last two days as we crossed the border and headed south to Iowa. He hadn't brought up the DEA operation or the "troubling developments," and I hadn't asked. Instead, we stopped at every curbside taco place, food truck, and donut shop between Two Harbors and Iowa City.

"Gotta support the restaurants," he said before demolishing a gyro and immediately savaging the quality of it like a feral Yelp reviewer. He was loud but he wasn't wrong. The falafel tasted like cardboard.

We passed a few pedestrians in masks, a few others standing six feet apart. The city looked apocalyptic, dead. What would Celina have thought of this? Would things have been easier or harder for her with the misery shut away and out of sight?

We picked someone up at a hotel—another officer, probably—and doubled back to the east. I didn't know where we were going, but my stomach clenched when we passed a boxy diner with an orange roof.

The Village Inn.

The place where I'd met Celina.

It had been later in the fall then, the nights longer, the air cooler. I'd passed the diner dozens of times without a thought of going in. I had a flavor bias. Give me spicy pad Thai or street tacos with lime wedges piled on the side. Greasy hangover food was not my thing. But one night I woke up two hours early for a scheduled 6:00 a.m. drop. I felt itchy for something. I couldn't fall back asleep, and I didn't feel like drawing or driving around or studying alone in my apartment. The only things open in Iowa City at 4:00 a.m. were a few donut shops or the Village Inn.

The last pack of after-bar frat bros were stumbling out when I got there, leaving the place pretty much empty. A few stoned guys dug into pancake stacks in one booth and a girl on the opposite wall nursed a carafe over a pile of textbooks. As far as company went, it was perfect.

"What can I get you?"

The server appeared without warning, smiling like she knew she'd caught me off guard.

"Uhh." I glanced at the menu stupidly. "Jalapeño poppers and coffee. Hot sauce, too, if you have it."

"Sriracha?"

"Sure."

I opened my textbook on genetic disorders. It was Sam's idea, me going to school. He said I couldn't run drugs all my life and had set me up at the thrift shop so I'd have easy access to campus. I took the tuition money, knowing there was another reason. With Sam, there was always a plan, even if you didn't know it yet. The thrift shop was a front to launder money. Maybe he thought it looked good having a student run the place. Maybe he wanted something else, but I was willing to play along.

I had no idea how much I'd like college. I took whatever classes I wanted—art, gym, science—and didn't give a fuck when advisors tried to make me choose a major. This was the first semester I'd taken genetics and it was weirdly comforting to read all the ways DNA could mutate and fail. I felt quantified, less alone.

The server brought my food out, topped up my coffee, and pulled a bottle of sriracha out of her apron.

"Can I get you anything else?" The way she said it was low and warm, almost musical, and my gaze snagged on hers.

"I'm good."

Her hair was long and black, framing white skin and pale blue eyes that lingered on me with a clear and fully present gaze. Twenty, maybe twenty-one, and definitely not a customer of Sam's. She was tall and sharply curved, like some benevolent Botticelli vampire working the graveyard at the Village Inn.

"Celina." She smiled and tapped a midnight blue fingernail to her name tag. "Call me if you need anything."

Something turned over in my gut as I watched her go, a flush of blood and nerves I tried to ignore. It had been a few months since my last hookup. That's all it was. But I kept stealing glances at her. Celina. It was a good, benevolent vampire name, a name to whisper in the dark. Around 5:00, a few anchorless old men drifted in, ordering eggs and coffee as they read their newspapers alone. Celina lingered at each of their booths, asking questions that told me they were all regulars and touching them on their shoulders before moving to the next table. I tried to focus on my reading assignment and not stare like some creep. The night was turning. It was almost time to get the drop, the week's cash I would funnel through the thrift shop, making it shiny and new.

"*Genetic Diseases Associated with Protein Glycosylation Disorders in Mammals,*" Celina read over my shoulder, making me jump. "Sorry."

She didn't look sorry.

"Yeah. Fun stuff."

"Premed?"

"No, I just find the biosynthesis fascinating."

"Fascinating." She repeated, looking at me, not the book.

"I mean, how our bodies function, how a microscopic, instantaneous fertilization decision can drive the makeup of an entire life."

I didn't know why I was telling her this. It was more than I talked to most people, but there was something about this girl, her flare of sudden and genuine interest. Was it genuine? Maybe I was just another old man to her, another shot at a decent tip. But before

I could say anything to save the moment, she spun the textbook away from me and started paging through it.

"It doesn't make sense, does it? That something so trivial, so tiny, could be the center of our entire identities. Like, aren't we more than peptides and proteins?" She looked at me like I had the answer.

"There's hot sauce, too. At least in my case." I grinned and she answered with a smile that made my mouth go dry. We looked at each other a beat too long, two beats too long.

"Does it say anything about neurological disorders?" Her eyes cut back to the book and she seemed flustered for the first time. I wanted to lean in and inhale it.

"Tons." Did she have a genetic disorder? Maybe we actually had something in common. The thought made me sit up straighter. "What are you looking for?"

A call from the cook interrupted us and Celina left to grab an order. The cook eyed me as he handed it through the window, saying something that made Celina laugh. That white skin flushed red and she refused to look at me as she delivered a side of hash browns to one of the newspaper guys. I turned back to the book and told my heartbeat to chill the fuck out.

After that, the section got busy with a breakfast crowd. I didn't have time for her to circle back, even though every single nerve in my body begged me to wait. I couldn't be late for the drop. I tossed two twenties on the table and left.

Two weeks. That's how long I lasted before going back to the Village Inn, although I could only take credit for a week and a half. I started driving through the parking lot at 3:00 a.m., looking through the windows for Celina's slash of dark hair and speeding off as soon as I spotted someone else hauling trays.

She beamed when she saw me walk in, pulling a bottle of sriracha out of her apron and setting it by my elbow. She remembered me.

"Hi."

She grinned and tipped her head to the side. "Couldn't get enough of those jalapeño poppers?"

We talked for hours. I pulled out my textbook at one point and we looked up neurological disorders—she was vague on which one she was actually interested in—while she leaned against the back of the booth, her hip grazing my arm. I doodled birds in the margins while she waited on other tables, realizing too late that she was wearing feather earrings and might think the drawings were about her. Which they were, I guessed, but I wasn't going to make it weird by admitting it.

The same old men wandered in at the same time, good as clocks. One of them had a walker and struggled to get into his booth. Celina helped him, chatting quietly as she braced his shoulders and eased him onto the vinyl seat. His face was pinched with pain. After he finally got settled, her eyes snapped closed and her head bowed slightly, like she was saying a prayer for him. She looked different when she came back to my booth, paler. She moved more carefully.

"You okay?"

"I'm fine." Her voice didn't sound fine. It sounded like she'd just taken a punch. I wanted to reach out, to do something to help her. "Just a headache."

I'd never had a headache. I imagined it was like waking up when everything feels distorted, but a distortion that wrapped around every thought and movement. Or maybe like nails were driving through your skull. But I wouldn't know what that felt like, either, not even if someone hammered them into my head.

"Pretty." She nodded at the sparrow I'd drawn, barely more than a few thin, quick lines. "There's a place by my apartment, on the river, where the birds swarm every morning like they're having a street market. I walk down sometimes after my shift."

"Yeah?" I didn't know what she was asking.

As she reached for my empty plate, our hands brushed. Celina didn't pull away. She looked at me strangely.

"That's weird." She brushed a finger along the back of my hand, and I felt the touch climb up my arm and spread heat through my entire body. "My headache's gone."

"I'm glad." Our voices had dropped to murmurs, barely audible above the pumped music.

"They never disappear so soon." She continued to brush a finger over my hand, and it took all my energy to stay still. "It must be you, making me feel better."

That couldn't be right. I didn't make anyone feel better, not in my whole life. But I smiled and said, "I'm actually sentient aspirin."

"My dream match." Our gazes locked and held and she gave me a small, shy smile. "Are you doing anything around six thirty? That's when my shift ends. We could go see the birds."

I wanted to wander along the river with Celina more than anything, to find out everything about her, to invent reasons to touch her and watch the sunrise light up her face. I imagined a whirlwind of birds over the water, the calls and cries and flurry of beaks and wings, and being caught up in it together. But Sam hovered at the edge of the scene along with all the reasons I couldn't afford to allow anyone into my world. Maybe this was what a headache felt like, the crashing of two things that couldn't exist in the same place.

The crashing sensation hit me again in the back of the DEA's car, driving through this city that was soaked in memories of Celina. It was a pain I couldn't breathe around, couldn't medicate. Every road led somewhere we'd been: a movie theater, a park, someplace where she'd laughed and slipped her hand in mine like she knew it belonged there. A lifetime of ghosts packed into a few months, and it all started with that doomed morning when I'd sat in a vinyl booth at the Village Inn and told her yes.

I slid further down in my seat, wanting to wrap myself around memories of Celina and being destroyed by them at the same time. Crashing again and again.

We pulled into the Coral Ridge Mall parking lot. Celina and I had talked about going here once—she'd wanted to ice-skate at their indoor rink—but it had been a holiday weekend. She always got more headaches in crowds, so we never went. Now the lot was practically empty. Only a few people walked in or out. The ones in bandannas and masks side-eyed the ones without.

"What are we doing here?"

"Welcome to headquarters." The agents got out and waited for me to follow. Morales handed me a surgical mask.

"At the mall?"

"Lot of ways in and out here. And you won't look suspicious coming to shop."

I looped the mask over my ears and pulled my hat down further, slouching into my hoodie. If I had a pair of sunglasses, I'd be completely anonymous, nothing but the gray outline of a blank avatar.

Morales waved across the asphalt. "Let's meet the team."

Max

The Coral Ridge Mall, like all malls in this country, had already been through the apocalypse. Malls were huge when I was a kid. There weren't a lot of them in Iowa to start with, so they felt like Disneyland whenever we made the trip with my parents or friends. I'd spent hours pumping quarters into arcade machines and hanging out at food courts. In the last two decades, though, the internet had pushed brick-and-mortar shopping complexes to the brink of extinction. And I got why. Like any sane person, I preferred to shop from my couch, buy something with a few clicks, and have it show up at my door two days later. No gas, salespeople, or pants required.

Entire YouTube channels were dedicated to abandoned malls now, recording footage of dark, cavernous spaces left to the elements like discarded children's toys. Coral Ridge Mall—the closest thing Coralville had to a downtown—had fared better than some. I walked through the mall corridors, masked and taking in the aging building. There were still chain stores here, advertising sales discounts and BOGOs next to their Covid policies and hand sanitizer stations. The pretzel place pumped out the same soapy steam smell while the kids behind the counter chewed on their masks and surfed their phones. But there was a jadedness to the empty storefronts and cracked floor tiles, an air of knowing where this pandemic would lead.

The task force headquarters was sandwiched in an empty storefront between a clothing store and a jewelry place. There were two ways in: either the storefront glass doors that were papered over with COMING SOON! signs, or a steel door in the back off a locked corridor for authorized employees only. I took the employee entrance and walked into a storage room full of masked people, folding chairs, and a complicated tech setup sprawling over shelves probably meant for retail inventory.

"Summerlin." Agent Morales saluted me from the front with a half-eaten soapy-smelling pretzel. I hadn't seen him in person since the day of the weigh station incident, but he looked the same. Big, tan, as imposing by sheer girth and volume as by rank. His mask dangled from his ear while he ate and started introductions. I was ten minutes early but the last to arrive.

Everyone introduced themselves by name, title, and home office. The two sitting closest to Morales were both DEA. They had the rumpled, unwashed look of being constantly on the road. The woman, Olson, was tech and the man, Grimes, said he was resources, whatever that meant. Behind them was a Des Moines investigator named Meyers I'd met briefly after Matthew Moore's murder and an Iowa state trooper named Pyle, who seemed ready to clap back at any Gomer references. A young woman in the back sat apart from everyone else, making no move to join the introductions.

My attention snagged on her. She leaned back in her folding chair, arms crossed and legs sprawled. Small and wiry, almost the same build as Garrett, she wore baggy clothes and a hoodie with no official designation I could find. The sides of her head were shaved and the hair on top swooped tall and dark over half her face. I could only see one of her heavily lined eyes over her mask, cataloging each person in the room with bored calculation.

When it was my turn, her attention turned to me, and the slight shift revealed the edge of a tattoo at her neck. It was some kind of plant or vine. She didn't blink, holding my stare until I looked away.

"Investigator Max Summerlin with Iowa City PD. I've been on the force fifteen years, investigations for eight."

"Don't stop there." Morales chucked his napkin and pulled his mask back on. "This is the officer who single-handedly busted Belgrave's semitruck shipment last December. Twenty-two million in street value and a few dead traffickers who won't be clogging up the penal system."

Nods and noises of approval came from around the room. "Nice work, man," someone said. It was hard to tell with everyone masked. The girl's boredom evaporated. I couldn't read her expression with so much of her face covered, but it wasn't congratulatory.

"All right, let's get rolling." Morales flipped on the largest screen and the DEA's logo appeared center stage in front of us. "Any questions before we tear into the meat of it?"

I raised a finger, still feeling the girl's gaze on me like a knife. "Why are we meeting here?"

He smiled, and even though his mask stretched wide, something more than good humor lit his eyes. "That would be due to the makeup of this particular task force. We have an informant with us who'll be our man on the inside for a key part of this operation. Kara?"

Kara Johnson. I whipped around to see her chin jerk up once. She didn't offer a single word to the roomful of law enforcement. I'd searched databases for this woman for months, trying to find out more about the college student/drug trafficker who'd helped save Jonah in that barn. But there was nothing. Other than her student records at UI, her past was as blank as her present. Wherever she'd disappeared to after December hadn't popped her up on a single radar as far as I could tell. Somehow, though, Morales had tracked her down.

"Obviously, Kara can't be seen going in and out of a police station or government building. This place has multiple entrances and exits and enough activity, even now, that she should be able to navigate check-ins here without raising suspicion. Speaking of check-ins . . ."

As Morales laid out the schedule for task force meetings, I stared at Kara Johnson. She shifted the hair out of her face and met my look head-on. Someone asked another question; I didn't hear what. This wasn't what I expected when I agreed to this assignment. I thought I'd be working with a team of like-minded investigators, cutting through the red tape and politics, tuning out the chaos of 2020 and focusing on questions we could actually answer. Arresting people like Kara Johnson, not sharing coffee with them. She might have had a moment of conscience in that barn, but that didn't mean she was someone who could be trusted. She could run again or turn on us. She'd already turned at least once. And there was another problem. I'd promised Shelley I wouldn't get shot again, and the people around Kara Johnson tended to end up with holes in them.

Morales cued up a video recording and I forced my attention back to the front. The monitor showed footage of a hospital hallway. The officer posted outside one of the rooms was the same one who'd been assigned to Matthew Moore.

"The perpetrator comes from the direction of the nurses' station. He obtained the fentanyl drip from the outside—our lab confirmed that—but he wanted to make it look like he was legit."

The man appeared. He was in profile and the footage was too grainy to make out eye color, but he was definitely white with light brown hair. A few inches shorter than the officer who stood up to let him in the room. Slim build. I jotted notes in a fresh notebook.

"He spends a little under five minutes inside"—Morales fast-forwarded—"more time than he needed to hook up the IV. Maybe he was looking through the room or talking to Moore. We're not gonna know now. Here he comes again."

The door opened and the man said something to the officer before walking directly underneath the camera. In a few seconds I would pass him in the hallway on my way to interview Matthew Moore and dismiss him just like everyone else in the ward.

"The nurses were having a shift change meeting when the perp administered the lethal dose of fentanyl. They said those meetings generally took between five and ten minutes and most if not all nurses in the ward would be present to review patient status and hand off assignments." Morales looked around at us. "Which means he knew that in advance. He'd been watching the ward, memorized the schedule, and knew exactly how much time he'd have alone with Matthew Moore."

Planner, I wrote under the physical description. *Will be hard to surprise.*

Morales flipped to a different shot, this one of the main hospital entrance. The man had gotten rid of the surgical gloves and mask and added a ball cap. He kept his head down, scrolling on a phone as he left the building. Morales froze the footage before he disappeared from the frame.

"Kara?"

Everyone turned to the back of the room. Kara perused the screen like she was checking her nails. Casual, killing time. "Haven't worked with him."

It was the first time she'd spoken, and her voice was just as hard and dismissive as I expected.

"Do you recognize him?" Olson, one of the DEA agents, asked.

She shook her head. "Not one of Sam's as far as I know."

She called him Sam, not Belgrave. I was taking notes on Kara, too, but these I kept in my head.

Morales pressed her on it. He was obviously counting on Kara to give him some info on this guy, but she shrugged.

"I didn't know everybody. Sam liked to keep us all in our own lanes, but when it came to stuff like this"—her voice strained and she paused, so quickly I wondered if anyone else noticed it—"he either gave it to Ash or he handled it personally."

Ash was Russell Ash, the one who'd ended his own life at the weigh station. I knew of at least one person he'd killed, a young woman who stored drugs for local dealers. If Russell Ash had been the unofficial hit man of Belgrave Operations, that could explain why he hadn't wanted to stand trial.

"That happened months ago, right?" Kara asked, her first show of interest in anything Morales was saying.

"December 22," I replied.

She didn't acknowledge that I'd spoken.

"You said there'd been some troubling developments." She mimicked Morales's booming tenor. "That stuff with Moore is from the before times. Older than Covid."

I couldn't imagine distilling a man's murder, no matter what he'd done, into "that stuff." I didn't particularly care for Matthew Moore. He'd taken every advantage in his life—a good career, a caring family—and wasted it for lies and money. But the way Kara Johnson spoke set my teeth on edge. The more she slouched, the taller I sat. I didn't trust her long enough to take my eyes off her.

"We don't know who hired Matthew Moore's murder, but it has every characteristic of a professional hit. We followed as many leads as we could, but nothing came of it and the perpetrator vanished. Until three weeks ago."

The screen switched from the frozen frame at the hospital to what was clearly a crime scene photograph, and this one wasn't grainy at all.

The photo had been taken in a living room where a brown sectional sofa took up most of the space. A ficus stood off to the side and the wall behind the couch was decorated with white framed photos in all shapes and sizes. In the middle of the room, the remains of a coffee table stood surrounded by glass shards and scattered magazines. A woman's body was shoved through the iron frame, vertebrae twisted so her bottom half faced the ceiling while her head and shoulders turned toward the wall. Her arms stretched along the carpet like she'd tried to claw away from the bed of broken glass. Dark blood covered her fingers. Lacerations crisscrossed her arms, her stomach below her shirt, and her head, but she would have survived that. The cause of death was obvious: a gaping wound that opened her throat.

She must have been found within a few hours. Decomp hadn't set in. My gut clenched when I registered her face. "That's the air traffic controller from Iowa City."

She'd diverted Jonah and Eve's plane last December, sending them into Belgrave's hands, and disappeared before anyone realized she was working for him.

"Gail."

Kara's eyes flashed with something before dropping from the screen.

"She was found in a trailer park in Missouri on July 29. Her next-door neighbors remember a man visiting her a few hours before she was discovered. White, light brown hair, medium height, slim build. He was alone. When we showed them the footage from the hospital, witnesses confirmed. The same person who killed Matthew Moore also killed Gail Whitaker." Morales paused, letting the image sink into the room. "Someone is ordering hits on the people who worked for Sam Olson, aka Belgrave. One by one, they're being taken out."

Kara got up and went to a counter where a coffee machine and box of rolls were lying out. She chose a donut covered in cereal, pulled off her mask, and bit into it, chewing as she stared at the screen.

"Why?" the Des Moines investigator asked.

"Given the timelines of both hits, we believe the killer was trying to get something from both victims."

My spine straightened as a memory pinged through my head. "When I visited Matthew Moore, the killer had already come and gone. The first words he spoke to me were 'I don't know, I said.' Like he'd been telling someone that before. When he realized who I was, he seemed confused."

"Exactly," a DEA agent chimed in. "We believe the killer was looking for information, and Moore didn't have it."

"Why didn't he sound the alarm when the guy was in his room? He could've hit the call button for the nurses' station or yelled for the officer at his door," Meyers, the Des Moines investigator, said.

"Unless he didn't feel threatened." I stood up and started to pace behind the chairs. "If he was sleeping when the killer hooked up the lethal IV, he might not have known he was in any danger. He wakes up. The killer asks him some questions. He's been answering questions all week, might not even think anything of it. He answers, knowing he's got the officer right there as a security measure, and drifts off when the drugs start to kick in."

"The killer spent a longer amount of time with Gail." Morales flipped to another picture of the trailer, this one of a galley kitchen with a table at one end. Morales pointed to the table. "Two cups of half-drunk coffee. Two chairs pulled out. One cup and chair were wiped clean of prints, likely after the murder."

"So she didn't feel threatened either," Meyers added. "At least, not at first. Maybe she knew him?"

"Money."

We all looked around to where Kara sat on top of the counter, holding a coffee. She'd put the half-eaten donut back in the box. Her mask lay forgotten on the counter. If I thought I'd get a better read on her without half her face covered, I was wrong.

"Gail didn't do anything for free. The guy would've offered her cash in exchange for what he wanted."

"Which was what?" I asked, looking from Kara to Morales. The two of them sized each other up. Kara took a gulp of coffee and tipped her head like she was waiting out the punch line of a long and terrible joke. Morales flipped the screen to the next picture. This wasn't footage or a crime scene photo. It was the entire state, from Nebraska to Illinois, a blank and open map.

"We know Belgrave was getting out of the business. He'd cut ties with several key members of his operation and stopped shipping product into his usual markets. We believe the semitruck shipment Investigator Summerlin intercepted was an off-load of inventory to a new player, someone who was taking over his operation.

"That buyer, whoever they are, didn't get their product. Any additional shipments would have been dead in the water as soon as Belgrave died. We believe the hits are an attempt to locate the stranded product and the rest of Belgrave's infrastructure to revive his operation. With lockdowns and quarantines and people losing their jobs right and left, the number of drug-related deaths is second only to deaths from the virus. We're on track for a 30 percent spike in overdoses this year, and that's entirely fueled by opioids. We can't afford to let another Belgrave loose in Iowa.

"The mission of this task force is simple: find the rest of the drugs before this player does and stop him before he gets started."

As Morales handed out assignments—forensics, tech, etc.— Kara drained her coffee and dunked the cup in a nearby trash can. At least I understood her role now. She must've been familiar with all the places Belgrave stored his product. She was the one who'd emptied the stockpile at Earl Moore's farm. How many other caches would she lead us to? But when Morales said as much, she bristled.

"That's not why I'm here."

The room went quiet. Everyone turned.

"I'm bait." Kara pushed herself off the counter and faced the front of the room, legs spread, arms crossed, cocking an eyebrow at Morales. "You need me to draw this killer out, figure out who he works for."

"You have a problem with that?" Morales asked.

She shrugged. "Not as long as you have the balls to say it to my face."

"Then we're clear. Put your mask back on."

She did eventually, and Morales turned back to the rest of the group. "We'll need a primary on-the-ground liaison for Johnson. Someone to help her with resources and cover. Summerlin?" My head snapped around. "That's you."

Kara

Drug dealers and cops were two heads of the same animal. None of them would admit it, but it was true. Men waving their dicks around, thinking their lives were important because they were part of something bigger, that they had cred, rank, or whatever. The mood might land a little different—Morales called it a hit, where Sam always said we had to take care of someone; Morales recruited me to a task force, while Sam called me family—but in the end their languages boiled down to the same shit. They played out their war games and secretly loved them. No matter what they called themselves, which head of the animal they looked like, they were the same kind of men. They needed enemies to feel alive.

It got more and more clear as the meeting dragged on. A roomful of guys spouting credentials like they were whipping them out to measure. They dissected photos of Gail's dead body, barely containing their excitement.

I knew Gail as well as anyone did, which wasn't much. She'd directed shipments in and out of the Iowa City airport for years, but she didn't make friends. All her emotional energy was reserved for her fucking handbags. Gucci. Chanel. She liked hanging designers off her arm. One of those trailer park neighbors was having a great day selling all those bags on Poshmark.

But one thing was obvious: I wasn't here because they needed a man on the inside. All that bullshit about justice for Celina, publishing an affidavit to tell her story, was just to get me here. I was bait to trap the enforcer. If I died in the process, Morales would probably get a promotion. And Celina's story would die with me.

For the past year, I'd been trying to fit myself into the person Celina wanted me to be, knowing I should be dead and she should be alive. Wishing I could die for her. Hating myself. Hating her. Hating myself more. Even when I was working with Matthew to turn Sam in last winter, I always hoped I would die in the process. There was nothing driving me, nothing to look forward to, until now.

Heat seeped into my gut, filling my chest as I watched Morales dismiss his team of wannabe Avengers. It wasn't the warmth I felt for Celina, that spark of possibility, the breathlessness of knowing someone like her existed in the world. This was the other head of the same animal, a more familiar fire.

I would live through this. I'd bring the enforcer in and whoever had hired him and shove them into Morales's face until he released Celina's story to the world. I would make this asshat keep his promise.

Morales walked over to me as most of the others filed out. One of them, the Iowa City officer who'd been assigned to babysit me, hung back and pretended to get coffee.

"We've got a place for you to stay."

"I'll find my own, thanks."

"There's a car—"

"No."

He shoved a phone into my hands. "This is nonnegotiable. We need to get ahold of you."

"How do you know she's not going to skip town again?" The guy, Summerlin, stopped pretending to stir his coffee. He'd spent the whole meeting staring at me, taking notes like I was a suspect he was pissing himself to arrest. He wore khakis and a pristine white T-shirt. His head was freshly shaved, and his notebook gave off strong teacher's pet vibes.

"She's not leaving. We have something she wants." Morales grinned at me, stretching the mask across his face until the paper threatened to rip. "Don't we?"

I left without answering.

The house hadn't changed. It was only blocks from Mercy hospital and the sorority and frat houses northeast of downtown. I'd caught a bus to campus and walked from there, dropping the DEA's phone at a curbside takeaway window in a taco place. If I wanted it later, I could grab lunch at the same time.

The house was old, a cramped white box with a single-car garage and a concrete slab off to the side for extra parking. Cobwebs chilled in the corners of the doorframe and gnarled shrubs lined the foundation. A faded wood privacy fence enclosed the backyard, with leaves and vines curling over the top. The front windows were dark, with shades drawn. No cars were parked out front. It didn't look like anyone was home and nothing about the place invited anyone to come see. A crow perched on a nearby tree, waiting to see what I'd do. I circled the block twice before picking the fence gate latch and slipping into the backyard.

Green met me, green for days. An overgrown raspberry bush almost completely blocked the gate. I stepped around it, looking deeper into the yard. There was no grass back here, just dirt rows that snaked through an ocean of plants. It was more jungle than garden. Tomato cages hung from a rusted clothesline, making a curtain of vines and ripe fruit. Peppers grew everywhere, gleaming in every color from waxy white to red to almost black. Beans covered peeling trellises, and sunflowers shot up behind them, their faces eating up the sun. A giant bush with five-pointed leaves and weird red cones stood almost as tall as me. I skirted it, careful not to touch anything or breathe too deeply.

I picked my way toward the house until a noise behind the clothesline made me stop.

"Phyllis?"

No answer. I took another path, winding around a bush covered in fat black dots. I knew that one. Belladonna.

Phyllis Reed sat on a low stool with a pile of weeds at her feet. Somewhere between eighty and a hundred and fifty years old, Phyllis had a hooked nose and tight, wrinkled skin that looked like it had already started the mummification process, probably from smoking Winston Lights her entire life. She was shorter than me, with a narrow frame and breasts that sagged down to her potbelly. Her hair was set in steely curls that she always covered with a clear plastic tie-on hood when it rained.

When she saw me, her hand relaxed on the trowel she was holding, but the other one stayed hidden beneath an apron.

"The prodigal daughter returns."

I scoffed. "You know women are only chattel."

She laughed, one dry cackle, before easing her other hand out into plain sight. I didn't feel much safer.

"You got a minute?"

"That's anyone's guess." She picked up a rag and started methodically wiping off her tools, nodding to the open back door of the house. "Go on in."

I did a quick check of the main floor. Of the three bedrooms, only the one with a patchwork quilt over the bed and a stack of large-print paperbacks on the nightstand looked occupied. The room directly across from it had a giant padlock sealing the door shut. So many questions I wasn't going to ask.

There was one toothbrush in the bathroom, a cracked plastic cup on the sink, and denture cream sitting next to it. In the hallway, four framed and yellowing photos hung on the wood paneling. Three boys and a girl. The boys had Phyllis's beady eyes and all of them—tragically—got her large, hook-shaped nose. The rest of their features were a grab bag of unfortunate genetics. No one knew if Phyllis had ever been married and her kids were all dead or gone before I was even born. It was sort of horrifying to think of her as anyone's mother.

Once, when I called her Grandma P. after we first met, she stirred Carolina Reaper mash into my coffee. She didn't let on when I drank the rest of it, but I could feel her watching me, waiting for some reaction I wasn't giving. All I said was "This tastes weird" before finding the residue in the bottom of the cup. After that, we both recognized something in each other, an entirely different person underneath the veneer of what we looked like to everyone else. A college student. A grandmother. The surface assumptions we both used to every advantage. I learned to respect what she brought to the table. I never left food or drinks lying around her again either.

I waited for Phyllis in the kitchen, a tiny space with dark wood cupboards and wallpaper left over from the sixties. When she came in, it was with the speed and flexibility of a glacier. She practically flattened me against the wall to hang up her gardening apron.

"Not worried about the virus?"

She made a disgusted noise and turned on a burner with a teakettle sitting on it. "Been breathing longer than anyone wants to. If this is what gets me, it'll be a goddamn relief."

She pulled a few leaves out of the pocket of her faded floral housedress and took a knife from the block, slicing them into shreds and sprinkling them into a cup.

"Did you do it?"

I didn't have to ask what she meant. Sam was our mutual boss, the only reason we knew each other.

"No." I didn't kill Sam.

"But you turned on him. After he got rid of that girl of yours."

I didn't answer.

"I told him. I told him to get rid of you if he knew what he was doing. But he couldn't do it, could he?"

"I'm sure he could've."

She sniffed, a wheezy sound that might have been amusement. "Knew it would be him or you after that. It was only a matter of time."

The way she said it was how people talked about reality shows: all-knowing, smug on their couch. But maybe she cared more than she was letting on. She'd known Sam a lot longer than I had.

"Did you make any bets?"

"With who?" The teakettle started to shriek and she poured boiling water into the cup with the leaves, filling the room with an earthy scent I couldn't place. It was tangy, like licorice. "Can't cash a bet with a dead man."

"No renters this semester?"

Phyllis had retired from Sam's family, as much as anyone retires from a drug trafficking ring. She'd been in charge of the thrift store and the money-laundering operation until she couldn't handle the volume anymore and I took over. Phyllis taught me how to cook the books, how to move inventory around and keep a steady stream of people actually shopping at the store to make things look legit. After she was done downtown, she rented out her house to college kids and spent most of the year in Florida, only coming back in the summers to tend her massive garden.

"They're all home, taking classes on the internet. Can't say I mind not having to sift through the lot of them looking for a decent tenant. More of these idiot kids pour into town year after year, each one shittier than the last."

"That include me?"

She made a dismissive noise. "You know how shitty you are. They don't have a clue."

She drained her tea or whatever it was and pinned me with her beady gaze. "What are you doing here? Place is a ghost town."

"Boo."

She didn't crack a smile, just waited me out until I got to the point. "You know Sam was trying to retire, too. He was getting out of the business."

"He sure did."

"Who was he selling off to?"

"He wouldn't tell me something like that."

"But he trusted you." More than anyone else, by the end.

"Trust is a dangerous thing. It'll blind you and rip you in half as easy as love. Sam knew that. And still he couldn't bring himself to kill you." She looked me over like she was trying to see anything worth preserving.

"Sam didn't love me."

Outside the kitchen window, a group of sparrows flitted through the labyrinth of plants, wanting to land but unwilling at the same time. The scents and colors all wrapped together, confusing them with calls of food and warnings of death. I wanted to shoo them off, to make the decision for them and break them out of their scared, hovering loops.

"That's the kicker, isn't it?" Phyllis pushed away from the table, standing up with a concentrated effort, and went to rinse out her cup. "You never know the how or why of love. No reason behind most of it. If anyone else had betrayed Sam like you did with that girl, they'd be rotting in a hill somewhere. You know that as well as I do. But he let you live, and here we are." She tipped the cup into the drying rack and tied her gardening apron back on with knobby, gnarled hands. "There's no one in town far as I know. Or there wasn't until you showed up."

I followed her back into the garden. The sparrows hopped along the top of the fence, behind a bush covered in delicate umbrella sprays of white flowers. Hemlock.

"Gail's dead."

"Good for her." Phyllis worked her gloves back on, easing them over her fingers, and started picking peppers.

"Someone's taking out Sam's people one by one."

"That right?" She sounded like it was the first piece of good news she'd had all year.

"I need a room while I'm in town."

"A thousand a month, cash only. Another grand for the deposit."

"What is this, the Hilton?" I pulled a wad of hundreds out of my sports bra and counted out twenty. It was most of what I had on me.

"It's a pharmacy fundraiser. Sam's stuff was a goddamn bargain compared to CVS." She pocketed the bills without looking up. "Take the room next to the bathroom. There's a spare key hanging by the back door. All the other bedrooms are off-limits."

Like the giant padlock on one of them wasn't a hint. "This includes vehicle privileges."

"Not on Friday. I need my pickup for the farmers' market."

"Deal."

I tossed my duffel bag in the bedroom, grabbed the keys, and left through the front door. My front door, for the time being. The pickup in the garage was half-rusted and older than me. It smelled like dirt and cracked leather, the seats patched with duct tape. I fired it up as Phyllis's dry, crackly voice replayed on a loop in my head. *You never know the how or why of love.* That was the problem. I never understood what Celina saw in me, why she picked me. Or maybe I did and just didn't want to admit it.

What would she say about this operation? She was the one who'd convinced me to become an informant in the first place. But that was different, information passed through phone calls and anonymous tips. Now I was spearing myself on a hook and floating in the water, hoping to outsmart the sharks. And I had to. Because if I didn't, Celina's story would die with me.

The sparrows clustered on the side of the driveway, hopping and pecking at a patch of gravel. I threw the truck in reverse and sent them scattering into the air. They'd be back in Phyllis's poison garden soon. They couldn't help themselves.

Max

Shelley wanted to take dance classes before we got married. She had this vision of the two of us waltzing around the Best Western ballroom at our wedding reception, and no amount of logic could change her mind. I mastered the art of swaying back and forth to the beat at high school formals, and the two of us might have done the electric slide at a bar once, but watching *Dancing with the Stars* every week didn't qualify us as dancers. She wouldn't drop it, though, and eventually I gave in. For six weeks I cold-sweated a one-two-three, one-two-three around a middle school gymnasium, stepping on Shelley's feet as the teacher shouted instructions and randomly grabbed my hips to "correct my form." The first time she did it I went for my handcuffs, which I wasn't wearing. Shelley couldn't stop laughing.

My first day on the task force was going about as well as dance classes.

After the meeting broke up and the DEA agents settled into their computers, I pulled Morales over to the retail side of the store, where abandoned display stands and shelves were covered in dust.

The glass front of the store had been papered over, but that didn't shake the feeling that I was on display.

"Sir, I'm not comfortable with this assignment."

"We need someone on the ground for Johnson, someone who has an intimate knowledge of eastern Iowa. That's you."

The state trooper, Pyle, was based out of Cedar Rapids. I didn't see how I was any more of an eastern Iowa expert than him, but it seemed petty to point that out.

"I wasn't aware we were going to be working directly with Belgrave's people."

"Trust me, she's not connected with anyone who could harm this operation or the people on it. Everyone she worked for is dead."

"As far as we know."

Morales leaned against a checkout station and pulled at his mask, clearly irritated at having to wear it. "She's the best shot we have at uncovering the rest of Belgrave's stockpiles. I couldn't have gotten clearance to pull this team together before we tracked her down."

"Where was she?"

"Not far. She wanted to be found. Another point in our favor."

I paced the displays, listening to the agents in the other room talking strategy and parameters. That's where Shelley wanted me to be, tucked behind a computer, fighting crime from the safe distance of an office or courtroom.

"Is she right? About being bait?"

Morales considered me. "Would it matter if she was?"

I stopped and looked him in the eye. "No. But I need to know that going in. And I'm not interested in hanging on the hook with her."

"I looked over your record, Summerlin. That weigh station bust wasn't a one-off for you. You like being in the thick of it. And from what I understand, you have plenty of experience working with unusual characters."

My jaw clenched. Larsen must have told the DEA about Jonah. I'd gotten used to being the department joke, the cop with a psychic best friend, and I'd only felt like more and more of an outsider as 2020 unfolded. I'd wanted to be something different on this task force, to feel like I was part of a team, but apparently I was an outlier no matter where I went.

"Get her resources and cover, and put the pieces together if she can't or won't. Watch your six. If this killer makes a move, I'm counting on you to help bring him in."

I nodded. "Understood. And, sir?" I stopped him as he turned toward the back room. "If I get shot again, my wife's coming after you personally."

He barked out a laugh and slapped me on my bad shoulder, sending nerves screaming up and down my arm.

I didn't trust Kara Johnson. Everything about her made the hair stand up on the back on my neck. But Morales wasn't asking me to put my faith in a drug trafficker; he was asking me to trust him. And whether or not my history with Jonah was the subject of interagency briefings, he was giving me the opportunity to do exactly what I craved. Find answers. Put this operation in the ground before it could be revived.

Resources and cover. That was my assignment, with one small problem: Kara Johnson had already vanished.

She didn't answer the phone Morales had given her—voice or text—and I tracked the GPS on it to a taco stand northeast of downtown. The owner hadn't seen her and couldn't tell me which way she'd gone. Great. Thirty minutes into my assignment and I was already failing.

I refused to contact Morales or my department. This woman was not shaking me, not after only my first hour on the job. I ordered some carnitas to go and canvassed the neighborhood. It was mostly residential, tucked away from the main roads, and the longer I drove, the more convinced I was Kara Johnson was nearby. If she really hadn't wanted to keep the phone, she could've tossed it in a garbage can in the mall. No, I was betting she left it somewhere she could access if she needed to. Morales said she wanted to be found, and it looked like she wanted to be able to find us, but on her terms.

I parked at the edge of a lot near Mercy hospital and watched cars pass as I jotted down Kara Johnson's résumé.

1. Drug trafficker.
2. Money launderer.
3. Student at UI. Implicated in affair with Matthew Moore, which turned out to be bogus but still got him suspended from the university.
4. Relationship with Celina Kendrick, which ended in Celina's abduction and death.
5. Turned on boss to save Jonah's and Eve's lives, then disappeared.

It was bare bones but enough to confirm one thing: Kara Johnson invited chaos. If anyone could draw a hired killer out into the open, it was probably her.

I put the notebook away and tried not to think what Shelley would say about any of this. The less she knew about this assignment, the better.

A rusty Dodge pickup sputtered out of the taco stand neighborhood and I caught enough of a glimpse of the person driving it to feel a surge of vindication. I hadn't lost Kara Johnson after all.

Pulling out a few cars behind the Dodge, I tailed it into downtown. She parked on a side street near the library and strolled toward the ped mall. She'd ditched the hoodie and the duffel bag she'd had earlier and was wearing a tank top and light-wash jeans. There weren't a lot of people out, but the ones she passed took note of the tattooed girl with the partially shaved head. She clearly wasn't hiding.

I followed at a distance, even though she never once checked her back. She paused in front of the empty storefront that housed the thrift store where she'd worked. In any other year the space would have already found a new tenant—a café or shop or bar—but with Covid practically closing the university, the ped mall was on life support, too. An anemic stream of people wandered warily down the cobblestone. Kara unlocked the storefront door and slipped inside.

Was there a drug cache here? I stiffened. The DEA had seized the entire contents of the store last winter. They would've found anything on the property. But the longer I stood outside, the less certain I became. Morales had brought Kara in because she had inside information. The DEA might have missed something.

She'd left the door unlocked and I opened it as quietly as I could. An AC condenser hummed somewhere in the building, but it was still hot as a sauna. The windows were covered, leaving the space in total darkness, and I waited for my eyes to adjust before moving further inside.

I hadn't taken two steps before something caught me in the kneecap and I went sprawling. I rolled up, automatically grabbing for the holster I wasn't wearing as light flooded the room. Kara Johnson stood next to the door, arms crossed.

"What are you doing?" She looked unsurprised to see me.

"Babysitting recalcitrant felons. You?"

"You're going to scare off your killer if you tail the bait everywhere. You want that, Captain America?"

I got up slowly, keeping plenty of distance between us. "Technically he's going to be *your* killer, and you can call me Max."

Her mouth twitched, but the stony expression she'd worn for most of the task force meeting chased it away. "Get fucked, Max."

"Visiting old haunts?"

She snorted and moved through empty clothing racks. Today was all about gutted retail establishments, apparently.

"We need to talk."

"No we don't."

She disappeared into the back room and I gave her a cautious amount of space, monitoring her noises as I looked around the front of the store. Every fixture was stripped and even the ceiling tiles had been ripped off and stacked in one corner. The DEA would've brought dogs through here, and it looked like they'd searched every inch of the place, but when Kara reappeared she was carrying a miniature backpack covered in dust and debris. Something they clearly hadn't found.

"What's that?"

"Personal effects."

She tossed it on the counter and nodded, daring me to search it. It held some prepaid Visa cards, a USB drive, a thousand dollars in cash, a Ziploc bag of underwear and toiletries, and a notebook half filled with drawings and columns of numbers that were mostly scratched out.

"Off-the-books books?" I asked, swiveling the notebook page toward her.

She wiped the bag on her pants and repacked it before shrugging it on. "Sam always told me to keep bug-out bags, to be ready to disappear." She looked like there was more to it than that but didn't add anything else.

"Were there drugs here?"

She shook her head. "This place was clean. Strictly a cash operation."

"Where are the caches Morales was talking about?"

"No idea." The answer was immediate.

"You worked for Belgrave for how long?"

"Long enough. But after the first bust, Sam got paranoid. He moved product and equipment, shut down some locations and opened others. No one knew where everything was except him. The only place he told me about was at Matthew Moore's family farm."

If that was true, she'd been right: all she represented to the task force was a means to draw out the killer. But I wasn't taking anything Kara Johnson said at face value. She could be planning to empty the caches herself, skip town, and sell them off to fund a ridiculously early retirement.

"You know more than you're telling."

She left the store, not bothering to lock it behind her. I followed her down a side street heading south, away from campus. We walked a few blocks that way, her ignoring me while I kept pace. She slouched into the backpack and kept the same lazy saunter as before, but at this range I could see it was an act. She clocked everything from the flies buzzing over garbage cans to the cars parked on the street. And she was sizing me up, too. Looking for weak spots. I leveled my shoulders and used my left hand to pull out her phone she'd left at the taco stand.

Typing in my contact information, I tossed it to her. She caught it without looking.

"You can call me anytime during the operation, day or night. I don't sleep."

She glanced at the contact page and snorted. I'd listed my number under Cap with a gold star emoji. "Cute."

"Keep the phone on you if you don't want surprise visits from me. And if you go looking for any drug caches, the team and I are coming with."

"My own stalker. This deal just keeps getting better."

"Let's get one thing straight."

"Oh, good." Her hair was in her face again. A puckered scar deformed the tattoo on her left shoulder, inches above her heart.

"I don't buy your reformed act. People are who they are and you"—I waited for her to look over—"are a criminal." Neither of us blinked. "You belong in prison. You're the reason the overdoses in this country are at an all-time high."

The muscles in her face tightened, but she kept the lazy pace. "I never forced anything down anyone's throat. Everybody makes their own choices."

"And you profited off those choices."

She glanced at an empty soda bottle in the ditch. "Just like Coca-Cola. Just like fucking Pfizer and AstraZeneca. Profiting off other people's bad choices is what this country is built on. You do it, too."

"Excuse me?"

"If we weren't out here playing the bad guy, you'd be out of a job. Your salary, your benefits, your pension, your Blue Lives bullshit—that would all vanish, and what would you be without it?"

Blue Lives wasn't my bullshit—it never had been—but I wasn't getting into that, not with Kara Johnson. And I knew one thing I would be even if I wasn't a cop. "A better person than you."

"You can't eat morality."

She stopped on a block full of off-campus housing and low-budget apartments, places that benefited from their proximity to the university and tenants who cared more about beer than working windows.

"Wait here." She shoved her tiny backpack at me.

"Where are you going?"

"To chum the water." She paused to look me up and down. "God, you reek of cop. Do you own anything that isn't starched?"

I looped the backpack over my shoulders and she laughed out loud before disappearing into a dark brick building.

I waited in the shade, tracking her phone to an apartment on the back side of the building, and logged the address so I could pull tenant records later. I had her license plate off the old pickup, too. Morales said she wasn't connected to anyone anymore, but clearly she still knew people in town. And the more of her network I could trace, the better chance we had of finding a connection that led to Belgrave's buyer.

The hum of the investigation buzzed through me like adrenaline. This was what I needed: the kind of case I hadn't had since the pandemic began. It felt like waking up, like the first time Jonah and I chased one of his dreams through the corners of this town. We'd tracked down a missing person then. This time I was looking for a shadow. And I couldn't wait.

A message popped up on my phone, a picture from an unknown cell number. It showed the back of a guy—white or Latino, with short, dark hair, in sweats—inside a shitty apartment.

Kara appeared on the sidewalk and walked past me without acknowledging my existence. Something about the way she moved looked different, wrong. I followed at a distance until she ducked into a bus shelter and joined her inside.

Her nose dripped blood, and red marks, spaced finger-width apart, lined her arm.

"What happened?"

"Follow that guy." She nodded at my phone, wiping her bloody nose on the inside of her shirt. "He's high as fuck right now, but he'll pull it together soon."

"Your shoulder." That's what had been wrong. One of her arms seemed fine, but the other hung limp at her side. She looked down and sighed. Bracing herself against the bus shelter, she gripped her sagging shoulder and wrenched the joint back into place, then stood up as if nothing had happened, holding her hand out for her backpack.

I gaped at her perfectly sober pupils and relaxed, pain-free jaw.

"What are you?"

Kara

"Do birds feel pain?"

Celina and I lounged in her bathtub, her on one side and me on the other, both of us shrugged down into the water, legs intertwined. It was December and we'd been dating for three weeks, finding every scrap of time we could to be together. No pretense. No games. The attraction was instant and we'd both been pulled in hard.

We took daily walks along the river after her graveyard shifts, shuffling through the white world and watching the wintering birds. She didn't know the names of any Iowa species but told me about the birds in New Orleans where she'd grown up, about the white cockatoo named Loki her family owned when she was a kid and how he strutted across her headboard in the mornings, waking her up as he danced just out of reach.

This morning when I met her in the parking lot, she complained that she smelled like the deep fryer, so instead of our usual route we went straight to her apartment and into the bath. I hadn't noticed any smells, too distracted by the way her pale skin flushed pink against the tiles. Maybe that's why her question caught me off guard. Birds and pain. My hands froze on her calf, soap bubbles popping between my fingers.

"I don't know. Why?"

"You draw them all the time."

"And?"

Celina knew I was a student and that I worked at the thrift store. With our opposite schedules, I'd been able to dodge sharing any more than that.

She sat up and found my hand, linking our fingers together. Her hair was piled onto her head, making her neck look longer and somehow regal. Untouchable, even as she pressed her knuckles between mine.

"I need to tell you something."

I sat up, too, my eyes pulling toward the door. I wasn't sure if I was ready to learn Celina's secrets. Especially if that led to her asking about mine. I'd been with people before who knew about Sam and what I did for him. Some probably hooked up with me because of the connection, thinking they'd get a free pharmacy out of it, but that wasn't Celina. I knew in my gut she wasn't the kind of person who would roll with a drug-dealing girlfriend. But I couldn't lie to her. And I couldn't make myself walk away. In less than a month she'd become my air, my reason.

"I'm training to become an intuitive detective."

Okay, hard left. I had no idea what she was talking about, even as she went on to explain that she'd moved to Iowa to study with her uncle, who was also some kind of detective.

"He finds missing people. He's found them all over the country, some alive, some dead."

I could hear the pride in her voice, the respect.

"He's a PI?"

"Yes, but we use unconventional means, a certain skill set we have that other people don't."

I was still tripping over that word, "intuitive."

"Jonah dreams about people who are lost. He says it's like sensing a square peg in a round hole, finding the point where the energy doesn't fit. He uses the details from the dreams to track them, and his other abilities, too."

"What other abilities?" I wasn't sure about any of this, and it probably showed on my face.

"He can sense emotions and sometimes thoughts from the people around him. It makes it hard for him to be in public."

"You said 'we.' 'We' have a skill set."

After Celina fell asleep in the morning and before I had to leave for school or work, I'd started drawing her while she slept. Most people relaxed in their sleep, but Celina's hands curled tighter and her brow furrowed like she was taking cover. I showed her one of the drawings and asked if she had nightmares. "You look like you're waiting for a storm to pass." She smiled at the drawing, shaking her head. "I'm waiting for one to come."

At the time I'd thought she meant me, and my stomach had dropped at the idea that she knew I was keeping things from her, hiding a huge part of who I was, which could rip us apart as easily as a tornado shredding a town. But now I got it, or I was starting to. I lifted our linked hands and brought her knuckles to my mouth. "Do you dream about lost people, too?"

"No. Or at least not yet. Jonah didn't realize he was dreaming until he was about my age. His roommate helped him figure it out, after he started talking in his sleep." She traced her thumb over my lower lip. "My abilities are different."

"What can you do? Besides make me come like a genie lives in your tongue?"

She laughed and pulled me closer, into that place where I relaxed and came alive, all at once.

"I can sense pain," she said quietly, near my ear. "I've always been able to, ever since I could remember. I know when someone is hurting, whether they're hobbled by shards of it or enduring a chronic, dull ache. And Jonah is teaching me to feel around the pain, to the emotions wrapped up in it. It's easier when there are fewer people around, so I can focus on individuals. That's why I work the graveyard. I'm practicing my craft."

She bracketed my shoulders and leaned back, looking straight into my eyes.

"You have no pain."

My mouth fell open. How could she know that?

"It doesn't exist in you, and I don't think it ever has. You've never known a headache." Her fingers traveled up to dance over my temples. "Or a sore throat." She brushed her hands down my neck and moved to the scar on my bicep, the place Jillian had stitched up the first time I visited the vet clinic. "This didn't hurt you." She touched various bruises down my sides and legs. "And you don't feel these."

"I think that's why my headaches go away as soon as I see you. All the pain I've absorbed from everyone over my shift disappears. You're my anesthetic."

"Sentient aspirin, remember?" I managed.

99

She focused on my face again and ran her hands along my jaw, before letting them fall loosely to my side. Waiting.

I swallowed. I could say this much: she knew most of it already. I could share the rest.

"I have CIP disorder. It's a congenital insensitivity to pain."

A genetic mutation turned off a sodium channel in my body that normally acted like a nervous system highway to warn the brain about danger and injury. I didn't have that channel. I never did. Physical pain was as strange to me as watching a movie in another language. You know it's about something. You know it's beautiful and important. And you also know that no matter how many times you watch it, the words will slip away like birds taking to the air and soaring beyond your horizon.

"It's rare. There's only a few people in the world who have it. My stepfather found out when I broke my leg and dragged it around behind me for a day. After the doctor told him what CIP was, he brought me home and tested it."

"Tested?" The first trace of emotion crossed Celina's face.

"He put my hand on a boiling teakettle and waited to see if I had any reaction. I just stared at him until he pulled my hand away." I lifted my right palm. "It's still a little shinier."

"Oh my god."

"My mom found out, somehow between her endless double shifts, and she kicked him out for good. She took me back to the doctor, though, and he wanted to do a million tests, to submit me for studies and take samples of my DNA. We got calls from all over the country and she signed me up for the ones that paid. I became grocery money, a guinea pig, until she met another asshole and I left."

"How old were you?"

"Fifteen."

"I'm so sorry."

"It's fine. The hardest part of it is the not knowing. It feels like I'm invincible, but my body's lying to me and I don't know when or how or where. Maybe it's lying now. I don't know."

"Thank you for telling me."

"Thank you for letting me." Tears pricked into the corners of my eyes and I tried to hide them. I couldn't show weakness or emotion with Sam's people, but Celina pulled me in, wrapping me in her arms. It felt like the two of us, together, were unbreakable. Maybe we were. Or maybe that was another lie.

Eventually her forehead drifted to mine, our breath mingling, warm and unsteady, as she ran a finger over the ink on my arm. "I wondered if that's why you like birds so much. Because they don't feel pain, either."

"It's more about the flying. No one tries to mess with them, and even if they do, the birds are gone. Out of reach." I ran my hands over her hips, every perfect inch of them. She arched against me. I didn't want to talk about birds anymore. "Wow, my psychic girlfriend."

Her mouth fell open, lips hovering just out of reach. "Girlfriend?"

"Mmm." I closed the distance and hitched her leg over mine, working my way into her.

Later, as the tub drained and we toweled off, she asked if I wanted to meet her uncle. It was hard to be casual about it and not run immediately out of the house. She wanted me to meet her family? And not just an uncle but a man who could sense when people were lost or didn't belong. An hour ago I hadn't believed psychics existed, and now I was afraid this guy would take one look at me and throw me out of his niece's life. And he would be right to do it.

What are you?

People stared at me with that question in their eyes my whole life. My stepfather, holding my hand to a teakettle. My mom scrubbing blood out of my clothes. Kids at the park, guys on the street, lovers, dealers, doctors, truckers. And now this cop, Max Summerlin, trying to pretend his own arm wasn't killing him as he watched me pop my stupid joint back into its socket. The whole fucking world was shut down and reeling while a monster virus killed more people than Sam could ever dream of, and somehow I was still the sideshow.

"I'll check in later." I shoved the DEA burner in my pocket and turned to leave.

He tried to stop me. He wanted to ask a million questions, to put me under a microscope like everyone else, but before he could get rolling a half dozen crows descended on the street outside the bus shelter, picking at the remains of a dumped take-out bag. Bobbing among them, completely out of place among their gleaming black feathers, was a pure white bird. Its Mohawk head feathers rose and fell as it hopped and scrambled for position.

"Hey, there's the cockatoo." Summerlin moved to the opening of the bus shelter. "We started getting calls about it last fall—someone's pet that got loose—but Animal Control's never been able to trap it. Everyone figured it would die over the winter, but the thing's still going strong. Now it's a Covid celebrity, gone viral." He started taking a video with his phone. "My wife loves the thing."

I couldn't move or even reply. The bird hopped up to the curb, tilting its head as a car passed. More cars came from the other direction and within seconds the whole flock was airborne, the cockatoo's white wings eclipsed by the black bodies surrounding it.

Summerlin was still talking when I stepped off the curb and walked into the middle of the street. Cars honked and brakes screeched around me. I didn't care. I searched the tops of buildings, power lines, trees, but it was too late. The bird was gone.

Max

After Kara Johnson snapped her own disjointed shoulder back into place and literally walked into traffic, I spent the rest of the day following the lead she'd tossed me. It was suspicious at first—she could've sent me down a rabbit hole just to get rid of me—but after checking the mailboxes in the building where she'd gotten knocked around, one of the names popped. J. Doyle. It was a guy I'd questioned last year during the ice storm, a low-level dealer who used to work for Belgrave's operation. At the time, he'd given me enough information that I reduced his charges to a misdemeanor, but this guy hadn't learned any lessons, picking up a DWI in February and an assault charge in May.

I got my car, pulled around to an alley across from Doyle's building, and waited. When he finally appeared, he didn't look great. His hair wasn't combed, his T-shirt was stained, and he was limping. Maybe Kara had won that fight after all.

Doyle climbed into an old Buick and I followed him out of town, heading east on the freeway long enough that I wondered if he was going to Chicago. He exited just shy of the Davenport-Moline border and went to a bar that could've doubled as a Harley dealership. I hesitated about going in, looking at my clothes and hearing Kara tell me I reeked of cop. I had on khakis and a T-shirt, which admittedly did look a lot cleaner than any of the jeans and leather jackets filtering in and out of this place. No one wore masks. This was red country, not exactly the crowd keeping the CDC website bookmarked. Before I could decide what to do, Doyle came back out with another guy.

They headed straight toward me through the parking lot. Doyle seemed to be doing all the talking. His friend was a head taller and had a solid seventy-five pounds on Doyle, which looked like mostly muscle. He wore a gold chain and a pinky ring, with slicked-back hair and a five-day beard. A few more people trailed outside, lighting cigarettes and watching the two move through bikes and cars. An entourage. I didn't recognize any of them, but they looked drunk and restless, never a good combination. I took a picture of the pair before they got too close, then flipped to Facebook and pretended to scroll as I listened through the cracked window.

"—straight up started to toss my place. She wanted to know where the stuff was."

"And?" The taller guy asked. I glanced up to see him looking in my car, pausing in front of the hood with the air of a man who owned the place. My pulse picked up. I made a show of digging at something between my teeth with a fingernail and went back to scrolling.

"I said I didn't know what the fuck she was talking about."

"Good."

"Then she threw a fucking chair at me."

They disappeared past the next truck, their voices fading until I couldn't hear anything else. The group in front of the bar tracked their progress, clouds of smoking rising against neon beer signs. One of them stared right at me. I jotted notes, fast and jerky, trying to get it all down. The next time I looked up, he was gone.

Heart pounding, I pulled out of the spot and cruised the lot until I saw Doyle and the gold-chain guy standing in front of an F-350, all black and jacked up on specialty shocks. Whoever this was, he wasn't low-key.

I left the bar. It was getting late, the sky turning twilight with a last strip of orange glowing on the horizon. I'd already texted Shelley that I wouldn't make it home for dinner. She hadn't replied. I knew I should go home and try to smooth things over, but home was an hour away, and there was someone else on this side of the state I needed to see.

The cabin stood on a bluff overlooking the Mississippi. From the driveway it was all dark wood logs next to a garage at least as big as the house. The front door disappeared into the shadows of the eaves where a NO SOLICITING sign was the only indication anyone actually lived here.

Trees and a long driveway insulated the place from its neighbors, but I still checked the perimeter as I walked up. The garage was closed. A van I didn't recognize was parked in front of it with Iowa disability plates.

Jonah answered the door, looking surprised and something else I couldn't quite place. "In the neighborhood?"

"Yeah, actually. Sorry I didn't call. You busy?"

I'd stopped by weekly since the lockdown started and we'd put away at least a few cases of beer on his deck together, watching the slide of water on the river below. Jonah was probably the best prepared person in the world for this pandemic. He was an early adopter of the six-feet-apart philosophy when we met in college, decades ahead of the curve. Afterward, as I moved through the world—getting married, having Garrett, getting promoted at work—he withdrew further and further from it. He ordered everything online and, other than me, his contact with the outside world was limited to working with clients. Not even Shelley could object to my visits here, which were socially distanced, outdoors, with the world's least likely man to contract Covid.

So whose van was parked in his driveway?

Voices came from further inside the house, and Jonah shifted uncomfortably. "I have company."

"Who?"

"Let's go to the deck." He disappeared inside for a second before leading me around back and grabbing beers from his fridge in the garage on the way.

He stopped at the railing of the deck that overlooked the Mississippi River valley, the wide-open expanse of trees, water, and sky. It was a hell of a view but not the one I was interested in at the moment. From the road the cabin was all dark logs and shadows, but on this side it was the opposite. A giant wall of windows stretched from the second-story bedroom to the open kitchen and living area below. Standing in the middle of the living room was Dr. Eve Roth. Her father-in-law, Earl, had parked his wheelchair next to the couch.

"We decided to bubble. She asked . . . she wanted to—"

A smile broke over my face and I struggled to keep it casual. "Bubble?"

"She's been alone with Earl this whole time. With his age and underlying conditions, they can't go anywhere except—"

"Here." I cracked open my beer and toasted Jonah at an angle only he could see. "Makes sense."

"It's not that."

"Isn't it?"

"Her husband just died."

"She was gonna divorce him anyway."

He took a drink, his eyes pulling toward Eve inside the glow of the house even as he shook his head. "She deserves better."

From the very beginning, something had been brewing between these two. I figured something criminal at first—job hazard—but it was more than that. They'd been through a car crash, a plane crash. Hell, they'd survived Belgrave together. It didn't make sense on the surface. Jonah dealt in dreams and emotions, while she spent her life with data in labs. Eve was polished, put together, while my best friend barely looked at himself in a mirror. Eve flew airplanes into storms, while Jonah kept the world at a distance, but somehow this gutsy scientist had found a way in.

She touched Earl's arm and said something before moving to the patio door and joining us outside. Her dark red hair gleamed in the porch light. She wore lipstick and some kind of flowy top. It was the sort of outfit that, if Shelley put it on, she'd ask me how she looked before we went out.

"Investigator Summerlin."

"Max," I corrected. "Sorry to interrupt your evening."

"It's fine. We were just about to watch the cinematic masterpiece *Jaws*." Her expression became amused as she shifted a look at Jonah.

I pointed my beer at her. "Watch it. That's sacred ground."

"See?" Jonah moved closer to her and they started bickering about realism in movies. On the other side of the glass, Earl watched the two fight. I wondered how the old man felt about his daughter-in-law getting into a new relationship less than a year after his son's death. It had to be complicated, but as I watched him he gave me a labored wink with his good eye. I drank to that.

"Look, I don't want to derail the dissertation, but I need to talk to you—both of you, actually—about something." I couldn't discuss the task force with Eve, but there was still something she might be able to help with.

"Kara Johnson's back in town."

The good humor on the deck instantly evaporated.

"Why?" was Eve's immediate question.

"She's assisting on a matter with law enforcement." That was debatable. I replayed the conversation I'd overheard at the biker bar. Kara must've been leaning on Doyle for the location of Belgrave's caches. Whether it was for the task force or for herself, I still didn't know.

"You were close to her a couple different times last December." I turned to Jonah. "Did you pick up anything strange off her?"

"Everyone's strange. Be more specific."

I told them what happened at the bus shelter: Kara's surprise EMT skills as she'd snapped her own shoulder back into place. "You said she acted fine after being shot in the barn. Like she was impervious to it. I assumed she was on drugs, but she was stone sober today."

Jonah closed his eyes and paced to the other side of the deck. It took him a minute while both Eve and I waited, watching.

"She wasn't medicated then, either. There was no fog, no altered perceptions. I felt nothing from her—a blank. Absence." He opened his eyes again. "Terminator."

"What does that mean?" Eve asked.

Jonah groaned. "God, I have so much work to do with you."

"So she's what, a psychopath? Sociopath? She can't feel anything?"

"A psychopath isn't capable of empathy," Eve said. "She rescued us in that barn. She wouldn't have done that if she truly couldn't feel."

"Eve's right." Jonah put a hand to his head, massaging the echoes of traumas I'd forced him to resurrect. "Kara's emotions were behind a wall, but once she found out I was Celina's uncle, it all crumbled. She was grieving. Utterly broken. The indifference I picked up when we fought and when she was shot wasn't mental; it was physical. Her body had no reaction."

I took another drink and the twinge of inflamed nerves raced a rutted highway up my arm, making my shoulder clench, the same muscles always tensing in a dumb, knee-jerk response. The doctor said nerve damage could take months or years to heal. Sometimes it never did, which meant the rest of my life would be a choice between pain and drugs. Even if I hadn't seen more than my share of addicts in this line of work, I hated the cloud prescription painkillers made of my head, the inability to focus or keep track of what was happening around me. They took away more than I was willing to give.

If Jonah was right—if I could trust what I saw in the bus shelter today—Kara Johnson never had to make that choice. I could hardly imagine a day without pain anymore. And this twenty-something drug trafficker got to waltz through life without feeling a thing.

"It might be a genetic abnormality." Eve had fallen into step with Jonah and the two of them traded theories. Eve offered to contact a biologist friend of hers to get more information. Then she noticed Earl trying to make popcorn and quickly excused herself. Jonah watched her go.

"Have you had any dreams lately?"

"Nothing clear. It's mostly recycled images, things I've seen before, or—" He broke off and shifted from foot to foot, eyes flashing inside the house. "Other, uh, normal dreams."

I finished the beer to hide my smile, but a twinge of disappointment shot through me at the same time. Not that I expected Jonah to dream about the guy at the biker bar, or Belgrave's successor, but it would have been another piece of information and I was always collecting information.

He walked me out to my car and we stood in the driveway. It was full night, the sun long gone and a banquet of stars stretching overhead.

"You're not telling me everything."

"Don't worry about it. I'm fine. You focus on this." I nodded toward the house.

"Max."

I sighed. Without getting into all the details of the task force, I filled him in on the murder of the air traffic controller and Kara's role in drawing out the killer. My role in shadowing her.

He went quiet and I knew he was dissecting whatever feelings or thoughts he could skim off me. But in the end, all he said was "Be careful."

"Let me know if you dream anything."

He nodded and leaned on the door as I climbed into the car. "This pandemic . . . it's different than anything I've felt before. People aren't lost in the world; they're lost inside themselves. Their certainty, their constructs, the things they used to dull their anxiety and fear—it's all been stripped away. What I hear at night is muffled screaming." He let go of the car door, backing away. "And it's getting louder."

Kara

Six days in Iowa City and no one had tried to kill me, if you didn't count Doyle or the hemlock I'd found in the vegetable drawer of Phyllis's refrigerator.

During the day I led a team of DEA puppies to random sites across eastern Iowa where I'd dropped product off or picked it up once upon a time. Empty grain bins, abandoned farm buildings, places where the trees stitched the fields together and the horizon stretched empty in all directions. The task force swept the fields like grandpas on the beach with their 3D ground imaging, which could find things that didn't belong in the earth. After six days they'd found the foundation of an old barn, a trunk full of hair and postcards, and three skeletons. Two chickens, one cow. No drugs.

At night I went on aggressive pub crawls, barhopping through town at the places that were still open—mostly outdoor patios and alleys with a few picnic tables and lights strung up to make the space look like some sad, half-assed party. I puked on sidewalks, started two fights, ended another, and my contact list in the DEA phone grew by two interested women making blatantly questionable decisions. I caught glimpses of my babysitter (deathsitter?) on the far side of patios and edges of parking lots, frowning at his own life choices. But no hit men.

It felt like the virus, waiting for an invisible killer that could show up anywhere at any time. Every decision could be my last decision. If I opened the wrong door or got too close to the wrong person, that was it. The end. Take your worthless bow and be grateful it was finally over.

But it wasn't over—not yet. The days kept going, the morning sun shining relentlessly into the shitty bedroom at Phyllis's house, sending that hollow punch into my gut every time I woke up and realized I was still here. Breathing in Iowa City without her.

Morales was so disappointed at my continued heartbeat, he called another task force meeting, which deathsitter Max texted me about five times. I showed up late, vodka seeping out of my pores, and drained the coffeepot while everyone else played Impress Morales with what they'd dug up so far.

When it got to Max's turn, he actually stood up to explain the lead I'd given him. He handed Morales a flash drive that had a dozen pictures of me, Doyle, and Doyle with some other guy in a parking lot.

"His name is Charles McAllister." He pointed at the guy next to Doyle, a trashy Jake Gyllenhaal knockoff. "Goes by the name Chase. He's got priors for possession with intent and had his license suspended a few times. Nothing violent on his record. Likes to race cars in the Midwest circuit. Doesn't keep a low profile." Max looked directly at me, nailing the eye contact portion of his presentation. "Friend of yours?"

I drained my third cup of coffee. "Never heard of him."

He didn't believe me—I could tell by the way his jaw twitched—but he kept plowing ahead. Getting to his five-point conclusion paragraph. "This is where Doyle went when Kara made inquiries about the drug caches. And from what I overheard, Chase seemed pleased that Doyle didn't tell her anything."

"What did you get from him?" Morales snatched the last donut before I could get any ideas.

"A bloody lip. And this." I pulled a Ziploc bag out of my backpack and tossed it to one of the DEA dudes, the lab guy. He lifted it so everyone could see the smaller bags stuffed with pills inside. There were probably a hundred altogether, nothing major, but everyone in the room perked up like dogs scenting their first ever bone.

"Belgrave's?" one of them asked.

I shrugged. White pills looked a lot like other white pills. It wasn't like Sam had a brand stamped on his stuff. Matthew had been the science guy in our operation, and he wasn't around to ask.

"That's why you got thrashed." Max was looking at me, not the bag of baggies.

"I did most of the thrashing."

He nodded, acknowledging it, but there was something else in his face, too—calculations, dissections. *What are you?* My stepfather's stare, holding my hand to a teakettle. The look every doctor gave me when pieces of my body randomly bruised, broke, or bled. Looking at me first like I was an idiot, and then—when it became obvious I couldn't feel their pokes or shocks or sadistic little tests—like an alien. I probably shouldn't have snapped my shoulder back into its socket in front of gold-star investigator Max Summerlin, but this guy's job was to watch me die, and he made it clear he not only understood but would enjoy the assignment. Part of me wanted to show him I couldn't care less—that whatever justice he thought the death of a drug trafficker would bring, I wasn't going to make it more satisfying by screaming.

I turned away while the rest of the bros made self-important noises about testing the pills. Morales took charge of the meeting again and Max sat down next to me.

"This guy Chase—what were his priors for?"

"Fentanyl."

Morales nodded. "He could be connected to Belgrave's successor. A mid-level guy." He switched out Max's pictures for a screenshot of a bank account and explained they'd been searching through Sam's finances, trying to trace any connections through the money. I laughed, drawing everyone's attention.

"Sam didn't funnel any of the business through his personal accounts." That was his first rule. Nothing traceable. He never left a trail—not on the drugs, not on the money, not even on the people. Not the kind of traces you could prosecute, anyway. Everything he did was wrapped in disguises and veneers: shell companies, fake product shipments, fake businesses. There were so many layers that when his mask came off, it was like a polar plunge. The instant shock of reality. Holding your dead girlfriend in your arms, rocking back and forth as she became colder, less recognizable, while he stood over you and patted your goddamn back, saying he'd taken care of you. Saved you from her.

Morales was talking. I could barely hear him. The room faded and swam, and no one seemed to notice except the deathsitter. He stared at me as sweat broke out all over my body. The coffee I'd guzzled rolled and pitched. I bent over the trash can and vomited up everything in my stomach.

When I finished, the room was quiet. Disgust, anger, and sour acid filled the space. Before I could say or do anything, Morales forwarded the presentation and started talking like nothing had happened. Every single one of them turned away. Except Max. He handed me a wet paper towel—slowly, like a zookeeper approaching a wild animal—and bagged up the garbage, taking it out of the room.

I moved as far from the coffee as I could and tried to pay attention to the columns of numbers on the screen, the cobwebs in the corners of the ceiling—anything besides the memories clawing at my head.

"These are Belgrave's personal accounts from 2013, the year his wife died and when the operation reportedly began." Three lines were highlighted, transfers that added up to over a hundred grand. I'd moved loads more than that through the thrift store on the reg, but I could see how it stood out from everything else at the time. In 2013, I hadn't even met Sam yet. I was cycling through dead-end jobs and dead-end people, running drugs for small-time assholes who commented on my fuckability like it was an actual prospect in their lives.

"The transfers went to a company owned by Frederick Nilsen. Belgrave wrote them off as farm expenses on his taxes, but the transactions never appeared again, before or after."

"Any money coming the other way, from Nilsen to Belgrave?"

"Not through these channels."

Morales switched the slide to a picture of an older, heavy dude with a sunburnt nose, snowy white hair, and Buddy Holly glasses. I froze.

"Nilsen has been involved in a number of businesses over the years, none directly criminal, but he's been dinged by the IRS and various oversight agencies numerous times. His longest-running enterprise is a slaughterhouse outside Waterloo. Contributes to a lot of political campaigns. Likes to golf with state senators and one U.S. congressman."

"What did Belgrave buy from him?" someone asked.

"Unclear."

"Do we know Belgrave was still associated with this guy?" Max asked. He'd finished getting rid of my barf and was leaning against the doorway to the room.

"He was." I spoke up. Everyone looked at me again. I swallowed the acid that lingered in my throat. "I met Frederick once with Sam."

"What was exchanged?"

I pushed away from the wall and got some water. "Sam didn't touch product or money directly, but he always passed information in person."

It was a few years ago, before I walked into the Village Inn and met Celina. I'd just enrolled at the University and was phasing out Phyllis at the thrift store. Sam rarely came into town, but he'd wanted an update so I'd gone out to the farm. No one else was there, just the two of us, and I was surprised to see a whole ass dinner sitting on he table. Beef stew and a steaming baguette fresh from the oven.

"Sit down," he ordered, pulling out a chair. "Eat."

Sam was a massive guy, the kind who wrestled farm machinery and did manual labor his whole life. The kind who intimidated people just by standing silently in front of them. If he put on a fur coat and walked through the woods, he could've generated some Bigfoot sightings. Seeing him in a kitchen wearing pot holders on his hands was enough to make me swallow a laugh.

"You think I don't cook?" He pointed a ladle at me, which made me laugh harder. "You think I survive on that garbage you call food? You need real meat if you want to put any meat on those bones."

I slid into the chair, knee wedged between my chest and the table, and ripped a hunk off the baguette.

"Watch it, that's still hot."

I held up my palm, which had turned instantly red but not shiny. "Seems okay."

He grunted and served bowls to both of us. Sam knew about my condition. I'd told him early on as a sort of offering, or maybe to ingratiate myself, knowing my disease would be useful to him on a number of levels. I'd never become addicted to pills—at least, not his brand—and wouldn't be tempted to lift any of his product. I couldn't be intimidated by threats or violence, and I won every fight I was in because I had a weapon no one else did. Telling Sam about the CIP helped him learn to trust me in those early days, but it did something else, too. Something unexpected. It created a bond between us, a weird sense of family. Every time we met, I could see him checking me for bruises and deformities. And he made comments like this when no one else was around, looking out for me, making sure I took care of myself.

"How's it going with Phyllis?"

"I mean, she tried to poison me. So . . . great?"

His laugh was like an explosion in the quiet house. I told him about the Carolina Reaper mash in my coffee and the rest of what I was learning at the store, but he waved off most of the details and asked about my classes instead. I listed my enrollments: a few art classes, biology, weightlifting, a completely random schedule with no common thread other than I thought the subjects sounded interesting. Sam mentioned a chemistry professor I should check out—Matthew, I would find out later—and I immediately agreed.

"Sure. The semester hasn't started. I can drop these and take different stuff if you want."

"Take anything you like. You can't run drugs your whole life."

"Are you firing me?" I asked, grinning.

Sam put his spoon down and looked at me long and hard enough that I started to squirm. "I'm not going to be in this business forever. I'm seventy-two years old."

"You don't look a day over seventy-one."

"Smart-ass." He shook his head, still staring at me in that weirdly intense way. "You've got most of your life ahead of you. You have to think about your future. Some of these guys? This is all they can do, it's all they're built for, and they'll keep at it until they die or get caught. You can do more."

A truck pulled up outside, saving me from the sudden choking feeling in my throat. I could toss shit back and forth all day, quips and threats and literal punches. Any of that was no problem, but I had no idea how to handle what Sam had just said to me. Not once in my life had I thought about having a future. Futures were for other people; I'd only ever had now, and the next now, and the next, and I got through them until I couldn't anymore. Until I hit the last now, the wall my body would forget to warn me about before I was flattened and gone. A lifetime supply of nows finally spent.

Sam went to the door, and by the time he reappeared with Frederick Nilsen, I'd managed to shove down whatever strange mess the conversation had stirred up.

Sam made the introductions. He turned to Frederick, who was probably a few decades younger than Sam but looked halfway to diabetes. He had cow eyes and a drinker's nose. "Kara's the bright light around here."

"Is she running the show now?" Frederick laughed at his own joke, looking at me like he was checking for pigtails while Sam went to his gun safe in the living room and entered in the code. I sat up a little straighter, my hand drifting to a steak knife. When Sam came back, though, all he had was a piece of paper, folded twice.

He handed the paper to Frederick. "She's got better things to do than take over this circus."

Frederick unfolded the paper, read it, and nodded. He peeled off a jump drive that had been taped to the inside. "This is everything?"

"Untraceable." Sam clapped him on the shoulder. "Let me know if you have any problems."

"What was on it?" Morales asked after I told the task force everything I remembered about that day.

"I don't know." Frederick had joined us, eating a bowl of Sam's stew as the two of them talked about the weather for the rest of the meal. He'd pocketed the jump drive and the paper as though the transaction had never happened. "I didn't see what was written on the paper and I never saw him after that."

"But he knew you were part of Belgrave's operation?"

"Yeah. Sam never talked about what anybody else did in terms of jobs or assignments, but we all knew. If someone was around Sam, you knew they were involved."

The agents made a bunch of self-important noises, going back and forth about the two players on the board and the likelihood of Chase versus Nilsen being Belgrave's suspected buyer, but nothing they said at this point mattered. I already knew my next DEA homework assignment.

Talk to Frederick Nilsen.

Max

Walking into ICPD with Morales by my side was a strangely similar experience to coming back after a leave of duty when I'd been shot last year. The station looked different—desks had been pushed apart and arrows on the floor directed people to walk in one-way flows; the front desk sergeant took our temperatures before letting us into the building past boxes of disposable masks and jugs of hand sanitizer—but the looks felt eerily the same. Nods and muffled greetings followed me through the building. Guys looked away when I tried making eye contact.

Last year I'd been a pariah because of my association with Jonah. Everyone thought my psychic best friend had finally become unhinged and shot me. I was the butt of jokes. Rookies were warned about me. The guy in Records, the one who'd had his cats taxidermied, smirked when I walked by. I thought the task force assignment would change things, but I felt like as much of an outsider walking through the station now as I had in my sixteen years on the force. Except instead of joking, the mood edged toward hostile.

Interagency cooperation was a fickle thing. It worked—it had to work—in order to protect and serve a country where crimes and jurisdictions were sliced into rubrics of responsibility, but there was a lot of posturing, prick waving, and politics. The DEA had poached two ICPD cases in the past year: the fertilizer truck and the Russell Ash semitruck. Both were connected to Belgrave, in retrospect, and the DEA was working with us now, but no one liked handing over credit for a prime bust. Department resentment still ran strong. I could smell it as we walked through investigations toward my desk, where . . .

My desk was gone.

"What the hell?"

"Needed to make room." Ciseski, a fellow investigator and human vacuum for vending machine snacks, piped up from across the one-way aisle. He wore a mask over his mouth but underneath his nose, which made me think of the underwear meme where the guy's dick hung out over the top of his Hanes. *If you wear your mask like this* . . . I shook my head, looking around. "Where is it?"

Ciseski shrugged, giving Morales a once-over. "I'm sure you and your hombre can figure it out."

"What did you just say?" I took a step across the aisle as several heads turned in our direction.

Ciseski grunted and went back to his computer. Morales got there before me and sat on a corner of his desk, crunching a bag of chips into the mess of paperwork littering the work surface. He leaned in, waiting until Ciseski gave up pretending to work. Morales's eyes were dark, expressionless, and Ciseski recoiled, scooting his chair back until it hit his own garbage can. The area around us had gone quiet.

"Your coworker asked where his desk is, amigo."

The question was a sugarcoated bullet. Morales's voice was soft, seemingly friendly, and everything about it set my reflexes on edge.

Ciseski glanced at me, looking for help. Fuck if I was giving him any. I always knew he was a lazy, half-assed investigator, but I hadn't realized he was a racist, lazy, half-assed investigator. He checked around, increasingly uncomfortable. After a silence that seemed to stretch from one end of the department to the other, he muttered something that sounded like "Check with Larsen."

Morales clapped him on the shoulder, hard enough to jolt Ciseski in his chair. Heat pumped through me, simmering in my gut as we walked to the field division captain's office. Eyes followed us on all sides.

A BLUE LIVES MATTER sign was taped to the door of Larsen's office. I looked at Morales, who grunted and shook his head. *You and your hombre.* For months I'd felt like I had no home in my own department, that I was caught between two worlds. I couldn't imagine how someone like Morales felt.

Larsen was expecting us. "How are things progressing?"

"Decent." Morales leaned back in his chair, hands clasped behind his head like the scene with Ciseski had never happened. "We've got two solid leads on Belgrave's successor, one of them thanks to your investigator here."

"You need surveillance? I can spare an officer or two. They'd be happy to have an actual assignment instead of having their every move filmed by protestors."

"Been bad, huh?"

"You'd think we were the goddamn Gestapo." Larsen jerked at his mask, irritation in every move as he adjusted it. I wasn't a small guy, but Larsen had a good three inches on me and he dwarfed most of the men on the force. He benched two-sixty and ran a marathon every year for his birthday. He handled situations head-on and he didn't pull punches. Something like this, a global movement for social justice, wasn't the kind of issue Larsen could bulldoze, and that was his main problem, because it came in the form of guys like Ciseski, twenty-year veterans of the force who flew under the radar and forgot how to protect and serve anyone beyond themselves.

Larsen asked for details on our two leads, clearly eager for a case with faces, names, and blunt action plans. Morales filled him in on Charles "Chase" McAllister and Frederick Nilsen.

"Sounds like Nilsen's got a lot of public interests. He should be easy to put a guy on."

Morales waved him off. "We've got them both covered for now."

I kept quiet. We'd discussed it on the way here, but I still wasn't happy with the way the assignments had played out. I got how it made sense for Kara to contact Nilsen. There was a relationship there, or at least a known association. Morales had her on the team so we could leverage those connections. My problem was with my assignment. I was the one who followed Doyle and unearthed Chase as a potential lead. I'd spent most of the night IDing the guy and pulling all available background information on him for today's briefing. And Morales responded by handing all my work to Pyle, the state trooper.

Pyle had grinned at the assignment—I could see his mask stretch—and took the intel without even a nod in my direction.

"You said yourself I know eastern Iowa. Why didn't you put me on Chase?" I'd argued on the way here, when it was just the two of us in the car.

"You've already got a job."

I was supposed to back Kara and prep her for the meeting with Nilsen. I'd already followed her around for the last week, nursing warm Bud Lights in seedy bars while watching for any sign of our killer. She'd brought us the link to Chase, the bag of pills from Doyle's apartment, and she was playing the part of bait exceptionally well, if public drunkenness and complete lack of Covid safety measures were any bar. What did that add up to, though? None of the sites she'd taken us to had turned up any stockpiles of drugs. It could all be a distraction, a carrot for the task force to chase while she emptied Belgrave's caches for herself.

Morales didn't seem worried about the possibility. "Trust me," he told me in the car, and I was trying to do that, but Larsen's reaction echoed my own instincts.

"I think you need more eyes here. You're leaving huge gaps in your surveillance."

"Nilsen doesn't have any priors."

"Neither did Belgrave," Larsen pointed out, and I couldn't help nodding. Until the day he'd been killed, no one could prove Sam Olson—quiet retired farmer—was a criminal drug lord.

"We'll take a desk if you can spare it," Morales said, sidestepping the point.

"Which desk?"

I spoke up. "Mine. Where the hell is it?"

Larsen walked us down the hall to an interview room. The table was full of my stuff: computer, stacks of unfiled paper, framed pictures of Shelley and Garrett smiling in the glare of the overhead lights. "When we rearranged again for the distancing, I had you moved in here. It's temporary, of course, but you can work on your task force assignments without interruption."

And without any human interaction. I glanced at the one-way glass, the scuffed and dented walls. It made sense to have privacy during this assignment, but it also felt . . . something else. Something I couldn't quite place. I'd been removed from the rest of the department and it didn't seem like it was purely for my sake. After Larsen left, Morales pulled out a bag of Skittles and peeled off his mask, popping them into his mouth one by one.

"There's a reason I wanted you on this task force, Summerlin."

I sat down and booted up my computer. "I have experience with unusual characters."

"That's not all." He sat on the edge of the table and offered me some Skittles. I declined. "You connected a few cases last year in an interesting way. Remember Binance?"

The cryptocurrency exchange. I'd traced transfers to and from Matthew Moore and Alexis Dwyer, and they'd both worked for Belgrave. "What about it?"

"Let's see if you can find any connections from those two cases to our current players. Belgrave wasn't using bank accounts."

"You think we can trace them through crypto."

"We're already working on it, but it never hurts to have another set of eyes."

"You don't have to throw me a pity assignment."

"I'm not." Morales smiled before putting his mask back on. "You know, I've been DEA for thirteen years and I was DHS for five years before that. I've been on every kind of investigation and worked with every type of person. There's the spineless ones like your friend out there, the hard-asses like Larsen, and every shade in between. You get real good at seeing people. Not for what they are—who gives a shit about that?—but for what they bring to the table. Evidence, connections, seizures. At the end of the day, that's all anyone's worth: what they get off their asses and do." He went to the door and leaned on the handle, glancing at the sorry spread of my things on the interview table. "Don't worry about the guys outside this door. Fuck 'em. We've got a motto on our team and it gets us back on track every time."

"'Eat your feelings'?"

It was out of my mouth before I realized it—all the hours I'd spent tailing Kara and listening to her burn-it-down attitude must have rubbed off on me—but where Larsen would've ripped me a new one, Morales just laughed as he opened the door.

"'When in doubt, follow the money.'"

Kara

"Watch it," Phyllis barked as I unloaded a cardboard box clanking with hot-sauce bottles, hitting it hard—and mostly accidentally—against the tailgate.

"I'm fine, thanks."

"Who gives a rat's ass? I can't sell you."

It'd taken a half hour of waiting in line for our turn to drop off Phyllis's farmers' market orders. The in-person market had been called off this summer, which she bitched about the whole way here while puffing on Winston Lights. "People order online now and do a contactless pickup, whatever the hell that means. Douse themselves in Purell to drive through a parking garage and get their organic kohlrabi."

Somehow during breakfast she'd forced me into hauling her shit up here and in return I made her lower my rent by fifty dollars this month. Not that I cared about the money, but she did and that was the point.

"Hi, Phyllis." A masked blonde bounced up to the truck. She had curves, PPE, and a ponytail that made me think of Jillian, but this girl's obvious interest in the human species set her apart from the veterinarian. Jillian probably hadn't even noticed a global pandemic was unfolding. The thought made me smile as the blonde wheeled a cart up to the tailgate.

"Is this your granddaughter?"

We both laughed shotgun loud, startling the blonde as she glanced awkwardly between us. She wasn't entirely off base. Phyllis and I were both short and thin, and we were wearing matching Day of the Dead skull face masks with roses blooming in the teeth. I'd found them in town and Phyllis had helped herself to the pack on the way here.

"This is my tenant, Kara Johnson." Phyllis piped up on the name and looked around the facility, as if hoping for a hit man to pop up from behind a pile of summer squash. An unlit cigarette stuck out beneath her mask.

I set the hot sauce on the blonde's cart and climbed into the pickup bed, kicking boxes of fat tomatoes toward the end. "No hemlock orders today?"

"What?" The girl had no idea what to do with us. She backed up a few steps and looked at the ground like the six-feet markers would tell her where she might be safe.

Phyllis grunted and lit the cigarette. I was half-sure she sold poison under the farmers' market tables. It would explain why she was so twitchy about the in-person market being called off for Covid. Harder to move belladonna tinctures when you had to advertise that shit in writing online.

Max Summerlin walked up as I pushed the last of the produce boxes to the tailgate. Phyllis clocked him from ten feet away, watching his every move as she ashed her cigarette. "Morning, Officer."

He stopped in his tracks, looking at his jeans and T-shirt before glancing at me. He was honestly clueless and there was no explaining to a guy like this that it wasn't the clothes; it was the tension stringing through his shoulders, the stance, the assumed authority in everything his white male gaze touched that gave him away.

He pulled a mask out of his pocket and put it on, nodding at Phyllis. "Ma'am."

"What are you doing here?" I had the DEA phone on me. It wasn't like I was hiding my location, but if they wanted to lure out a killer, it was an objectively bad idea to drape deathsitter Captain America on my arm for everyone to see.

"It's a nice day for a drive."

I paused. So they'd located Frederick Nilsen and wanted me to go in. Sure, why not? What else was I doing today other than painting a target on my back and waiting for someone to notice. I nodded and kicked a box full of beans. "Give me a hand, then."

He picked it up and a twinge shot through his face above the mask. He smoothed out the expression, burying it immediately, but it was too late. I'd already seen the thing he was trying to hide.

"Can I use the truck?" I asked Phyllis.

"I already told you, not on Fridays."

"What else are you doing after this?"

"None of your damn business."

Max finished loading the boxes, saying something to the now extremely nervous blonde as Phyllis and I bickered like the half-dead crones we both were. He interrupted only after the girl wheeled the cart away and the truck waiting to unload behind us honked in frustration.

"I've got transportation. Are you okay to drive this on your own, ma'am?"

The look Phyllis gave him was one hundred percent acid. I was still laughing halfway down the block when Max pointed out an old Chevy sedan. "It's DEA. Untraceable. It won't give you away."

"Doesn't really matter when you're around, Cap."

He didn't comment on that as we headed north out of town. The city fell away as soon as we hit the freeway and I leaned into the window. The radio was off. Neither of us talked. After a week of trying to live as loudly as possible, the quiet was a relief.

Summer fields played like a silent soundtrack on the horizon, rising and falling, flashing their endless, precise rows as the car sped down the road. There were no towns, no gas stations or rest stops, only a couple of stray buildings on the horizon. Even the exits were few and far between. The world out here was distilled to green below and blue above. A Rothko meditation in a landscape, the Calm app manifested in corn.

In the last year I'd tried to fill the empty spaces inside me— with drinking, with drawing, with vengeance. Nothing worked. Even this task force, something I could actually do for Celina, was only a temporary distraction. The void was still there, a black hole in my chest. But at least I could face the emptiness out here, look at it head-on. It was a relief to drive through Iowa, this endless, open country, a place that could swallow me and my misery whole.

I needed this. There was an extra layer of sucking sadness this morning, the reason I'd said yes to Phyllis's stupid demand to help haul her produce. I'd wanted something—anything—to keep me busy. Today was my goddamn birthday.

I'd never had a ton of great birthdays. My mom took me and a few cousins to the quarry to swim one year and it stormed the whole afternoon. Another year a kid threw up on me. When I turned sixteen I got my first ink and the guy did such a bad job I had to design the vines over my arm and shoulder just to cover it up. I didn't even remember my birthday last year; I was too lost in grief and guilt. And now it was here again, reminding me that I was still breathing, still wasting space on this planet where Celina no longer existed. I never made birthday wishes—they seemed as pointless as the rest of the pretend-land of childhood—but as I stared at the ocean of corn whipping past the window, those beckoning, swallowing rows, I wished the killer would hurry up and find me.

After a half hour, maybe longer—long enough that I startled to hear his voice—Max spoke up.

"So. CIP disorder."

I didn't move from my slouch against the window, but the comfort of the land instantly vanished. "What about it?"

"A friend of a friend looked into it after I told her about you. It explains a lot."

"Gold star for you. Now you've got something to put in my obituary besides felonies."

"I'll mention your attitude, too."

"'Criminal Bitch Dies, Feels No Pain.'"

He grinned and shook his head, but the smile faded from his face almost instantly. "Must be nice."

"People like you always think so."

"Who, cops?"

I turned to face forward, legs sprawled. "People with chronic pain."

He didn't say anything to that, but his jaw clenched. He wasn't happy that I saw the thing he wanted to hide. The hand on his bad arm was a little redder than the other one, pretending to drive while the other hand did all the work. The cornfields behind him rose and fell with the hills and I tried to breathe with them, to lull myself into the emptiness again, but he'd ruined the moment.

I picked at a hole in the scratchy old fabric of the seat. Maybe it hurt. I didn't know.

"There was a kid in Pakistan who worked as a street performer," I said. "People came from miles away to see him. He would walk barefoot over hot coals and drive daggers through his arms."

Max glanced at me, then looked at my arm, as if a dagger might be hiding in the ink.

"The kid collected his earnings after every show and went to the hospital to get treated for the wounds and burns. The next day he did it all over again."

"What was his name?"

"I don't know." Nobody ever reported it in any of the stories I'd found. Why would they? He was a freak, something to be pointed at and studied, and by the time the researchers swooped in it was too late. "One day he fell off a roof and broke more than the hospital could put back together."

"He died?"

I nodded. "He was thirteen years old, which in CIP years is practically middle-aged. Most of us never make it past twenty-five."

Max made a noise. "So be more careful. Don't work for drug traffickers or shove knives through your arm."

"Easy for you to say. You hit something and it hurts. You put your hand too close to the fire and it burns. I don't have that. I have to check myself every night for fresh bruises, to see if my joints still bend the right way, whether I have a fever or not, because this body tells me shit on its own. I don't know where the boundary is between healthy and hurt, between living and dying. How do I skirt a line I won't ever be able to find?"

The energy in the car changed. We drove in silence the rest of the way, but I couldn't see the fields anymore. The waving green stalks turned into feet smoking over hot coals. Burning flesh filled the car, the singe of hair and blistering skin. A hand pressed to a hot teakettle. The sticky surprise of blood, dark and staining.

I was twenty-seven years old today and long past my expiration date. I should've been dead by now. Cold in a grave, my name forgotten, just another story about some freak of nature. If I'd died at twenty-five, like I was supposed to, Celina would still be here. She'd be training with her uncle, soothing the aches of old men who came in for 5:00 a.m. coffee at the diner, falling in love with someone else. Someone better than me.

She had so much to live for. They probably all did. Matthew. Gail. The kid in Pakistan, driving knives through his arms, had a thousand better reasons to be on this planet. Yet somehow I was the one sitting here, on my way to reunite with one of Sam's friends and see if he was a drug lord who maybe, fingers crossed, wanted to kill me.

The slaughterhouse was ten miles outside Waterloo, a chain of stained white metal boxes surrounded by dirty paddocks and a parking lot of cars that made Phyllis's pickup look reliable. We'd stopped at an abandoned gas station with broken windows and potholed concrete to meet up with the DEA agents, who put a wire on me and told me how to get here. Max hung back with the DEA, and I'd driven the sedan to the slaughterhouse.

They said Nilsen would be here today. I didn't know how they knew that, considering the ten-foot fences surrounding the property and the guard station out front, but I pulled up and said I had an appointment with the boss. "Tell him Sam Olson's representative is here."

The guard called it in, making me wait off to the side for ten minutes before getting the reply that I could enter. I smiled at the security cameras as I drove through the gate.

A tired-looking woman met me at the front door. Instead of going to an office, she led me to a locker room bisected with plastic sheets hanging from the ceiling.

"Distancing." The woman explained before making me take off all my earrings and other jewelry and sealing everything, including my phone, in a Ziploc bag. She tossed me a bag with a blue jump-suit, gloves, a hairnet, and elastic booties that slipped over shoes. "Keep your mask on and change into that."

"Why?"

"You can't be on the floor otherwise."

"The floor?"

She pointed to a door on the opposite end of the room and left without any further explanation.

I changed into the prison lunch lady outfit and went the way she'd pointed, through a solid metal door plastered with signs covered in four-point font talking about health, safety, and OSHA codes. On the other side was a long, dark hallway. A man stood in shadows at the opposite end.

It was noisier here, the screech of high-pitched machinery mixed with white noise coming from somewhere nearby. It got louder as I walked down the hallway.

The man waited, watching me, and it wasn't until I was a couple feet away that I knew for sure. Frederick Nilsen.

Even with the mask, he looked the same as I remembered. Round and squat, those same cow eyes peering from behind thick black glasses. It felt like we could've just stepped out of Sam's kitchen together and the déjà vu of it made my skin crawl. I fought the urge to look behind me and see if Sam was here, waiting in the shadows, ladle raised to bash my head in.

"Kara Johnson." He tipped his head and pushed open another door behind him, waving me into a bigger room lined with rows of carcasses. Pigs, I thought, skinned and gutted. They hung on hooks from metal chains snaking across the ceiling and my breath fogged through the mask.

"Long time, Fred." I glanced behind the animals as we walked through an aisle of bodies, checking the edges of the room.

"I didn't think you were alive."

"It's debatable."

He laughed the same wheezy chuckle I remembered over beef stew, but the thought of meat right now made my stomach flip and the butcher shop blood smell tinged with chemicals wasn't helping. The machinery noise kept getting louder. What would Jillian do in a place like this? She wasn't the type to crumble or record secret footage for some PETA exposé. She'd more likely set the penned animals free and light the place on fire.

"How's business?"

He waved a hand around. "We process twelve hundred hogs an hour. Not a single Covid outbreak." He said it like he thought I'd challenge him.

"I meant your other business."

"Why? Are you looking for a job?"

"No." The blood chemical smell was clogging my throat. I dug the heel of my hand into my chest and the wire taped to my skin. "I have a message from Sam."

"Is that so?"

We entered another room and I could see the source of the noise now, or at least one of them. Workers stood in a line, cutting up carcasses with what looked like mini buzz saws. The ceiling chains snaked through here, too, moving the animals down the line as pieces were carved out of them.

Frederick stopped in the middle of the room. None of the workers looked at us, but their spines straightened and their movements became precise in the way of people who know they were being watched. My own back tensed as I realized this was the place he wanted me, full of saws and people too scared to look and so loud I could barely hear him. So loud the wire became useless. A man dressed in the same blue uniform appeared in the far door. He was tall and broad, not the same build as the guy in the hospital footage but muscle all the same. A guy waiting for instructions. The hair on the back of my neck stood up.

Frederick leaned in and his mask brushed my ear. "What does Sam want me to know?"

It was an effort not to shove him away, to stand absolutely still and let his coffee breath seep through his mask and into my skin.

"He wants you to have what's yours."

Frederick didn't say anything, didn't give up a single tell. In front of us, an animal carcass jerked as a worker sawed into it.

I swallowed. "I know where it is."

"Smart girl. And you haven't run off into the sunset with it?"

I moved in slow motion, turning until I could see the whites of his bulging, unblinking eyes. If Frederick was Sam's successor, he'd lost tens of millions of dollars when everything went down last winter. He'd kill to recoup the product he'd paid for and never gotten.

"Sam kept his promises." I kept turning until we faced each other a foot apart, nothing between us but the shriek of saws and smell of blood. "And so do I."

Max

We left the DEA team at the abandoned gas station outside Waterloo as they argued over the recording. One of them thought they could clean it up to make the last part of the conversation distinguishable, but Kara told them to forget it.

"He didn't tip his hand."

"Didn't you get anything?" The agent looked disgusted.

"A new appreciation for vegans." She reached under her shirt and ripped the wire off, tossing it at a tech before striding past me out the door. "Let's go."

We let the team sweep the other vehicle for any bugs or trackers and took a different car back to Iowa City. She obviously didn't want to talk. She leaned into the door, watching the fields again as I checked the rearview mirror for tails and even exited the freeway a few times to make sure we weren't being followed. She sniffed at one point, unimpressed by my driving tactics, but didn't say anything. And that wasn't how we were going to spend this time together.

I picked up some coffee from an operating gas station and handed her a cup as we got back on the road.

"What happened after you told Nilsen you had a message from Sam?" That was the point when the background interference became too much and no matter how the DEA agent tweaked the frequency, we couldn't make out any of the conversation after that.

"Nothing."

"He said something. Tell me the rest of the exchange word for word."

"I baited a hook and he didn't bite, okay?"

"What did he say?"

"I don't know." She shrugged and turned on the radio.

I turned it off and repeated their entire interaction up to the point when the saws became too loud. She ignored me. It was almost cute how she thought that would be all it took to win this argument.

I turned onto a county road and drove until there was nothing but corn surrounding us in every direction, pulled to the shoulder, and cut the engine.

"What is this?" She looked around.

"Word for word." I slipped my mask down and took a sip of coffee like I had all the time in the world. She glared at me. I smiled.

The wall of corn next to us was taller than the car, its tassels touching nothing but clouds and blue sky. Without warning, she shoved the car door open, chucked her mask behind her, and walked directly into the field.

"Hey!"

She didn't turn around. I pocketed the keys and went after her.

Green closed in around me. After only a few steps I couldn't see anything except stalks, leaves, and golden tassels waving in the breeze. Kara had completely disappeared except for the rustling sounds ahead. I followed the noise.

I hadn't been in a cornfield since I was fifteen years old on a detasseling crew, but the memories of getting up at five in the morning and taking a bus out to the fields came flooding back. Getting soaked by the dew in the morning and scorched by the sun in the afternoon. Eating salt tablets, hunkering in the shade of the truck for lunch, the foreman yelling whenever we missed a stalk. It was three weeks of hot, hard work and one of the only jobs we could get as kids during the summer.

I was the only one who wanted to know why we were pulling the tops off a sea of cornstalks, who researched plant pollination and made diagrams in notebooks during the gray hours of the night. When I explained why preventing cross-pollination improved seed corn yields to another Clear Lake city kid who got bused out to the fields, he moved away and wouldn't talk to me for the rest of the day, which, in a cornfield when you're a teenager, is a long time.

I wasn't getting ignored in a cornfield again.

Leaves whipped against my face and arms, cutting tracks into my skin. I caught a glimpse of a dark head darting through the rows and picked up my pace. Where the hell did she think she was going?

When I caught up, she whirled on me, shoving me so hard and fast I stumbled back. My hand went automatically for a non-existent holster. She caught the reflex and her eyes narrowed. Moving in again, she feinted right, and when I moved to block her, she punched me in the left shoulder. My bad shoulder. Shock waves of pain ricocheted out from the spot. I grunted and a surge of anger shot over the pain, coating it in slick, red heat. I hooked a foot around her leg and took her feet out from under her. By the time she got back up, I was out of arm's reach, holding my shoulder and waiting.

She brushed herself off, daggers in her eyes. "I don't work for you."

"No, we're supposed to be working together." I kept my voice flat, my face relaxed despite the screaming nerves tightening every muscle and tendon in my shoulder. "A concept you've obviously never heard of before."

"You're not working with me. You're waiting around for someone to kill me so you can chase after the bad guy because you think it means you're good, that playing your righteous little gun games makes your life matter."

I opened my mouth, ready to deny it, to tell her how fundamentally skewed her entire worldview was, but nothing came out.

Christ, was she right? I'd been desperate for this task force, for the promise of a new investigation. It was something different, something to focus on beside this goddamn pandemic, but it was more than that, too. It was the hunt. My mom always said I couldn't let anything lie. I needed the how and whys, whether it was a waving tassel on top of a cornstalk or a tipped-over semitruck stuffed with pills, its destination unknown. I needed explanations for all the questions I still had about Belgrave and Matthew Moore and to make sure everyone associated with them ended up either behind bars or dead. I hadn't cared which one, because this wasn't about them. It was about me. Jonah called it my hero complex. Fuck.

A crow flew overhead and Kara tracked it, momentarily distracted by the shadow of wings that flickered over her face. When she looked down again, a deep resignation seemed to have taken all the fight out of her. "You like having answers, don't you? Because you think it means you're in control. That you're not spiraling into oblivion like the rest of us. But you're looking for the wrong fucking answers. Nilsen didn't say shit. And you want to know how exactly he phrased it." She laughed, humorless and choking in the oppressive August air. "So you found out I have CIP disorder. Congratulations. You still know nothing about me."

I dropped my arm from my shoulder. "I knew her."

"Who?"

"Celina."

She looked like I'd gut punched her. "How?"

We hadn't been more than acquaintances. I was a forty-year-old cop and she was an eighteen-year-old girl; the only thing we had in common was Jonah. But he lived on the edge of the state and she had no immediate family in town when she moved to Iowa City. I started dropping into the diner before my shifts, grabbing a coffee and a roll for breakfast and checking on her.

Celina Kendrick looked a lot like her uncle. She had the same pale skin and dark hair, but where Jonah avoided the brunt of humanity, Celina embraced it. She lit up with a smile every time I came in and always asked about Shelley and Garrett, whether he'd gotten to play shortstop at his latest game. The rest of the staff loved her and she knew every regular by name. The last time I stopped in before she went missing, she'd been dancing behind the bakery case, laughing as she got down to the Bon Jovi song that pumped through the sound system.

"Living on a Prayer." All the blood drained from Kara's face as I told the story. "She sang the lyrics as she handed me my take-out bag. I was surprised she even knew them."

"The music got recycled every few days. She always had one of those songs stuck in her head."

Celina Kendrick's face filled my mind: the young woman who was barely older than Garrett, just beginning to find her place in this world.

"You're right. I don't know much about you and you're probably right that it doesn't matter. Neither of us matters. But I know she deserved better."

We stood facing each other while corn leaves whipped our arms and the sun beat down on our heads. Kara's throat worked and she blinked, looking away.

"Nilsen asked me if I killed Sam, if I'd taken him out in order to take over."

"What did you tell him?"

"The truth. That someone got there before me, but I'd wanted to. I wanted him dead, even though I knew it wouldn't bring her back. Killing him wouldn't help. Nothing does." Her throat closed up and she breathed for a second, taking unsteady gulps of air. "This DEA thing—Morales promising to go public with Celina's story—it's something to do for her. Something she would've, I don't know, been proud of? Stayed with me because of? But I hate it. I hate every minute of it even though I don't know what else to do. What even is there? What am I good for, if not this?"

Her words caught me square in the gut, in the place that had been twisted up for months every time I walked into ICPD. It was the question underneath everything else, the thing that sent me running into this task force and barreling into this cornfield when I could've been home with the people who actually mattered. The ones I hadn't lost—not yet.

Kara shrugged and turned away, taking another ragged breath. "Nilsen gave me shit, okay? Nothing. So apparently I'm not good at this, either."

I stared at her back for a minute, the vines snaking over her arms and puckering into the exit wound of a bullet, before walking through the cutting leaves of the cornstalks and leaving her alone in the field.

Kara

It took me a while, standing alone in the cornfield, to realize he was waiting for me. The engine started and idled in the distance, unmoving, until I emerged from the rows and climbed into the car.

Max dissociated to hideous classic rock for most of the way back to Iowa City, which was good because I didn't have any idea what to say to him now. He'd known Celina. He'd heard her laugh and watched her adorably terrible dancing and glimpsed pieces of her life I'd never seen. And the worst part was that Celina would've liked him. I knew it on a gut level. She would've seen right through his patriarchal protector bullshit and befriended him anyway. She would've asked about his job or his dog or whatever crap he'd unloaded on her the day before and curled toward his pain, absorbing what she could, no matter what it cost her. The force of knowing that, of feeling the echo of her feelings, landed like a three-ton weight on my chest. I could barely breathe around it.

We were both covered in shallow cuts from the whiplike edges of the corn leaves, bright red slashing across our skin. I drew a finger over a slice across my forearm, tracing the line from one end to the other, back and forth over the break in my skin. I wished that just once it would hurt, that I could gouge the skin open further and feel a bite of warning, that sudden animal focus. Anything to distract me from the sucking hole inside my chest. But there was nothing. I could cut my arm off and my body would barely shiver. All I had was the ripping feeling inside me, telling me over and over again that Celina wouldn't have knocked Max on his ass in the field. Celina would have been better—was better—in every way. Sitting next to someone who knew her and had seen how amazing she was just rubbed acid into the wound.

In Iowa City, I gave directions to Phyllis's house, but when we turned onto her street, my hand shot to the radio and flipped it off. Silence fuzzed in my ears.

"What?" Instantly tense, Max slowed the car to a crawl.

"The window." The far window on the front of the house—the window to the room Phyllis kept padlocked and refused to even look at when she toddled down the hallway—was cracked open. That window had never been open, day or night, in the seven days I'd been staying here, but it was lifted off the sill two inches now, paint flecking into the still-closed plastic blinds.

I looked at anything else, pointing out where Max could drop me off, and kept my expression neutral. There were no lights on inside. This time of day Phyllis usually napped or sat out in her garden listening to true-crime podcasts, giving epic critiques on everything the criminals did wrong. "Stupid sons of bitches, you can't burn a body in an open pit."

After everything that happened in the cornfield, after I'd punched him and insulted him and mocked his life choices, I wouldn't have been surprised if Max yeeted me out of the car at twenty miles per hour, shouting, "Good luck." But he pulled into the driveway and let the engine idle, his eyes sweeping every corner of the property as he pasted a fake smile on his face. "What is it?"

"Probably nothing. Do you have any weapons?"

He hesitated and I didn't blame him. I wouldn't trust me, either. After an awkward pause, he reached into the console and slid a switchblade across the seat. I flipped it open and pocketed it in my hoodie, got out of the car, and raised my voice. "Thanks for the lift, Cap."

"See you tomorrow?"

"Fuck if I know." I slammed the door and pretended to check my phone, listening to the house as Max drove off. A dog barked somewhere down the street and the air conditioner whined in the side yard, but inside there was only silence. I unlocked the door and stepped into the living room.

Nothing looked out of place. The remote sat in the middle of the spindly-legged coffee table, next to the stack of *Readers Digests* I'd never seen her read.

No one was in the kitchen. Two mugs sat on the table, one in front of Phyllis's spot and the other by the window seat where I'd had breakfast this morning. Phyllis's chair was pushed back against the wall, angled out from the table. A wet napkin lay on the linoleum floor. It was wrong—all of it. Phyllis washed every cup and put them in the dish rack to dry. She would never leave mugs on the table or trash on the floor. The hair rose on the back of my neck as I flashed to the crime scene shots of Gail's mobile home, the two half-drunk cups of coffee. Her body shoved through a glass table.

"Phyllis?"

The sliding glass door to the garden was unlocked. I didn't see her outside, but that didn't mean she wasn't in the jungle of trees and bushes somewhere. I opened the door. "Hey, Phyllis!"

Nothing.

I doubled back through the living room, creeping on the floorboards I'd tested the first day I moved in, the ones I knew wouldn't squeak. My hand slipped over the knife handle in my pocket. A pipe in the basement clanked.

At the end of the hallway, opposite Phyllis's bedroom, the door to the off-limits room stood half-open, its padlock hanging from the latch. Not breathing, I drifted toward it, checking the bathroom and my room as I went. Both spaces were dark and empty.

I drew the knife and pushed the off-limits door open, revealing the room by inches.

It was a time capsule. A twin canopy bed stood in the middle of the room, made up with a quilted yellow blanket decorated with orange and olive flowers. Dark green shag carpeting swallowed my feet. A dresser stood in one corner, covered in picture frames dripping with ribbons and a brass necklace hanger topped with two birds. The pictures were mostly of dance teams, but one shot showed two hooked-nosed women in front of a brick building. The younger one had long brown hair flowing over her graduation gown. The older woman, standing tense and unsmiling in a trench coat with the exact same skull-hugging curls she still wore fifty years later, was Phyllis.

The door creaked. I spun around as a black blur caught me in the temple, sending me into the dresser. I grabbed for it, but before I could get my balance, another blow to the back of my head put me facedown on the carpet. A foot stepped on my back and another pressed into my cheek. Drool leaked out of my mouth. I couldn't see past the dresser, but I made a grab for the ankle that was grinding into my skull.

"Uh-uh." A voice tsk-tsked me, singsongy and quiet, as the pressure changed. Something thin and sharp pressed against my throat. "Let go."

I held on a minute longer, weighing the bony feel of the ankle in my hand and the possibility of ending everything right here, pouring my throat out on a green shag carpet and never having to wake up without Celina again. No more exploding birds. No more playing nice with cops. No more jumping through hoops and pretending to be something I wasn't. It was almost enough to squeeze the ankle harder and wait for the release of the knife, for the white cockatoo to fly down to my side, feathers gleaming and mischief in her eyes.

But.

But something about that singsongy voice grated. The stink of earthy breath hit the side of my face, making me gag. I wasn't going out by the hand of a guy like this, someone who waited in an old lady's house and clocked you from behind, who wouldn't even look you in the eyes. Fuck this guy.

I let go of his ankle.

"Good." He shifted his stance and the pressure of the knife at my throat eased. A whir of plastic sounded above me. Zip ties. "Put your hands behind your back."

Slowly, I dragged my hands along the carpet and slipped them up to my lower back. He breathed unsteadily and in the silence of the room his stomach gurgled. He wasn't that heavy. One forty, one fifty at most.

Where was Phyllis? Where was Max? Was he calling in the team for reinforcements or just sitting around the block, listening to music and waiting for a guy with a bloody knife to come strolling out of the house?

When the guy pulled my hands together to wrap the zip tie around them, I flipped, rolling as hard and fast as I could. He lost his balance and hit the bed post with a crash and a grunt. Scrambling up, I grabbed the knife out of my hoodie pocket and backhanded a slash into thin air as I spun around.

He stood up, too, the knife he'd put to my throat in his hand, and I got a good look at him for the first time. He was short and wiry, with dark brown curly hair and a completely forgettable face except for his eyes, which were too round and bright. They practically glittered as we faced each other. He wore a black hoodie and jeans, same as me, and with a jolt I wondered how long he'd been casing the house, if he'd watched Phyllis and me leave for the farmers' market this morning, put on the exact same outfit as me, masked up, and walked inside without any of the neighbors looking twice.

This was the guy who'd taken out Matthew and Gail, the reason I was here.

"Took you long enough. I was getting bored."

He smiled, flashing small, sharp-looking teeth. "My apologies. It's hard to find you without your DEA pet following you around."

So he knew about Morales and the task force. Had he seen Max dropping me off?

"What do you want?"

His eyes traveled over me, pausing at pulse points, the places I would bleed out the quickest. "Information."

"*Jeopardy!*-style, or are you more the Trivial Pursuit type?"

"You're not telling the DEA everything."

"I don't tell anyone everything." His stomach gurgled again and I snorted. "Should we do this over lunch?"

"The codes. Where—" A creak behind me stopped us both. It came from the hallway. The guy's eyes glittered hot and angry. They bulged even rounder and I thought of a fish, a piranha's mouth dilating as it went in for the kill. I barely had time to process what he said before he lunged full speed into me. Fuck, he was quick. I dodged and swiped at his knife hand with my own. The blades clashed like swords as we both hit the wall next to the door. My head cracked against the plaster. He twisted me around at the exact moment Max appeared in the doorway. Max's legs were spread wide, gun drawn and pointed at the guy's head, two inches away from mine.

"Iowa City PD. Let her go."

The guy dragged me back a step, holding me like the dumb human shield I was. He wrenched my hand behind my back and pressed both knives into my spine.

Happy fucking birthday to me.

Max

I knew something was wrong the second Kara switched off the clashing guitar riffs on the radio. I'd spent a week watching her and she gave off more tells than she probably knew about or would admit. Her face went stony, void of any emotion, which meant her Spidey sense was tingling. Usually it did that right before she spotted me in the bar or tailing her home. She stopped fidgeting and slunk down in her seat, too, slouching like she did at the task force meetings when she wanted to appear indifferent but was actually soaking up every word and detail.

Nothing looked off about the house to me—no sign of anyone inside or out—but I didn't know this place the way Kara did. Despite the misgivings I still had about her as a person, I trusted her instincts.

After handing her the knife, I drove away and called Morales as soon as I left the block.

"What kind of situation?" he wanted to know.

"I don't know, but she was spooked. Can you send Grimes and Olson?"

He grumbled about pulling them off their current assignments for nothing more than some "scared-ass felon who's probably playing you," but he dispatched them anyway and came back on the line. "You think this is Nilsen?"

I doubled back, turning into the alley behind the houses, and killed the engine. "Can't be. He didn't know she was around until this afternoon, and no one followed us out of the slaughterhouse."

"Maybe Chase, then. Pyle's been tracking him in Dubuque all day but he could've sent someone local." Morales sounded like he was chewing. "Has Doyle marked her since she made contact with him?"

"No." The local dealer would be motivated, after Kara had beaten him up and taken his stash. I'd kept an eye out for him all week, but he hadn't surfaced anywhere.

The alley was quiet. I clipped my badge to my belt and drew my gun as I approached the fence to the backyard where Kara was staying. Tree branches and vines spilled over the top, like the fence was barely holding them back. "I'm going in."

"Sure." He didn't sound worried, which was the opposite of Larsen whenever I went off script at ICPD. Larsen wanted to know how my arm was, how my head was, the status of all my pending cases, what I had eaten for breakfast, everything. Morales seemed more interested in finding a soda. "The guys are en route. ETA ten minutes."

I hung up and unlatched the gate, creeping through the craziest garden maze I'd ever seen in this city and listening for any sound beside the rustle of birds in the trees.

The sliding glass door to the house stood open. An invitation.

I slipped inside, letting my eyes adjust to the dark. Voices came from the other end of the house and I cleared spaces as I moved in that direction. The kitchen, empty, the yawing door to the basement with a long set of concrete steps, dark. No one was in the living room, and as I moved through it, I started to make out what the voices were saying.

"You're not telling the DEA everything."

A man. Calm, soft tones I didn't recognize. I stopped halfway down the short hallway, hovering against the wall and waiting to hear more.

"I don't tell anyone everything."

Hearing it out loud—hearing Kara admit that she was keeping things from the team—sent all the hair on the back of my neck up. I missed what she said next, though, because something caught my eye in the room directly opposite the one with the voices. I thought it was a mouse at first, inching out from behind the dust ruffle of a neatly made bed, but when it moved again I made out fingers. It was a hand, scraping unsteadily against the carpet. I stepped toward it without thinking and the floorboards creaked beneath my feet.

I froze. The man's voice cut off. There was a beat of silence, followed by a crash and the sounds of bodies struggling. I pivoted off the wall and into the doorway.

"Iowa City PD. Let her go."

The man hid behind Kara. All I could see was his arm, hair, and one bright eye peering out from behind her ear. He held something to her back.

"Back up. Slowly. Now." He spoke in the same calm, controlled tone, like he was placing a curbside order for a meal he didn't particularly care about. Kara stood rigid, staring at me. She looked angry, but as the moment drew out, something passed over her face and her gaze dropped to the gun.

"Do it."

She wanted me to shoot. Her or him, I didn't know.

"Back up," the man said again. Kara's chest bowed slightly, as though he was pushing something into her back. Her face didn't show any pain or fear. It wouldn't, though, not even if I pulled the trigger.

I hesitated, heart pounding. My bad arm started to shake. Kara's eyes bore into mine, daring me.

No.

I lowered my weapon and moved into the hall. Kara shook her head, looking disgusted. For every step I took backward, the man pushed her forward the same distance.

"Let's talk about this, okay?"

"In there." He nodded at the bedroom behind me, the one where I'd seen the hand on the floor. I complied without taking my eyes off him, moving slowly into the room. When the back of my legs hit the bed, I heard a noise: a shallow, rattling breath coming from the space between the bed and the wall.

"We can cut you a deal."

The man acted like I wasn't even talking. "Sit down and kick the weapon over here."

I lowered myself onto the quilt. Where the hell were Grimes and Olson? It had been at least ten minutes since I'd requested backup. Stretching the moment out, taking as long as I dared while my heart thudded in my ears, I bent to the floor to set the Glock down.

Then everything happened at once.

Behind me, something hit the bed. The man's eye widened and Kara's face split into a grin a heartbeat before she was being shoved in my direction. The man bolted. A gunshot exploded, missing him by inches and shattering one of the framed pictures in the hallway. Glass and plaster flew everywhere. Without missing a beat, Kara rebounded off the bed and sprinted after him. The woman from the farmers' market leaned against the wall, a smoking shotgun clutched in her hands. Grabbing my gun, I raced after the other two.

A muffled cascading crash came from the kitchen, like a noise at the end of a long tunnel. My ears rang, and as I sprinted through the living room, I saw a car pull up to the front curb. Grimes and Olson, I hoped. But no one else was in front. No suspect. No Kara.

The sliding door in the kitchen was still open and I got there in time to see the man disappearing into the jungle of the backyard. I barreled after him, zigzagging around rows of bushes and trellises, ducking under tree branches. I couldn't hear anything except the thudding of my own feet. When I reached the gate, I stopped short. It was closed. And latched.

Mulch crunched behind me. I swung around in time to see a knife arcing through the air and leapt back a fraction of a second before it would've sliced open my neck.

I stumbled into the gate. Before I could recover, he had my gun hand pressed against the fence and was raising the knife again.

"You don't want to do this."

His eyes gleamed as they peered up into mine and a smile curled his mouth. Everything became crystal clear in that moment. The world dilated and each detail came into painfully sharp focus: the gate splinters scratching my head, the clammy vise of the man's glove on my hand. I could count every black spike of the eyelashes that ringed the man's eyes, like spider legs braced in their web. And somewhere deep in my head Shelley's voice broke, telling me to be careful. Telling me I didn't know what was going to happen.

But I knew. I knew from the spark in the hired killer's eyes. They were pure black, dilating the world back at me.

"Beg me." The knife twitched and I flinched. My heart filled my ears, pounding like a madman. He laughed, low and light.

A shovel arced into view, catching the sun as it swung around an overgrown bush, bringing Kara behind it. She raced in a strange, uneven gait, every move playing in slow motion in my head. I saw the killer's smile freeze, felt him tense as he pushed the blade into my neck, planning to end me before he dealt with the threat behind him. But he didn't get a chance.

I lurched away as the shovel connected with his head in a dull crack. His body hit the gate. He slumped to his knees, and like that we were both on him. I twisted his arm until he dropped the knife while Kara flipped the shovel to the handle end and shoved it repeatedly into the back of his neck and spine until he was coughing up dirt in the closest flower bed. I cuffed him as she tried to step on his head, saying something that might've been "How do you like it?" but I wasn't positive. My ears were still ringing from the shotgun blast.

Blood dripped down my neck, and my bad arm throbbed from pinning the guy, but I couldn't feel a thing. No pain. All I knew in that moment was that I was alive.

Then I realized what Kara was doing. I shoved her off the guy's head. He was white, but accusations of police brutality could stick with any suspect and I wasn't invoking that shitstorm, not in this investigation.

She stumbled back, one leg dragging on the ground with her foot pointed in at an unnatural angle. I tracked up from that foot, over her leg, and all the way to her neck, where a thin slash of red bloomed next to her windpipe.

"You're hurt."

"You too." She nodded at my own neck, which felt wet and sticky. This son of a bitch liked slitting throats.

"No, your leg."

But before I could explain—because apparently she had no idea her leg was broken—Grimes and Olson appeared. They secured the scene, ignoring Kara, and started reading Miranda rights to the man who'd almost killed us both.

Kara

The inside of the house was dark. I stalked past the open door to the basement, where that asshole had thrown me down the concrete stairs, and back to the bedrooms.

Phyllis wasn't in her room. The shell blast she'd unloaded had left an ugly hole in her ugly hallway wallpaper, and the last photo in the lineup of her kids lay obliterated on the floor. I picked up the remains of the picture—the only girl—and crunched over the glass to the unlocked bedroom.

Phyllis sat on the canopy bed, holding the shotgun in her lap like a baby. Her head listed to the left and one of her eyes had already started swelling shut, the wrinkles bulging and swallowing her eyeball. It was pointless asking what had happened before I got here, how long the guy had been in the house. I'd get more answers from the obliterated girl in my hand.

She didn't look over when I stepped into the room but kept staring at the framed pictures on the dresser. "You get rid of him?"

I shook my head. "Cops have him."

She huffed out a thin, shaky breath. "I would've nailed him square between the eyes if it wasn't for this damn glaucoma."

"They've got weed for that, you know."

"Wouldn't improve my aim." Her good eye snagged on the shredded photo. Her mouth pinched and the skin on her neck seemed to quiver. "Get out." I started to say something else, but her grip on the gun tightened and she straightened so fast the fabric of her housedress rippled. "Now."

Moving slowly, I propped the remains of the picture against the necklace hanger with the brass birds perched like guardians on top of it. I wanted to say something, to comfort her somehow, but it felt completely beyond my skill set. Carefully, I adjusted the half of the face remaining in the picture and left her alone in the room.

My chest buzzed like I was over-caffeinated. My hands shook and my body felt strange and off-balance. I couldn't sit down or stop moving, and my head kept replaying the moments with the rat-faced guy over and over. Since I'd come back to Iowa City, I'd spent every second of every day waiting for him to appear out of the shadows, and now that he had, I didn't know what to do. I could still smell the stink of his breath and the must of that ancient carpet even as I paced in front of the living room window and watched him get loaded into the back of a DEA car.

The agents climbed in front and drove away, leaving Max in the driveway. He came back to the house and stood in the open doorway, looking at me for an uncomfortable amount of time. I didn't want to hear what he was thinking because I was pretty sure I already knew what it was.

I'd asked him to shoot me. I'd stood there, bait finally caught in the predator's jaws, and told it to swallow. And we definitely weren't going to talk about it.

I kept pacing, avoiding his silent cop-laser stare. "What now?"

"ICPD is sending a crime scene team."

"Sounds like a party."

He watched me for another minute before turning to clock the street and surrounding houses. A few neighbors pretended to garden or get their mail while they gaped at Phyllis's house. People didn't get cuffed and hauled away much in this part of town. "You'll need to come to the station and give a deposition. Both of you."

"Good luck getting Phyllis there."

"But we're going to the hospital first."

"No." I stopped dead in my tracks. "No hospitals."

"Your leg is broken."

I looked down and took a few test steps, noticing for the first time how the left leg dragged behind me. It was harder to lift that foot off the floor. Fuck.

He moved further into the living room, cautiously, like I was some injured animal that would run or attack. "What happened?"

"Asshole threw me down the basement stairs when I went after him. That's what slowed me down getting to the yard."

"Thanks for showing up when you did."

I glanced up from the stupid leg. Max was closer than I thought and he looked awkward. Oh. Right. I'd forgotten the part about saving his life.

I nodded, meeting his eyes, and we stood there for a minute, with our matching attempted throat slashes. Something shifted in the air between us, a song changing to the next key. It wasn't anything I recognized or knew what to do with.

Luckily, Phyllis appeared with her shotgun in tow. Max flashed his badge, like they hadn't already met this morning at the farmers' market, and explained what was going on. Phyllis's face grew tighter with every word, contracting around the growing goose egg on her eye, until she unleashed, telling him exactly where he could stuff his crime scene team. It dislodged whatever that moment with Max had stuck in my chest, and I hid a smile as she cursed him out.

While they argued, I grabbed my bug-out bag from the front closet and snagged the truck keys off the hanger. "I'll meet you at the station."

Max moved to block me. "Where are you going?"

I didn't glance back at either of them on my way out. "My own hospital."

The sanctuary wasn't easy to find. A farmer must've sold them a back plot because the paved road ended a half mile before the GPS said I arrived. It took two turns onto gravel and dirt before I saw the small wooden sign for Wild Hearts Sanctuary. Another sign underneath it said NO TRESPASSERS. Fences lined both sides of the driveway, and as I bumped over a concrete cattle guard, I noticed the black eye of a security camera mounted high on a light pole.

Pastures surrounded the buildings and wind turbines lined the hills, churning steadily as I pulled into the yard and cut the truck's wheezy engine. A herd of pigs grunted from the base of a nearby hill, rooting through dirt as they looked for snacks. Two cows stared at me from a barn trough, their mouths working as they clocked the visitor. Before I could decide whether to try the barns or the house, a girl appeared, wiping her hands on her overalls. Three cats trailed behind her.

Out of habit, I pulled the ball cap low over my eyes.

"Tours are the first Saturday of the month. Masks required."
Bright blue hair flowed beneath her bandanna and her cheeks carried a residual layer of baby fat. She scooped up one of the cats, perching it like a parrot on her shoulder. Major witchy energy on this girl.

"I'm not here for a tour." I kept my weight on the good leg and slammed the pickup door. "I'm looking for Jillian."

"Jillian?" The girl was surprised, and I couldn't tell if there was a sense of possession laced in the question or if she was just shocked that Jillian had a human visitor.

"Yeah." I hoped to god she was around. From the little Jillian had shared over the years I knew she spent most of her time here during the week before going to the veterinary clinic on the weekends. "I'm a customer of hers. In Des Moines."

The girl nodded and told me to wait as she picked her way through a pasture.

A pig wandered away from the rest of the herd toward the fence, grunting like it expected food. It was the strangest pig I'd ever seen, with a black body and tufts of hair curling out of its ears. Straw clung to the gray hair fuzzing its back, like it had spent most of the afternoon rolling around in a pile of it. I dug a handful of lint and sunflower seeds out of my pocket and walked over, dragging the broken leg behind me like a bad crutch.

"Hungry?"

The pig inspected what I tossed over the fence, looking up at me with unmistakable judgment. Not a lot of warm welcomes at Wild Hearts.

A noise from the barn drew my attention and I watched the blue-haired girl walk out with Jillian, the two of them chatting side by side. They straddled the fence and the girl detoured back to the house, where the cats circled and rubbed against the foundation, waiting for her.

I'd never seen Jillian outside the clinic, I realized as she walked over. She wore skinny jeans tucked into work boots that came up to her knees and were covered in dried mud. Her shirt was dirty, pit-stained, and looked chewed at the hem. A straw-colored cowboy hat was planted on her head. Something in my stomach flipped over. It was nothing—just a reaction to the cowgirl thing. I didn't know I had a cowgirl thing, but whatever. Her eyes—I couldn't help noticing—looked brighter here, her cheeks flushed red and alive, and a smile almost twitched over her face as she stopped in front of me and planted her hands on her hips. Almost.

"Serafina, meet Fluffy."

I turned to the pig, who was nosing my pants through the fence, probably hunting for something better than lint and sunflower seeds. "Hi, Serafina."

"What are you doing here?" There was no warmth in the greeting, not that I'd expected any.

"Checking on my goat barn. Making sure you named it in my honor."

Her eyes narrowed, raking down me until she saw I was keeping all my weight on one leg. One perfect eyebrow cocked under the hat.

"And I might need a cast."

She didn't say anything for so long that I realized what a mistake this was, a complete invasion of her privacy. She'd never told me I could come see her at the sanctuary, had only given me the address so I could send her payment for sewing up the bullet hole in my shoulder. Everything about the place screamed, *Stay out*. Signs, surveillance, Gen Z workers shooing people away. And the last time I'd bothered her, the cops had practically tossed her business looking for me.

"I'm sorry. I shouldn't be here." I half walked, half hopped toward Phyllis's truck, trying to keep my weight off the bum leg.

A loud sigh came from behind me.

"Fluffy. Wait."

I turned back. Jillian leaned on the fence, one boot braced against the slats, the cowboy hat tipped at an angle. "The goat barn still needs solar panels."

She smiled then, slow and wide, before coming to thread an arm under my shoulder, acting as my crutch as she led me to the house.

Jillian ordered me to take off my pants in a treatment room that smelled like animal musk and antiseptic. She had as much equipment here as in the clinic in Des Moines. Large kennels lined one side of the space, and locked cupboards and machines filled the other. I sat on the exam table in a T-shirt and my underwear.

"You're lucky you're not sharing the room. I had a goat with a cheek abscess in here earlier." Jillian positioned a machine over my leg.

She didn't ask how I broke the leg. She never asked, which meant I never had to lie, and I was grateful. I didn't want to think about this day anymore. Nilsen's rancid breath in the slaughter-house with carcasses hanging and bloodless behind him, the killer's foot grinding into my head, Max's Glock pointed at me, my body cartwheeling down the concrete steps of the basement as things inside me crunched and snapped. I'd been so close to done so many times, but somehow I was still here and it was fucking exhausting. Lying here, pushing air in and out. The weight of my skull, my chest, the shards of my numb, voiceless leg, all dragging me deeper into a pit that never bottomed out. A wet trail leaked down my temples into my hair and I scrubbed it away.

"It's a complete fracture. I can set it here. You'll have to wear a cast for four weeks. Or longer, if you keep being you."

Her face popped into my view of the ceiling, her eyes over the surgical mask even bluer than normal.

"Okay."

"Is anything else broken?"

"I don't know."

"Let's check."

Hands ran over my body, testing each bone and tendon. She didn't watch my face for signs of pain—she knew better than that—instead focusing on each body part intently, checking my range of motion, sometimes closing her eyes as she felt the length of a bone through my skin. It had been a year since anyone touched me this thoroughly, a year and a handful of days, and the simple physical connection acted like a lightning rod, taking me back to the last night with Celina.

The night before she was murdered, we'd lounged in bed, watching the sun go down through her bedroom window. Her graveyard shift started at eleven and I wouldn't see her afterward because Sam was having me run to the other side of the state for a pickup first thing in the morning. It was strange—I hadn't been a mule for over a year—but I didn't question it. I never once wondered why he wanted me out of Iowa City that day. I lay in Celina's bed, running my hands over her skin like it belonged to me, like it was an extension of my own. It was August, the dog days of summer, with its heavy, sticky air that sat in your lungs and coated your body with sweat even in full air-conditioning. And even then I couldn't stop touching her, couldn't pry myself from the miracle of this person in my life.

"Don't go to work." I tried convincing her to call in sick every night, to forget the diner and its sad, yellow-lit patrons and stay with me instead. She never did.

Nuzzling into the hollow of my neck, the place she liked to burrow when she pretended to hide from the world, Celina groaned. I felt the vibration of it in my own throat.

"Take me somewhere," she murmured.

My fingers slid into the curve of her waist, lingering. "Where do you want to go?"

"Anywhere. Lake Michigan. A cabin in the woods. Bali."

I could. I could buy plane tickets to Bali and rent a thatched hut on the beach for weeks, a month. I had that kind of money now and the feeling of it, of being able to whisk Celina away and satisfy her every whim, seeped through me like a drug.

"Today or tomorrow?"

She rose up and straddled me, her hair tumbling around her face, smiling with a kind of joy I still wasn't familiar with. The drug in my veins doubled. Then the expression faded and the shadows came. Those I understood.

"You can't leave today."

She was right. I couldn't. I had a job to do.

"Tomorrow, then. I'll book the tickets." I bracketed her thighs, trying to call the fantasy back, but Celina was wide-awake now and sober with the reality of our lives.

"When will you be back?"

"Tomorrow night. I think." Sometimes plans changed at the last minute. A shipment that was supposed to go to Dubuque got rerouted to Hannibal, Missouri, at the last minute. You never knew the end game, could never trust the instructions beyond the next minute. With Sam, it was always follow the leader. I was still waiting to see why he'd sent me to school, other than the excuse of being a student who could run the thrift store business.

But Celina and I had changed the game. When I finally told her what I really did for a living, she said she needed time to process it. I didn't hear from her for three days—three of the longest days of my life at that point—and I'd gone almost feral thinking that she was going to end it. Then she showed up at the thrift store. She looked around at the place like she was seeing it for the first time. No one else was in the building, and when she reached over and pulled my hand against her heart, I almost melted into the counter.

"I love you," she said, and things broke inside me. Her hands shook against mine. "You're better than this."

I wasn't. Of course I wasn't, but Celina wanted me to be, and I would be anything she wanted me to be. She had a plan. Together, we contacted DEA Agent Morales—telling him I had information to pass on. I met with him a couple times, but when I got cold feet about sharing details, feeling like Sam was watching from every corner, Celina was right there. She handed me her phone to call in the fertilizer truck bust—anonymous, she said, through a tip line—and law enforcement intercepted the whole thing last month.

Sam went into a full rage and Celina had gotten more and more worried that I'd be discovered as the informant. The shadows crept into every conversation. This wasn't the first time she'd mentioned leaving town, and I knew where it was coming from.

"I'll be fine. Don't worry about me."

"I can't help it." She leaned over, covering my body with hers and hugging me so tight, it would have been painful for someone else. When she pulled back, her blue eyes looked liquid, like a bright, bottomless sea. "You're my air. I can't live without you now."

A chug of emotion tripped in my chest. Little explosions fired everywhere under my skin. I didn't know this existed, that love like this happened in the real world, and part of me worried that someday she was going to look at me and see what I actually was, a money-laundering dealer who didn't deserve to even touch her.

"Not air." I kissed the wet streaks beneath her eyes, trying to pull myself together. "Sentient aspirin."

"Air," she murmured into my mouth, sending the words into me. "You're my air."

"Sit up."

I startled and blinked into the bright exam light, jerked back to the present.

Jillian didn't seem to notice my distraction. She traced my lower ribs from my spine around to my breastbone, listening to my unsteady breathing with a stethoscope. If I'd been an anesthetic to Celina, I was probably a curiosity, or maybe a challenge, to Jillian. She'd never given me a full-body exam before. I'd always come in with some obvious cut or fracture or gunshot wound and she just sewed up whatever part was oozing. This was different.

When she accidentally brushed the underside of one breast, she paused, clearly hearing the hitch in my lungs, and examined that rib more thoroughly. I stared at the most boring piece of equipment on the wall and tried to read the tiny font on the label, willing my body to ignore its proximity to Jillian's. I didn't have any right to feel this way, to have a single reaction to anyone ever again, especially not a doctor who'd let me crash her life with my shit show way too many times.

"This wrist is swollen."

I looked down to see her cradling both of my hands, face up, in hers. The left wrist looked redder and thicker than the right.

"Does it feel any different than the other? Maybe slower to respond?"

I rotated both, slowly, careful not to cause more phantom damage. "Not really."

She x-rayed it and studied the results. "I think it's just a sprain. I can't see any fractures, but I'm not one hundred percent sure."

"What the hell am I paying you for, then?"

"If you were a goat or a pig . . ." She shrugged and her mask moved, like she might be smiling again. I forced myself not to return it.

The examination complete, she started patching me up, starting with the leg. I stared out the window, eager to focus on anything beside the lean, strong hands setting my thigh.

The largest barn stood framed in the distance. It looked new, with graceful arches and solar panels lining the southern side of the roof. Add in the wind turbines, and this place was probably totally sufficient off the grid. Hedgerows boxed in the yard to the house, neatly trimmed, and a cascading water feature made out of limestone decorated a nearby pasture where the sow, Serafina, now lounged, her tufts of gray hair blowing gently around her face. A gleaming bronze sculpture in front of the barn seemed to double as a goat playground.

"This place isn't what I expected."

Jillian scoffed. "Let me guess: a few lazy hippies, two pigs, and a farm that should've been razed in the seventies?"

"Something like that. I don't know." I'd never really thought about Jillian's life outside the clinic. She'd always seemed one with the antiseptic and undead hours.

"Remember the game girls used to play with those paper fortune tellers? How many kids you would have. The person you would marry. The house you would live in."

"The fuck are you talking about?"

She shook her head. "Millennials." She started wrapping, winding the cast material around and around my leg. "It was a deeply problematic game, but I remember the house part. I always wanted to get a farm. Zero kids. Zero spouses. And a giant fairy-tale farm for me and all my animals to live forever."

"Looks like you got it." I looked out the window again. "It's beautiful."

I wasn't lying. Sam's farm—and all the farms he used for product storage—had a hard, deliberate layer of neglect and poverty, the kind of farm that made you want to look away so it could slide immediately out of your mind. Jillian's place, though, lived up to its name. It was a sanctuary, full of strength and beauty and a thing I'd rarely known: peace.

"It's my life's work." Her hands paused and she leveled me with a look. "And I'm not going to let anyone jeopardize it."

"No one knows I'm here. No one would ever look for me or be able to track me here." Her gaze narrowed, and I swallowed. "I promise."

She nodded and kept working. We fell silent for a while, until she moved on to my wrist, and something started scratching the door. Jillian ignored it, but the door began rattling, like some tiny demon was raging on the other side. Finally, Jillian sighed and opened it, letting in an orange and gray cat I recognized from the last time I was at the clinic. Maleficent. The cat that took down a rooster.

The cat rubbed against Jillian's legs while glaring at me like I had personally wronged it. When I stuck my tongue out, the cat jumped onto the exam table and stared me down, tail twitching.

"Malley. Settle down."

I couldn't see the scar on its leg anymore. The shaved fur had all regrown, hiding whatever damage remained, and the cat didn't favor the leg at all. It was too busy willing a slow death on me.

"Do all animals feel pain?"

I didn't know where the question came from, but suddenly it was there in the room between us. Jillian's eyes flashed up. We'd never discussed my condition before, but she knew. She never seemed surprised by or even interested in my lack of pain. The doctors I'd known growing up had treated me like a rare find, a fascinating case study. They could barely contain their excitement over the freak in their midst as they drilled me with questions and tests, some subtle, some not. Jillian's disregard was probably one of the things I liked most about her, and the fact that her attitude clearly had nothing to do with me. She disregarded humans in general.

"Most species do. Studies show that injured animals will choose food that has painkillers in it over food that doesn't. Reptiles, amphibians, and fish all have the neuroanatomy necessary to perceive pain, and there's no indication that they don't in some form, or any reason to believe the experience wouldn't be as useful to them as it is to us."

"To keep them alive."

"Exactly." She finished wrapping my wrist and secured the gauze.

I swallowed, looking at the parts of me covered in casts and bandages, the puckered scar shriveling the tattoo on my shoulder. "So I'm alone in the universe?"

She stared at the cat and then me, thinking, still balancing my wrist lightly between her hands. "Naked mole rats."

I blinked. "Huh?"

"East African naked mole rats are impervious to acid and capsaicin." Her mouth twitched. "And they're cute as hell."

She went to a door that led into the rest of the house. Slowly, she peeled the surgical mask from her face and dropped it into the garbage, her eyes never leaving my face. I left my own mask on, frozen as she deliberately breathed the same air as me, mixing our germs, our viruses, our defenses and fears—everything that stained the air between us.

"How do you feel about enchiladas?"

Max

Jonah called right as the crime scene team arrived. I ignored it, but because it was Jonah he didn't leave a message or text me like a normal person. He kept calling until I got the team up to speed, packed Phyllis off to the hospital in an ambulance, and could finally pick up.

"Are you . . . Max?" Was his greeting. He sounded like he'd just sprinted a mile.

"Last time I checked. I'm in the middle of something here."

"But you're okay."

"Why? What did you see?" I walked to a quiet part of the front yard where nothing needed to be processed for the scene. There was a pause on the other end of the line and I could hear a voice in the background, low and female.

"I didn't see anything."

Bullshit. "Were you dreaming?"

"Not really. We were out on the bluff." It took a minute for him to piece himself together, but I was used to that. Jonah, first thing after a dream, was a scattered, bewildered mess. He had to find himself again and painstakingly separate what was him apart from whatever horrors he'd seen. It was something I could relate to at the minute. After he calmed down, he told me the story.

He and Eve had taken a picnic out to Jonah's backyard, on the bluff overlooking the Mississippi, and were lazing on a blanket afterward, relaxing in the sun. Eve watched the clouds. Jonah had drifted off, dozing, until a searing dread shot him bolt upright in the middle of the wildflowers.

"It wasn't a dream, just a feeling."

"Of what?"

"You. Dead."

I glanced at the barely contained jungle of trees and plants behind the faded rambler. I could still feel the splinters of the fence digging into my back, could see the pure black of the killer's eyes as he pressed the blade to my throat.

"He had you cornered. With a knife."

"Thought you said you didn't see anything."

"I could feel it happening, like I was there but with a blindfold on. It was the same when I was a kid and knew what Jason was up to, even when he was playing across town."

I didn't know what to say. Jonah's psychic abilities had been connected to his twin from birth. The idea that he could sense me like he could with his own brother left me momentarily speechless.

He took a jerky breath. "What happened, Max?"

I told him. I always told Jonah about my cases, regardless of ethics or protocol. He was my sounding board, and—except for a while last year after I'd been shot—had been since the day I joined the force. He was the reason I'd joined the force. I'd even considered—when I was finishing the academy and didn't know how things like mortgages or insurance worked—skipping the force altogether and becoming Jonah's partner in his PI firm. The two of us together, choosing our own cases and being our own bosses, felt like what I was meant to do. But ultimately Shelley talked me out of it. I'd put on the uniform, helped Jonah as much as I could on the side, and he'd done the same for me.

Jonah listened to my rundown of the case, not interrupting until I brought him completely up to speed.

"You don't know who he works for yet?"

"I'm heading in to the station now to interview him."

"Be careful, Max." Jonah hesitated. "He's connected to you."

"Yeah, trying to murder someone might do that."

"No, it's more than that. He's connected to your life."

"I'm on the task force that's been hunting him."

Jonah didn't reply, but I knew he was stewing over something.

"Let me know if you see anything else, okay? I gotta go."

There was another noise in the background, a female voice. It was jarring, but in a good way. Jonah had never had anyone other than family and me. He'd never had a romantic partner that lasted longer than a few weeks, and knowing Eve Roth was there for him—that she'd shared a picnic on the bluff with him this afternoon—made the parts of me that were still shaking start to quiet down. At least this pandemic had done one good thing. It had brought Jonah a person—two people, actually—who understood and accepted exactly who and what he was. I didn't even know if I had that.

Jonah let me go, but not before warning me again to watch my back.

"Why? I've got you for that."

He swore and hung up.

When I got to the station, Larsen was already deep in an argument with Morales in my office/interview room.

"—going to just stand aside."

"I'm not asking you to."

With masks muffling their points and covering half their facial expressions, it took me a minute to catch up.

"This is a joint task force and ICPD is represented." Morales clapped me on the back, bringing me into the middle of what I realized was a pissing match.

"You're DEA," Larsen said, taking a step closer to tower over Morales. "The task force is a drug operation. This is attempted murder in my community, a felony assault of a senior citizen minding her own business in her own home. If you think we're taking the bench for this one, you can go fuck yourself."

"ICPD isn't taking a bench. Your investigator helped arrest the guy, for Chrissake. The suspect is being held in your station. How many more sound bites do you want me to hand-feed you?"

"ICPD takes this investigation."

"The guy's a hit man for a kingpin. He's ours. He's been ours the whole time."

The two couldn't have been more mismatched—Larsen's military alpha against Morales's chill foodie persona—but the fight for jurisdiction brought out the same steeliness in Morales he'd shown with Ciseski the last time he'd come to the station. Neither of them was giving an inch.

Finally, Morales turned to me. "Max will back me up on this." He looked at me expectantly. Larsen did the same.

The thing was I could see both sides. Every move the force made was being dissected and dragged through the media. A new crime was on the rise this summer: kids stealing cars and taking them for joyrides, leaving them wrecked and abandoned for the owners to find later. It seemed like a policeable situation at first, a crime that could be investigated and stopped, but 2020 made everything a hundred times more complicated. If the police pulled people over for traffic stops, we were profiling. If we didn't, we were sitting on our asses, not doing our jobs. There was no winning.

And there'd be no winning with this case if ICPD didn't have a clear and visible presence in the investigation. It might be DEA jurisdiction, but the citizens of Iowa City weren't going to appreciate the department's *cooperation* when a little old lady had been attacked in her home in broad daylight. Even though it wasn't a random attack by any means, there also wasn't a clear connection between the victim and the perpetrator. And even though the suspect was in custody, he was part of a larger threat that still loomed. We couldn't call it an isolated incident. This kind of crime resonated for years. It would become a suburban horror story, passed out like Halloween candy.

On the other hand, I knew this was one of the primary objectives of the DEA task force: find the killer who'd been taking out Sam Olson's network. This hadn't started today. It went all the way back to last December, when I passed a faceless orderly in a hospital corridor who'd administered a lethal overdose to Matthew Moore. This killer was a critical piece of the task force's objective.

"It's not up to me but, for optics, it would look best if ICPD owns the case and everyone understands it's a joint investigation with the DEA. We're clearly signaling it's not isolated or random, and we're putting the weight of multiple departments behind it. The public will find that assuring."

"For optics?" Larsen cocked an eyebrow. I shook my head, ducking the shit he was trying to give.

Morales grumbled but eventually agreed to the plan as long as I was named the investigator in charge, which was fine by me, but Larsen objected again.

"Conflict of interest. This guy nearly killed Summerlin."

"As I was trying to arrest him. That's not a conflict. It's a hazard of duty."

"There's no deal if Summerlin isn't point." Morales moved next to me, shoulder to shoulder, making it clear this was a package agreement. And in the end Larsen didn't have a choice. DEA could take full control of this case anytime they wanted to, and everyone in the room knew it.

"Fine."

I left my office/interview room/cage match arena and went down to Holding to find out who exactly I was investigating. On the way, the officers I passed nodded, offered congratulations, and made high fives in the air.

"Nice going, man." A guy from evening patrol broke the six-foot rule to slap me on the shoulder and danced down the hallway singing "Bad Boys." Everyone around us laughed like it was happy hour. They all knew what had gone down this afternoon, and suddenly, instead of being the pariah banished to the interview room, the cop with the psychic best friend—the guy who'd snubbed them all to join the DEA task force—I was a hero. I smiled through the mask, waved awkwardly, and kept moving.

The truth was I'd almost become another victim, another cop fallen in the line of duty. Kara Johnson was the real hero today, a fact that sat as comfortably in my head as Larsen and Morales sat in a room together.

In Holding, the booking officer pulled me aside.

"He's got no ID and he's not talking."

"Fingerprints?" A guy like this was a career criminal.

"No match."

"Are you kidding me?"

She handed me a copy of the file. "Congratulations, it's a John Doe."

The guy in the mug shot stared at the camera with complete indifference, his beady eyes blank, mouth relaxed, more like he was waiting for his curbside pickup at Starbucks than someone who'd tried to murder three people today. The only indication of any stress was a shiny line of sweat across his deathly white forehead. If this was the first time he'd been arrested, that meant we had nothing. No known associates, no connections, no information that would bring us any closer to his boss, unless by some miracle we got him to talk.

He's connected to you, Jonah had said. *He's connected to your life.*

I snapped the file shut. "Where is he?"

In the holding cell corridor, a masked and gloved detention officer walked me to the last cell on the left. "He's been quiet."

"Yeah, that's gonna be the problem."

John Doe was curled up on the bare mattress in the back, facing the wall. Not exactly the professional hit man attitude I'd been expecting. The officer and I glanced at each other, our confusion clear above our masks. The officer banged on the door. "Hey, dude. You got a visitor."

No response. He didn't even move. Gripped with a sudden dread, I stepped closer. "Is he breathing?"

"Yeah, he was breathing fine when—" The officer cut off as John Doe rolled over and vomited all over the cell. "Goddamnit."

He jumped back, even though the mess hadn't sprayed near the door.

"Does coronavirus make you barf? I heard you can barf from it." The officer glanced at me, panicking. "What if he's got it?"

John Doe barely resembled the man who'd smiled and held a knife to my throat hours ago. He was pale, shaking, and covered in sweat. His eyes darted back and forth without focusing on anything.

"Get an ambulance here now."

The detention officer sprinted toward his station as the other detainees watched silently. None of them were masked. If John Doe did have the virus, he could've already spread it to half the people in here. On the other hand—I turned back to the cell as he grabbed for his stomach, rolling toward the wall—it could be a ruse. He had plenty of practice getting in and out of hospitals unnoticed, as he'd proven with Matthew Moore. He might be playing us, faking symptoms to get transported to a lower-security, more easily escapable situation. But if he did have coronavirus, he could die before we learned anything from him.

The possibilities warred inside me as I called Morales. The detention officer jogged back with a coworker in tow, masks on and batons out. They opened the cell and rolled John Doe over, checking his vitals.

"He's not breathing."

Kara

A door slammed. I jerked up, instantly alert and confused. I was lying on a couch in the middle of a massive room. In front of me was a fireplace flanked by a pair of chairs. A giant king-sized bed stood on the far wall. A sink and coffee station built into an antique dresser stood next to a door that opened into the cool white tile of a bathroom. Eaves on both sides of the room held window seats piled with books and blankets. Outside, a pink glow faded into blue. A musty animal scent hung underneath the woody library smell of the room, and that's when my brain clicked everything into place.

The stairs creaked and Jillian appeared, fully dressed with her hair pulled back in a ponytail. She stopped at the top of the stairs and stared pointedly at my hand, where the pocketknife Max had given me flashed in the early morning light. I dropped it on the coffee table.

"Sorry." I sat up fully and rubbed sleep out of my eyes. "I forgot where I was."

She went to the bathroom and shut the door. I sighed.

This had been a terrible idea. By the time we finished dinner last night—the enchiladas were insanely good, full of fire-roasted jalapeños, spicy beans, and smothered in a verde sauce that I actually licked off my plate—it was after nine o'clock. Jillian shocked me again while we washed dishes by offering to let me crash on her couch.

"I don't have a guest room because I don't have guests. The downstairs bedroom was converted to an animal treatment room. Janelle lives on the property, too, in her own house." Janelle, the blue-haired Gen Z worker, had grabbed an enchilada to go and shot me some side-eye before disappearing for the night. "But there's a couch upstairs."

An objectively terrible idea. I knew it immediately as something hummed in the air between us. But I didn't want to go back to Iowa City. Not yet. I wasn't ready to sit in a roomful of cops and talk about the rat-faced guy who'd almost killed me yesterday. Almost killed Max. Almost killed Phyllis. My gut clenched as I felt the heel of his shoe crush into my cheek all over again, pinning me to the floor. As I saw him holding Max against the gate, a knife gleaming at his throat. That little shitbag could rot. And it was still my birthday, the longest birthday in human history. I decided I'd earned one present.

So I stayed. Jillian made me bump up the stairs on my butt like a freaking toddler while the cat, Maleficent, stalked me with a twitching tail and murder eyes. I fell asleep practically the second my head hit the couch, stomach full, adrenaline long gone, knowing that no one could follow me here.

When Jillian came out of the bathroom, her face looked red and freshly scrubbed, and she was wearing a different shirt. I'd piled the blanket she must've draped over me last night on the far end of the couch, put the knife away, and zipped up my bag, ready for her to say, *Look, I was making bad enchilada-fueled decisions last night, and you need to get the fuck out of my life. Forever, preferably.*

But she didn't. She came over to the couch and sat down, unwrapping the bandage on my wrist and checking it as thoroughly as if I were a goat or a golden retriever. Something worth checking.

"The swelling's down. You need to rest it for a few days. Aspirin and ice compresses will help." She looked at me and her eyes narrowed. "Do you own an ice pack?"

I kicked the bug-out bag with my good foot. "Could be one in there."

She made a noise and ordered me to bump back downstairs to the kitchen, where she gave me a crutch, iced the wrist, and checked my temperature. Farm noises filtered in through the open windows—rooting pigs and the occasional bleat in the distance—as the wind turbines rotated slowly and silently in the sky.

"Is the clinic open?" Iowa had followed shutdown protocols over the spring, but the state government was back to business as usual, ignoring the mounting death tolls and infection rates in the name of jobs and the economy.

"Has been the whole time. We're essential workers. We mask during our shifts and transport the animals from the parking lot. We don't let the owners come inside."

"And they say the virus is a bad thing."

She laughed once and flipped the ice to the other side of my arm. There was something different about Jillian here, the morning light transforming her face. She was cracked open, unguarded. It was totally unexpected and impossible to look away from.

For a second, I could see exactly how her life would play out, and it had nothing to do with the clinic in Des Moines. That was just work. This, here, I could see it now; this was her life. Early, quiet mornings. The simple, hard work of feeding, cleaning, and caring for the animals. Jillian bent over, checking the progress of wounds and conditions, easing each animal into another day. The two of us drinking coffee, arguing over goat barn roofs, working side by side.

I blinked. How had I slipped into that frame?

Shifting the ice pack, Jillian's smile faded as she glanced up at me. "Are you . . . still in business?"

"No. This"—I nodded to the cast and the swollen wrist—"is just wrapping up loose ends."

"It doesn't look like it's wrapping up well."

"I tried to leave. Last winter. I took your advice to get away while I still could. But I got pulled back in."

"So leave now. Nothing's stopping you."

"I can't yet." Not until I made sure Morales would keep his word. "Soon, I hope." Maybe they were interviewing that savage little shitbag right now and getting the information they needed.

Max was probably furious I hadn't turned up yet. I could see him pacing the task force headquarters with his bad shoulder tensed up and the bulge he got between his eyebrows when he was mad. Only now he had a cut beneath his jaw, the same as I did. I should go, check in. I needed to see how Phyllis was doing, too, make sure she was okay. She'd charge me for the damage to the house and bitch for days about how I took off with her truck, but I didn't care. I was kind of looking forward to it. Strange how my entire world had been a formless blur for an entire year and now these faces stood out so clearly. Max. Phyllis. Jillian.

Jillian set the ice pack aside and rewrapped my wrist, winding the wide bandage between my fingers and thumb, positioning my arm with her light, nimble touch. "I hoped you'd listened to me last time, that you'd left town after you were shot. But I wondered." She spoke to my hand, not looking up. "When you didn't show up at the clinic and months had gone by, I thought maybe you were dead . . ." She trailed off, fastening the end of the bandage and holding my arm in her hands. She'd drawn her chair close to mine, and my uninjured leg was somehow notched between her knees.

"Don't worry. I'm sure I'll fuck right out of your life soon."

Her eyes finally lifted to mine, the irritatingly faultless blue shining with . . . . something. My breath caught on the something, trapped in the back of my throat.

"It's weird. Maybe it's the pandemic"—her gaze dropped to my lips and suddenly my entire body felt like it was on fire—"but I like knowing you're around." Her voice dropped to a scratchy whisper. "I'm glad you came."

A gust of wind blew in from the open window. Somewhere a cat yowled, but we were both frozen, eyes locked on each other. Her thigh pressed against my knee and her mouth curled wide and lush. My heart thudded, fuzzing in my ears.

I couldn't help it. I needed connection. Strength. Healing. I needed everything Jillian was and I wanted it in gulps and great aching gasps, at once, now. I reached for her jaw, slid a hand back to cup her head, and closed the electrified space between us. She was stiff for a second, not moving, and I hesitated. Had I read this all wrong? Then, like a switch had been flipped, she angled her head and fit us together.

The kiss was a light, a beacon. There was no tenderness in Jillian and I didn't want any. This was taking, both of us wide-open and trying to find the limits of what the other could stand. I twisted, trying to grab a better hold of her, and she jerked my hand back, keeping my arm prisoner, not letting me move the injured wrist. I made do with the other hand, winding it around her back and pulling her onto my lap, finding her spine underneath the shirt, the flexing muscles in her back as I pulled her down into me.

Everything inside me felt like it was clawing its way out: the loss, the grief, the rage, and the bright, hard truth that I was alone, even now, with Jillian breathing life into me, sending every stunted nerve into aching awareness of what this body could and couldn't be. I was alone and would always, without Celina, be alone.

I broke away. "I can't."

"Why not?" Jillian murmured into my neck. Her breath, hot and quick, stirred the hair behind my ear, but she pulled back when my hand dropped.

It was too much. The curves, the smell of soap and salt and sweat coming from her, that ridiculous blond hair falling into my face and begging my hands to run through it. I closed my eyes, trying to block everything out. I didn't have any right. None. What the fuck was I thinking?

"I'm sorry." I pushed her off and stumbled up, limping away as fast as the cast and crutch would allow. My body screamed with every step, urging me back to take exactly what she was offering. But my head. Fuck. Tears pricked into my eyes and I hated myself for what I'd done and what I didn't do, for how I was destroying a moment I used to fantasize about in explicit detail. But that's what

I did. I destroyed moments. I destroyed people. And the faster I got out of here, the less I would ruin Jillian's life, too.

I grabbed my bag and bumped back down the stairs as Maleficent sat at the kitchen door, ears back as she glared. I should've listened to that cat from the beginning.

I left through the front door, but Jillian had already beat me outside. She leaned against the front of Phyllis's truck, one boot hooked on the bumper and a cowboy hat shading her eyes. The only thing I wanted in that moment was to walk straight into her arms and the hugeness of that want terrified me in a way that almost dying yesterday couldn't even touch.

She waited until I reached the truck. "Well. That was interesting."

I tossed the bag into the truck. "I can't do this. It's me. You deserve way better."

"How would you know what I deserve?" She had a point. For all the years I'd been coming to the clinic, we barely knew each other. I'd never even told her my name.

She moved to the door as I climbed in, holding it open with her hip so I couldn't leave. I sat frozen in the driver's seat as forces inside me pulled in opposite directions, threatening to tear me apart. "I'm all fucked-up."

She nodded and her gaze dropped to my shoulder, the scar of the bullet hole. "That's the only kind of animal I see."

The buzz between us was undeniable, but there was something beyond that. A hardness, a no-fucks-given recognition that no one else had ever understood. Not even Celina. I knew that if I pushed Jillian, she would push back harder; that if I set the world on fire, she would add lighter fluid and watch it all burn.

Janelle appeared in the yard, leading a pig that looked like it weighed as much as her. Jillian released the door and stepped back as I started the truck.

"I'll send you the payment for this." I touched the cast, looking anywhere but at her.

"Bring it yourself. After you wrap up those loose ends."

I left without answering.

Max

"Hey, stranger." Shelley stopped in the kitchen doorway, clearly surprised to see me, and I felt a flash of guilt. I'd been working night and day on the task force, throwing myself completely into the assignment. I'd probably seen Shelley asleep more than awake in the last few weeks.

She wore leggings and her "I Like Big Books and I Cannot Lie" T-shirt. Her hair was piled up in the messy bun that had become an extension of her head in the last six months. School would be starting soon, but it didn't look like she was going in today unless there was a coronavirus dress code update I hadn't heard about.

"When did you get home last night?"

Technically, I'd gotten in this morning, sometime after 2:00 a.m. My regular shift had been ending when the murderous John Doe vomited all over his cell and stopped breathing.

The attending officers started CPR and pumped oxygen into him until the ambulance arrived. Morales and I rode along to the university hospital, using hand- and leg-cuffs to secure John Doe to the gurney. In the emergency room, I didn't let his body out of my sight.

They tried inserting a breathing tube down his throat. He came to long enough to dry heave again, but there was nothing left in his stomach except bile. For the first time, I was grateful for the masks. His cuffs clanked against the bed rails as his body went limp and he passed out again.

"Overdose?" one of the doctors asked me.

"I don't think so." The killer had seemed stone sober in the old woman's house and garden. No shakes or tremors, no balance issues or disorientation. "Dilated pupils; that's all I noticed." It was all I kept seeing, too, those ink-black eyes hovering in front of me as he smiled, his entire face wrapped tight with excitement as he pressed the knife to my throat.

I breathed deeply and slowly, forcing myself to focus on John Doe's face in the middle of the sea of masked and gloved bodies—his jaw slack, eyes rolled back, and vomit smeared over his face. That's all he was now, just a barely breathing failure on his way to life in prison. I kept repeating it, trying to replace the image in my head with the one in front of me. I'd gotten him. Kara had gotten him. We'd done what we set out to do and this phase of the job, at least, was over.

They finally got the breathing tube in and the doctor was ordering toxicology panels when another voice came from behind me.

"Ma'am, you can't be in here." A pause and then, louder: "Ma'am!"

Behind the emergency room door, a nurse tried to steer a stooped figure away from the window. The woman seemed oblivious, and at first I assumed it was a dementia patient wandering aimlessly through the hospital, totally unaware of coronavirus protocols, but then the scraggly gray curls and lined face came into focus.

Phyllis, the woman Kara was boarding with. I'd sent her here in an ambulance less than two hours ago. She must have been ninety if she was a day and was standing on her own two feet, ignoring direct orders from the staff. She wore a hospital gown and a mask. A purplish bruise colored one side of her visible face, and something was wrong with her eye. She stared at the body on the gurney even as the nurse pulled her away from the door, and her eyes narrowed, swallowed by wrinkles that grew deeper, sharper. Just before she disappeared from the window, she glanced at me and winked.

I pulled Morales back into the room, interrupting his phone call, and told him to watch John Doe.

"Where are you going?"

I didn't answer.

Running down the hall, I caught up with the nurse and Phyllis just as they reached her room.

"Sir, you can't—"

I flashed my badge. "I need a few minutes." And took them, guiding the old woman to her bed and standing between her and the door.

"What did you do?"

She plucked at her mask like she was trying not to chew it while she talked. "Not a damn thing. When can I go home?"

"We talked about this, remember?" The nurse squeezed between us while still acting like she could remain six feet apart by virtue of her full hazmat suit, gloves, mask, and face shield. "We're finding you a room for observation tonight for your concussion."

"Wasn't talking to you, girl."

"And you"—the nurse turned on me—"need to follow PPE protocol or you can have your few minutes through that window." She nodded to a view of an alley and a dumpster.

I complied and went through what felt like a twenty-step procedure to wash, sanitize, and cover every exposed part of me before she let me back into the "high-risk patient's room." By then Phyllis was scowling out the window, picking apart her ID bracelet with gnarled, twitching fingers. The welt on the side of her head stretched from her hairline down into her mask. Up close, I could see what was wrong with her eye: the white had turned red where a blood vessel had burst and flooded it.

"How are you feeling?"

"Still alive." She sniffed, and I couldn't tell from the noise whether she was happy or disappointed by that.

"We're going to go through what happened today. Every detail, as much as you can remember. But first . . ." I waited for her to look at me, and when she didn't, the silence drew out uncomfortably long. Eventually I stepped between her and the window, forcing her attention. "What happened to him?"

"Got what he deserved, didn't he?"

"The courts'll decide what he deserves. What did you do?"

"I was fixing my tea when he showed up, thinking he was smooth as a damn fox, and I asked him if he wanted a cup." The mask shifted like she was smiling underneath it. "Might've brewed that second cup a little stronger."

I remembered the empty mugs on her kitchen table: two of them, just like in the photographs of the air traffic controller's trailer. He got them comfortable first so they'd talk. But did that mean John

Doe was targeting Phyllis, too? Was this little old lady part of Sam Olson's network? Or maybe John Doe had simply been positioning himself in the house for when Kara showed up. Enjoying some hospitality before he took her out.

"He drunk pretty near all of it before he started to notice something was off. When he went to check the teapot, I hightailed it to the bedroom for my Ruger. He beat me there. Clocked me square in the side of the head. I remember falling and thinking that was it until I came to, heard voices, and had to save your fool hides."

"Yeah, thanks for that."

She sniffed again as Grimes from the task force showed up at the door, covered in head-to-toe PPE and ready to do her full interview. I nodded him in.

"And the tea? What was in it?"

The mask crackled as it stretched wide across her battered face. The iris in her blood-swamped eye gleamed, dark and wet. "Just some herbs from my garden."

Digitalis, also known as foxglove. The plant originated in Europe but spread throughout the States and was even considered an invasive pest in the Northwest. It grew up to five feet tall and bloomed in cones of bell-shaped flowers, purple on the outside with fuzzy spotted tongues sticking out the middle. The name came from an Irish legend where foxes put the flowers on their feet to muffle the sound of their steps. A power move if I ever heard one: wearing poison to better slip through the shadows.

And that poison thrived in Phyllis Reed's garden. Taken in small doses, the emergency room doctor explained, digitalis was actually good for you. It was a cardiac glycoside, which treated heart failure and irregular heartbeats, but a large dose to a healthy heart could be fatal. I'd looked up the symptoms and it wasn't pretty. Confusion, blind spots, blurred vision, nausea, vomiting, diarrhea. Poor, poor John Doe.

They stabilized him sometime around midnight and began treating him for digitalis poisoning. Morales and Larsen both posted officers outside the room—interagency cooperation—over the arguments of hospital staff, and I went back to the station to log as much of the day as I could in my interview room/office. The night shift wanted a full firsthand replay, but I begged off and drove home.

I had no idea how to sum that up for Shelley, though, and if I started the story of yesterday—from the farmers' market to the hospital—I might stray too close to the part where my throat was almost sliced open. That wasn't a conversation we needed to have, especially not in the kitchen where Garrett could wander in or overhear. I'd heard the Xbox fire up in the living room an hour ago. This house had thin walls.

"I got in late" was all I said. "Slept better than I have in a while, though."

That part was true. On a good day, most of my rest came in the distorted twilight of consciousness, hovering an inch outside myself and trying to focus on nothing except the gentle rise and fall of Shelley's ribs next to me.

Last night I slept hard, blacking out as soon as I hit the pillow and waking up with a start over four hours later, the orange August sun baking the window blinds. The day must have taken more out of me than I'd even realized.

"Are you taking time off?"

She glanced at my laptop and the empty coffee cup in front of me. I'd had almost a full pot since I'd gone down the foxglove rabbit hole this morning, looking up everything I could about the plant and its effects.

"No, but I can take a late start. We had a lot of developments yesterday."

She poured the last cup from the pot and sat across from me. The morning light slanted across her face, turning her brown eyes into glowing amber. "What happened to your throat?"

The cut from John Doe's knife wasn't deep. If we had a cat, I could've passed it off as a scratch. "It's nothing. I promise."

She waited for me to say more, and when I didn't, the silence stretched out. I closed my laptop, avoiding that plumbing gaze as it felt like the temperature in the room cranked up at least thirty degrees. It was easier to avoid questions by text or phone call. Sitting across from her, feeling the weight of her worry, was torture. She had so much pressing on her already: Garrett, her work, the chaos of the entire world pouring in daily from her phone. She didn't need to carry this, too.

"How are you holding up?" I tried turning the conversation around, and after a beat she allowed it. She and Garrett had gone to the park yesterday. They'd hiked through the woods and argued about wearing masks. That's where they would have been when the call came. The thought was immediate, visceral, and I muscled it away. There was no call. I was fine. Everything was fine.

"He has to mask at school. It's required, right?"

"Not school. This fundraiser on Saturday. I still don't think he should go. I know it's outdoors, but there's going to be a ton of people. They were saying on the neighborhood chat it could become a superspreader event."

"What fundraiser?"

Her gaze narrowed. "Are you joking?"

I got up to put some space between us and went to the calendar on the wall by the fridge, the "Goats in Trees" calendar Shelley thought was hilarious when we looked through clearance bins in January, maskless and laughing in the middle of the after-Christmas-sale shoppers at Coral Ridge Mall. It felt like a lifetime ago.

"There's nothing on here for Saturday." Shelley still wrote all the family events on the paper calendar, and this Saturday's box was empty, like every box of every day for the last five months.

"Because I haven't said he can go." She kept her voice down, but the anger was bright and brimming. "We talked about it on the phone during lunch the other day. You agreed it wasn't a good idea."

I probably had. I agreed with 90 percent of what Shelley thought when it came to Garrett—not just because she would debate me until I gave in but because she was usually right. My parents let me and my brothers run wild for most of our summers as kids. They owned rental cottages on Clear Lake, which kept them busy from April to November. As long as we did our jobs for the business—sweeping, emptying garbage cans, and hosing out the fish-cleaning station—they didn't care what else we did as long as it didn't bother them and we showed up, relatively clean, in time for dinner. But Shelley was a teacher. She had a master's degree in elementary education and an evolved perspective on parenting that neither my parents nor I could ever claim.

"It's been a long few days." I rinsed out my coffee cup. "Remind me what this thing is."

"It's a community fundraiser. They're having food trucks and a craft fair and holding a charity Little League game that Garrett's coach is organizing. He asked Garrett to play."

It sounded familiar now. Charity thing, food trucks. I'd been hungry when we talked before and had started placing an order for take-out gyros.

"Masked?"

"You know those kids aren't going to mask, not while they're running around and crowded onto the benches together. Breathing hard right in each other's faces. The whole thing is a terrible idea."

"I agree." And I did, but . . . "On the other hand, all he's been doing this summer is sitting in front of that television playing Xbox."

Instantly, Shelley stiffened. "What else can he do? It's the only way he talks to his friends."

"And he's going back to school in, what, a week?"

"Nine days."

"Yeah, so in a little over a week he's going to be around kids again one way or the other. This might be a good test of how well he'll follow the rules while we're there and can watch him."

"Oh, so you want all of us to go so we can all catch coronavirus and spread it to more people together?"

"It's outdoors, right? We'll mask up. We can wear gloves, bring hand sanitizer."

"I can't believe you." Shelley grabbed a bag of bread off the counter and shoved two slices in the toaster so hard, I was surprised they didn't rip. "First you don't remember the fundraiser after we discussed it multiple times, and now you want to send our only child into a superspreader event. The Big 10 canceled their entire season. Even football understands you can't have mass gatherings right now. It's not safe."

"Nothing is safe."

"What?"

I paced the kitchen, rubbing my throat as the familiar jolt of abused nerves sizzled through my arm. "You want to wrap Garrett in Bubble Wrap and keep him away from the entire world, but you can't. *We* can't. You have to go back to work and that means Garrett has to go back to school and I know you hate it, I know you're scared, but it's been five months and it could be five more of this shit. We don't know what this virus will become or who it's going to kill. We can't live in a box, Shel, cut off from everyone and everything, or what will it even matter? What is it we're trying to save?"

The toaster popped up like a gunshot. Shelley stood in front of it, frozen, like I'd pulled a weapon on her. Her face was shocked and furious, looking at me like I was the enemy, as if I'd become the virus in human form, invading her house disguised as her husband. Foxes tiptoeing on poison flowers.

Goddamnit. This wasn't what I meant to do this morning. After everything that happened yesterday, I'd fallen asleep with Kara's question from the cornfield whispering in my head. *What am I good for if not this?* It echoed down the hospital corridors, in the machine beeps of John Doe's vital signs, through all the interviews and briefings, while the answer sat dark and wordless in my gut. I wanted to be good for something else. I wanted to start today like the second chance it was. I'd planned to make breakfast for everyone—pancakes and bacon—and thaw out a can of orange juice for vitamins. I was going to challenge Garrett to a *Mario Kart* race and drive down to the fossil gorge afterward so we could look at dead things and remember we were alive. I was going to tell them I loved them, how the two of them were my world. It had gone so well in my head.

My phone vibrated on the table. "Shelley—"

"What am I trying to save?" Her voice was strangled and slow, choking on every word.

"You know what I mean."

"No, Max." She spit out my name, hurling back my tactic of using someone's name to deescalate the situation, which I hadn't even realized I was doing. "I *don't* know what you mean."

"Look, this isn't—" The phone buzzed again, and without thinking I grabbed it and pulled up the messages. Kara was texting me from the task force headquarters, sending pictures of donuts she'd arranged into ghoulish faces and asking where the fuck I was. When I didn't respond, she kept texting.

I'm the MVP now, Cap.

Hand over the shield.

Plates slammed on the counter, pulling my attention away from the phone.

"Go to work." Shelley's face had turned to ice as she spread peanut butter onto toast. "You'd rather be there anyway."

"I'm sorry." I didn't know whether I was apologizing for what I'd said or because, deep down, I knew she was right. I wasn't good at this. I was a fox bringing poison into my own house.

Kara

I saw *Outbreak* once as a kid, and mostly I remember the monkey and a guy hacking his lungs out in a crowded vintage movie theater, but the hazmat suits Max and I were wearing took me right back there. We had on full scrubs, masks, gloves, looking ready to play with nuclear waste in a lab somewhere.

We stood outside a janitor's closet, getting the side-eye from every masked nurse and orderly who walked by, waiting for the clearance to interview Rat Face. Morales wanted it to be the two of us, and Max's boss—who sounded like Siri cosplaying American patriarchy—agreed as long as we recorded everything and had a live call going for any questions that ICPD wanted to add. While we waited, Max glanced down at my leg and the cast bulging underneath the scrubs.

"So you went to a doctor?"

"It's amazing what you can do with napkins and papier-mâché."

He scoffed. "Right."

"YouTube tutorials are everything."

I'd been doing everything possible to avoid thinking about my doctor, driving twenty miles over the speed limit until the whole truck began vibrating, making donut art, remembering pandemic movies. Fuck, I'd even voluntarily showed up at DEA headquarters, hoping for some irritating job to distract me. Because the second I stopped doing other things, I felt Jillian slide into my lap, I heard the catch of her breath against my mouth.

I rapped the back of my head against the wall of the hospital corridor—not gently—making Max eye me as suspiciously as the hospital staff. I ignored him until he checked his phone for the twentieth time since we'd been standing here. The home screen was just as blank as the last time he looked.

"It's still on."

He glared. The fluorescent lights flashed off his head. "Thanks."

"Is it that time of the month or something? You're all bloated and crabby."

"Just another day in paradise with my felon of a partner."

Whatever I was going to say next died on my tongue. We weren't partners. That's not what this was, but arguing it felt like admitting something I wasn't ready to admit.

"Pull up naked mole rats."

He was surprised but obliged, pulling up a picture of something that looked like a skinned fetus with a pig snout and beaver teeth. I hit my head on the wall again.

"New pet?"

"My spirit animal, someone said."

Max snorted and put the phone away. Naked mole rats had put him in a measurably better mood.

"Remember, you're going in first, alone."

I pointed at my chest. "Bad cop."

"He wanted information from you. That's what we know from the victims so far. He talked to both Matthew Moore and Gail Whitaker before killing them. And Phyllis confirmed he was asking questions about you when he showed up at the house."

"While she was poisoning him." The woman was an icon. If I could've lived to a thousand, too, I would've wanted to be just like her. Phyllis was life goals.

"Did he say anything to you before I got there?"

I shrugged.

Max shifted, sandwiching me between his Cap stance and the wall. "I overheard him say you're not telling the DEA everything."

"Maybe you heard wrong."

"And you replied," he continued, "that you don't tell anyone everything."

I pushed off the wall, limping on the cast until we were toe to toe. "And, what, you do? You journal your entire day and share it with your wife before bedtime?"

A shadow flickered over his face and I knew I'd hit home. But I remembered something else, too. Rat Face had said something just before Max gave himself away in the hallway. Codes. He wanted to know something about a code.

The nurse came over and said we could go in, but not before laying down a long list of restrictions. Rat Face had been on a ventilator, which seemed like a waste of a lifesaving machine, and even though he was off it now, he still wasn't masked. We had to stay six feet back, exchange no objects or touch anything he'd come into contact with. Blah, blah. I tuned out after a while and studied the bird patterns on her scrubs. Funny how the hospital acted like a virus was the worst thing in that room.

"Everyone clear?" she finished, looking pointedly at me.

I nodded—"Love the finches"—and limped down the hall to the room where two officers were stationed. My DEA phone had a live call in progress, connected to both Max's phone and the task force headquarters, where they were recording everything.

Inside, Rat Face was strapped and chained to his bed, surrounded by machines and watching the door. He clocked the cast through my *Outbreak* costume and his attention sharpened. A predator sensing injured prey.

I dragged a chair to the window—we were on the fifth floor but it still seemed like a terrible idea, giving this bastard a potential escape hatch—and dropped into it, stretching the cast leg out in front of me and hooking the other knee over the arm of the chair. I made a show of stretching my arms overhead, taking my time about it, because I could. I hoped his restraints were giving him a rash.

"So, would you say this was your best week ever?"

He didn't answer but kept staring at me with those creepy, sunken eyes.

"Let's see. You get cornered by an Iowa City cop, assaulted with a shovel, arrested, and—my favorite—poisoned by a hundred-year-old lady." I ticked off each thing on gloved fingers. "You completely failed to kill a single person or get any information for your boss. You don't happen to have a flaming case of hemorrhoids right now, do you? Maybe an STD burning through your crotch?"

Silence. The guy didn't have eyelids. He hadn't blinked once since I'd been in the room.

"I'll just hope for the best on that one. Maybe you'll get Covid while you're here and you can suffocate."

I pulled the DEA phone out and scrolled headlines. After a few minutes of complete silence, I looked up. "Does suffocating feel like having your throat slit in slow motion? I would love that journey for you, getting to live your special kink."

Nothing.

What am I supposed to do now? This guy's a creepy statue. He's giving me nothing.

Go over your conversation at the house, came the reply from Cap ☆.

I had been, replaying those minutes in my head since Max brought it up, but I wasn't going to rehash it in front of an inter-agency audience. You don't tell the DEA everything. Rat Face got one thing right.

I shoved the phone back in the scrubs pocket. "How long have you been following me?"

Nothing.

"Did you wait until I was talking to Nilsen before you went to the house? You figured you'd have time to take out Phyllis before I got back?"

"Nilsen?" The soft, high voice almost made me jump, like a ghost had floated up behind me and whispered boo.

I pushed out of the chair and limped to the end of the bed. "He could've called after I left, given you plenty of time to beat me back to Phyllis's house."

Rat Face smiled in a way that cut right through the hazmat suit, making my skin crawl. I'd worked with plenty of shitty people—mostly idiots, with the occasional vicious dick tossed in for fun—but the people Sam used all knew how to play nice with others. They had to, to get the job done quickly and quietly. This guy got jobs done quietly—Max said he had no priors—but there was something objectively wrong about him, a monster barely hiding in that small frame and pointed face. This was a guy who would've killed me with or without a paycheck. All my instincts told me to back away, slowly. That or put a pillow over his face, push down, and wait.

"I don't know a Nilsen." His lips barely moved when he talked. I couldn't tell if he was lying.

"Who are you working for, then?"

The smile grew wider, revealing those small, sharp teeth. "I'm off the clock."

"Permanently. They've got you, just like they got me. Your only leverage here is what you know. It's time to cooperate."

The restraints clanked as he leaned up, rising an inch off the bed until the tendons in his neck stood out. "Do they really think you're cooperating?"

The phone felt heavier in my pocket with the weight of listening ears. I leaned over the bed rail—so close, his bloodless fingers twitched. "Check the welt on the back of your head. That's me playing along."

"He told you, didn't he? Where it is."

I was surprised he'd turned a question on me, but maybe the guy couldn't help it. Maybe he still thought he could get what he'd been hired for.

"Sam didn't tell me shit, as you would've found out if you were any good at what you do."

Restraints bit into the tubes and wires on his chest, and his fingers slipped over the bed rail like snakes contracting. "We'll see."

I don't know how long we stared at each other. The next thing I knew, someone pulled me away from the bed. Even though I didn't register him consciously, I let the hand guide me backward. "Six feet, remember?"

Max launched into his side of the interview. He listed the charges and the maximum sentences for each, other stuff I wasn't paying attention to. Rat Face didn't seem to register it, either. He was still looking only at me.

"It's open-and-shut. We've got you on the security cameras outside Matthew Moore's room before and after the murder." Max sat in the chair I'd dragged to the window. Sunlight glared off his head—the only part of him that wasn't covered in blue—and I wondered if that's why he shaved it: to blind the people he interrogated. "Kind of full circle, don't you think? You killed Matthew Moore in a hospital, and here we are again. What's the word for that?"

"Stupid." I leaned against the wall by the door.

"That's it." Max's mask stretched as he shot finger guns at me. "And what was really stupid was how Matthew was still alive when I went to see him. How he talked to me before the overdose kicked in." Max turned toward me. "Don't professional killers make sure to silence their victims before leaving the scene?"

He was waiting for the quippy comeback, for my bad-cop banter, but all the air had been sucked out of the room and it felt like I'd been sucker punched. I wasn't in the hospital anymore; I was crouching on the floor of a broken barn, holding Celina's body while her blood and tissue soaked my clothes. She was lukewarm, hardening in my arms into something not Celina. Something silenced.

I blinked. Max was still looking at me, waiting for me to say something. The only sound in the room was the hum of the machines.

"Yeah, real killers get the job done."

I dropped the phone on the table and left the room.

Max

The door slammed shut, echoing off the white walls. It took a beat to register that Kara wasn't coming back. She'd stalked out in the middle of the interview after we'd spent the better part of a day getting clearance to even be in the hospital. Hours of work, dozens of hoops and endless forms, all wasted. I thought the balance between us had changed yesterday. We'd come through for each other. We'd worked together to bring the killer down. But maybe none of that meant shit to her. Why had I thought it would? That Kara Johnson would do anything other than lay me out flat or walk into traffic or just disappear?

John Doe lay strapped and cuffed to the bed, watching me watch Kara leave. His skin was pale and drawn, eyes sunken into his skull, hair greasy on the pillow. He looked like a different person from yesterday, but no less of a sociopath. His gaze dropped to my neck. "Trouble with your partner?"

"She's not my partner. It's Take Your Criminal to Work day. I'll buy her some ice cream later and give her a tour of the holding cells."

He didn't react, not that I expected him to. The phone Kara had dropped lay on the table, showing the call in progress. I moved closer to him, six feet and one inch away from the bed.

"I overheard you yesterday when you had Kara trapped in that bedroom. You said she knew things she wasn't telling the DEA. What did you mean by that?"

When he didn't answer, I threw my arms out wide. "I'm a senior investigator for the Iowa City police. I've got a nice suit and a welcoming demeanor. Trust me when I say I make a star witness and I look forward to telling a jury every detail about yesterday. Your only hope here is to work with us."

The laugh caught me by surprise, soft and shuddering, rattling his handcuffs against the bed. "And what do you think you can offer me, Investigator Summerlin? Are you going to cut me a deal?"

"If you know enough to make it worth a deal."

"Your fantasy trial is never going to happen. Apologies. I'm sure the suit is charming."

"You're not getting out of this."

He looked at my neck again. "All good things come to an end."

"Fuck your riddles. What are you trying to say?"

He tipped his head, daring me to come closer. I glanced at the door and the back of the officer posted outside. The phone was across the room, recording the hums and beeps surrounding us, the static of my indecision. I took one step forward. He lay perfectly still, tracking me, waiting as I took another step and another, until I was near enough to the hospital bed that he could've reached out and brushed me with his caged fingertips. The hair on the back of my neck stood up and I fought the instinct to reach for my gun.

When he spoke, it was hardly more than breath, nothing the phone recording could pick up.

"She knows where it is."

I knew it. I knew Kara had been hiding something this whole time. I kept my voice as low as his. "The drug cache?"

His eyes refocused, and for the first time he looked surprised.

"You think this was about drugs? You already have the drugs, Investigator Summerlin."

"What?"

"I wasn't hired to find drugs." Something spread over his face and I knew, in the pit of my stomach, he was telling the truth.

"Then what does Kara know? What were you hired to find?"

John Doe smiled as the door to the room opened.

"The same thing you were."

Morales wasn't at task force headquarters when I got there. One of the guys who'd recorded the interview gave me a look I couldn't read over his mask and said he and Larsen had gone to grab lunch. He didn't know where.

I skirted the people shopping, some in masks, some not, and went to the food court. Morales's phone went straight to voicemail. He wasn't at Panera, Panda Express, or Sbarro. I kept calling, ignoring texts from Jonah and Shelley as a few kids in hockey gear poured out of the ice rink, laughing and talking all over each other like this was 2019. Their parents eyed me, jaws fixed, daring me to saying anything.

Then I spotted a short, round silhouette with a taller one. They were leaving the mall. I ran, hitting the doors with my bad shoulder because I wanted the pain, I wanted the bright stab of it zinging through me, unleashing what lived inside.

I ripped the mask off and followed them to a park bench.

"What is he talking about?"

Morales didn't answer.

"He says there's no drugs."

"When? I didn't hear that."

I briefed them on the end of the interview, how John Doe signaled me closer to the bed and spoke too low for the phone to pick up. "Is he right? There's no drugs left?"

"That's not in line with our intel." Morales chewed his pizza like this was casual lunch conversation.

"Kara said the same thing, right from the beginning."

"Christ, Summerlin." Larsen shook his head. "First you believe in psychics, now drug traffickers?"

"I hate to be the one to tell you this, but criminals lie," Morales added.

"None of the sites she's taken us to have panned out. It's a wild-goose chase."

"Consider the goose," Larsen muttered.

"I've been reviewing Belgrave's operations, too. The volume Matthew Moore said Belgrave was producing doesn't add up to some hidden stockpile of drugs. Maybe a small reserve somewhere, but that's it."

"Matthew Moore was cut off. He didn't know shit when he died."

"He was in on it for years. He helped create the goddamn thing. And he obviously knew enough to be John Doe's first target. Whoever wanted him dead couldn't even wait until he got out of the hospital before they moved in."

"Summerlin's got a point." Larsen rubbed his chin, thinking.

"John Doe said we already have the drugs, and we do, don't we? The weigh station seizure was the biggest in Iowa history."

"Courtesy of ICPD," Larsen added, squaring up against Morales. "If this interagency cooperation is going to work, you better tell us right now everything the DEA knows."

"I can't reveal all my sources," Morales said.

"One of my men almost died in the line of duty yesterday." It took me a second to realize Larsen was talking about me. The captain got in Morales's face as he tried to shift away. "He has a wife and son. What were you planning to tell them?"

"Don't get hysterical. Summerlin's fine and we've got our link to the buyer."

"You've got a dead end. We can't even ID him." Larsen swung on me. His face had gotten red, which everyone in the department knew as a sign to put your head down, agree, and get the hell out of the way. "He didn't tell you anything else? If he wasn't after the drugs, what has he been killing Belgrave's people for? What was he hired to find?"

The same thing you were.

The killer's voice whispered through the back of my head, weaving through everything I'd worked on for this case. Where this had all started.

I looked at Morales, who'd gone quiet. He hadn't looked me in the eye once this entire conversation.

"At the weigh station, you said it was a twenty-million-dollar bust."

"Give or take. Market prices have gone up because of the pandemic."

"So where's the twenty million?"

The corner of Morales's mouth twitched up and something pitched in my gut, rolling with nauseating clarity. Everything was suddenly so fucking clear.

"You told me already, didn't you?"

"What are we talking about here?" Larsen asked as I stepped closer to Morales.

"You told me what you were after and I wasn't listening."

"It's one of our objectives," Morales hedged.

"What is?" Larsen demanded.

"*Follow the money,* you said. That's what you've been doing this whole time. That's why the DEA is here."

Morales shook his head. "How do you think this agency is funded? What do you think allows us to implement community outreach programs and get the resources we need to fight the flood of fentanyl and other synthetics coming into the U.S.? Asset forfeiture gives us the ability to attack the financial structures of drug trafficking. We seize bank accounts. We liquidate and distribute assets. Do you know how many ready-made undercover cars the DOJ has distributed to police departments across the country?"

"Why didn't you tell me?"

"You had your assignment. Kara Johnson. And you did it well."

"You're looking for twenty million?" Larsen asked. "The amount paid for that truckload of opioids?"

"Yeah."

"There's more than that." I shook my head. "I've been through Sam Olson's file a hundred times. He had a few bank accounts at the county credit union, an IRA with a couple hundred grand, and a hundred and fifty acres of farmland to his name. To *that* name, anyway. But he was laundering cash for years. There must have been a river of money coming in."

Larsen squared up next to me, shoulder to shoulder. "How much?"

Morales bit the inside of his cheek, hesitating, before he sighed. "We can't know for sure, not until we locate the assets. But Sam Olson wasn't a guy who lived large. He bought his clothes at farm supply stores and his food at Walmart. He didn't travel, didn't splurge. He'd lived through lean times: droughts, storms, supply shortages, recessions. From what we can tell, he hoarded most of the profits."

"How much?"

"A hundred, easy."

"And you think it's here in Iowa?"

Morales nodded. "I know it is."

One hundred million dollars, just waiting to be found.

Kara

"What's her name?"

A bush I didn't recognize was creeping into the pepper patch, with long, spiky leaves and flowers that looked like fuzzy purple corn dogs. Phyllis sat on a stool on the opposite side of the peppers, inspecting a habanero plant. Garden tools littered the ground around her, along with a pile of plastic Hy-Vee bags and a rifle. She squinted at the bush through the massive welt on one side of her head, lips pursed, annoyed by my interruption.

"Anise hyssop."

"Funny name."

"You should talk."

"Is she poisonous?"

Phyllis sniffed and plucked a shriveled, bright orange pepper. "Everything's poison at the right dose."

I scooted down the row on my ass, dragging my cast through dirt and pebbles, and hunted for jalapeños. When I got back last night, all traces of the cops were gone and the time capsule bedroom's door was closed and locked again. Phyllis was watching infomercials in the living room with the rifle next to her—her new best friend, apparently—and a glass of clear liquid sitting on the coffee table. I didn't ask. She wouldn't say if she had a concussion, but she held on to the walls when she finally went to bed and swore at me when I told her to get a walker. Today she demanded I help her cook a batch of hot sauce, which was as close as she'd probably get to admitting she wasn't okay. I agreed as long as she knocked a hundred bucks off my rent. We settled on fifty.

We picked our way down the rows, filling the Hy-Vee bags and sweating in the sun while chickadees flitted along the fence. Phyllis wore gloves, while my hands grew bright red. I wondered if they were burning.

Every time a car stopped anywhere on the block I paused, listening. I hadn't heard from Max since I'd walked out of the hospital yesterday, and it was only a matter of time before he descended. I didn't know what would happen when he did.

Everything was different now. The DEA had caught their killer and I already knew there were no drugs to find, but I had to convince Morales of that to get him to make good on our deal. To tell the world what happened to Celina. How was that even possible after yesterday? After that asshole smiled and said—on record for every DEA agent in the world to hear—*He told you, didn't he? Where it is.*

Sam told me a lot of things. And then he'd ripped my life apart. I was still trying to figure out what was real and what was bullshit.

The first property he'd ever shown me was on the south side of the state, on a relentless summer day like this one, not a cloud in the sky, no hope of shade, the air so humid you could practically drink it.

I'd been working for Sam for less than a year, muling, making the run between Iowa and Missouri as a driver for a maid service.

My name tag said "Maisie." There was a website and everything. I'd learned already that Sam Olson preferred women to make his deliveries because we got pulled over less as the rule-following, inconsequential gender we were. The truck was too light to have to stop at weigh stations, holding only a bunch of mops, cleaning supplies, and enough pills to supply our St. Louis dealer for a few weeks.

Sam wasn't the biggest game in the market and he didn't want to be, flying under the radar in every way possible. I was twenty and as happy as I'd ever been. "Happy" wasn't the right word, though. "Comfortable," maybe. I made enough money to live wherever, drink whatever, and do whoever I wanted. I felt secure, like I'd finally carved a place where I could breathe a little and that, obviously, was when it went to shit. A bigger player in St. Louis found our dealer, who set me up the next time I came into town. Two guys from the competition shoved me in the back of the van, held a gun to my head, and demanded I take them to Belgrave.

A few hours later I pulled up at an old farm outside Keokuk.

"Glad you found the place." Sam sat on the broken porch steps when I arrived, wearing stained overalls and eating an apple. I'd texted him from the burner phone, telling him I needed to meet. He'd replied instantly with an address, nothing else.

A few guys stood in front of a barn smoking, glancing at me every few seconds. The other buildings looked dark and empty, all the doors closed. "Want one?" He offered a basket when I reached him. "They're from my friend's orchard. Galas."

I took a piece of fruit and bounced it from hand to hand. He surveyed my uniform—brown splatters down the front, name tag hanging at an angle—as he took another bite, chewed slowly, and swallowed.

"You said it was urgent. Let's have it."

I went to the back of the van and opened it. Sam followed. The guys in front of the barn perked up, but he waved them off, eating his apple as he took stock of the interior.

A body lay in a heap of brooms and blood-soaked mops. A second man slumped on the other side, one eye swollen shut, hair matted and wet, hands zip-tied to the frame. He blinked blood out of his good eye and said something into the duct tape covering his mouth.

"They asked to see you." I bit into the apple, nodding toward the tied-up guy. "That one can still sort of see."

For the first time since I'd known him, Sam smiled.

A few weeks later, Sam invited me to his house. His actual home in the country where farm dogs ran around and bees hummed in an overgrown flower bed dotted with gnomes he said his wife picked out. I didn't see a wife anywhere. I didn't know much about Sam then and I was wary of all the open space, the silence on the horizon, and lack of any other people around.

We drank Bud Light on his porch while a mosquito zapper buzzed next to the screen door and he asked me questions like the world's strangest job interview. Where I grew up. What I wanted out of life. Did I use. What I liked to do.

"Birds."

Sam's beer paused in midair and I could feel him looking at me. I waved at the garden. Now that the dogs settled down on the porch steps, the birds had swooped in. A few robins and starlings hopped through the leaves, looking for dinner, while crows cawed to each other from the trees. "I like drawing them. Watching them."

"Most kids your age don't notice birds."

I shrugged. "I guess that's why I like them. They have their own world, like aliens all around us. They're everywhere and no one fucks with them."

Sam was quiet for a while.

"Ever killed anyone before?"

"No." The birds appeared and disappeared in the bushes, all graceful movements and cocking heads. The guys sent by the St. Louis competition had moved differently: confident at first, then jerky and desperate as the situation spiraled out of their control. "It was easier than I thought it would be."

I'd had to put more force into the knife than I'd guessed at first. Hit them hard and quick. Keep moving. I was a fast learner. The noises stayed with me the longest, the squelching sound of the knife ripping tissue and tendon, and the smell, too. The hot coppery stink of a threat turning into . . . not a threat.

"You were mad. That helps."

"You been mad at anyone else on that farm?"

He laughed, surprising me. It was a big, gravelly sound that boomed over the darkening lawn and garden gnomes, and I found myself grinning back.

"Might have been. But there's other things that fit in the ground. Nice thing about Iowa: all this land. Enough space to bury just about anything, and no one will ever come looking. Folks mind their own around here. But you still need to be prepared."

He drained his beer and went into the house. Alone with the view, everything around me shifted one click lower. I'd never really looked at the ground before, to the gravel and dirt and rocks under my feet. There was always too much happening above it, the birds drawing my gaze forever up, but now I saw. Beneath the sunset and the bleeding sky, beneath the rustle of cornstalks in the wind, beneath the cracked foundation of the house and the choke of flowers and weeds in the garden. The ground stretched beneath it all, dark and inviting, a solid ocean of secrets.

I'd helped Sam put two bodies into the ground and all I'd thought about was my stepfather's grave, if he had one, and whether it was worth finding so I could tag it with an honest epitaph. Here lies human garbage. But now I remembered how chill Sam was about the whole thing, like it happened all the time. Maybe it did. Maybe he'd dug and filled holes all over the state. What else had he buried in the belly of Iowa?

The beer sweat into my hand as a door opened and shut inside the house. Sam came back out holding a duffel bag. He set it down between us and the dogs lifted their heads from the porch steps as he pulled things out one by one. A couple of shirts, a plastic bag holding a passport, some papers, and a roll of hundred-dollar bills. A gun. A phone.

"This here's a bug-out bag. You keep it handy so you can leave at the drop of a hat."

"You don't seem like the leaving type."

"I'm not." He handed me the plastic bag with the papers and money. I pulled out the passport and opened it to see my own face staring back at me. I read the name out loud. "Kara Johnson."

"Why not? Sounds like a nice Iowa girl, doesn't she?"

I'd been Maisie the cleaning lady for almost a year, and someone else before that. A name that had been collected in medical databases and spat from the mouths of other people. It never belonged to me, never felt like the person I was. Sam had become someone else, too—had taken the name Belgrave, because Belgrave could do things Sam couldn't. Could bury things where the Sams of the world would never find them.

I looked at the picture again and smoothed the condensation on my thumb over her face.

"Kara."

I jerked as a pair of clippers bounced off my chest. "What?"

Phyllis had the rifle cocked against her shoulder. I swung toward the direction of the barrel where Morales stood with his hands up at the end of my row. I hadn't heard him come through the gate.

"I surrender." He smiled, but he was sweating, too, his forehead glistening as his eyes darted back and forth between me and Phyllis. He had a shoulder holster on, the first time I'd seen him armed since he found me in Canada, but his hands were empty.

"What do you want?" I asked at the same time that Phyllis demanded that he get off her property. She shifted for a clearer shot, nosing the barrel away from the leaves of a plant.

"Technically it's part of a crime scene, ma'am, but that's not why I'm here. I need to speak to Kara."

Moving slowly, he pulled out his badge. Phyllis grunted before lowering the gun to her lap.

Morales stumped a few paces down the gravel path, stopping well short of the pepper patch. "Is that a different Ruger than the one we took as evidence? You didn't tell us there were any other firearms in the house."

"Get him out of here," Phyllis grumbled, turning her attention back to picking.

I took Morales out the back gate, limping on the crutch into the shadow of the garage where thistles as tall as me hugged the siding. There were no DEA vehicles in the alley and I hadn't heard a car stop out front.

"Phyllis Reed." Morales grinned and smeared the sweat on his head with a forearm. "She family of yours?"

"No."

"Sure seems to like you."

"Phyllis doesn't like anyone. Where's Max?"

He leaned against the garage and pulled a wadded piece of paper out of his Bermuda shorts, unfolding it. "Phyllis Annette Reed. Born May 3, 1935."

A Taurus. No surprise.

"Married twice, both husbands dead. One in combat, another from a heart attack when he had no previous heart conditions." He paused, arching his fat eyebrows and letting the implications draw out. "Four children. The oldest is in prison for embezzlement and the two other boys have been in and out of rehab and picked up on minor offenses over the years. A very interesting family."

A sour taste built in the back of my throat. I knew it wasn't important, but I couldn't help asking. "The girl?"

"Drowned in the Iowa River when she was eighteen. No foul play there."

I paced back into the sun. "You must be really bored. No more killer to chase and I didn't die in the process, so you lost that office pool. Now you're running background checks on old ladies? Sad."

"We both know what we're looking for. Why we're here." Morales folded the paper in his sausage fingers as sweat continued to drip down his face. "You've taken us to three storage locations, two that we already knew about, and we've found shit."

"Maybe—and hear me out on this one, because I know it's hard for you to follow—because there's nothing to fucking find."

I didn't realize how loud I'd gotten until the chickadees on the fence scattered.

"That's not what our John Doe says."

"You don't even know the guy's name and you're jumping on the John Doe truther wagon?"

"Someone hired him to murder you and not just because you're a complete waste of society's resources." Morales stepped out into the sun, getting in my face without a mask, so close I could smell the sweat on him. "There are other Belgrave locations, more properties. You know where they are and you're going to take me to them."

There was at least one more location, and coronavirus could choke the whole planet to death before I took Santiago Morales to that farm on the southern edge of the state, the place where two bodies, covered in my DNA, were buried.

"I might know more." I smiled into his big, overheated face. "How's the affidavit for Celina coming?"

"I don't know what you're talking about."

"The affidavit. Our deal."

"Celina?" He shook his head, like he was trying to place the name. "Sounds like some girl who was in the wrong place at the wrong time. Bad luck."

"You can't." Everything in me went white hot. "I signed the papers. There's a record of what you promised me. I have it—" My voice died as I realized where I had it: in Phyllis's house, where the police and the DEA had dusted, logged, and searched everything for their crime scene.

Morales pulled a tin of mints out of his pocket and popped a few into his mouth, chewing lazily as he watched me figure it out.

I looked past him, scanning the garages. There was no one in the alley, no one to see me beat a middle-aged Mexican guy to death with my cast and a crutch.

"Always interesting what turns up at a crime scene. Take your friend Phyllis, for instance. We found a lot of correspondence between her and Sam Olson, stuff the DA would be very interested in reviewing. A five-year sentence would probably mean a life sentence for her. She's a tough old girl, but the virus is running like wildfire through jails and prisons."

"What do you want?"

He dropped the paper of Phyllis's life story on the cement and every trace of humor congealed on his face. His eyes were bright, feverish.

"A hundred million things."

Max

The house was dark when I pulled into the driveway. I sat in the car for a minute, eyes closed, shoulder throbbing a dull beat against the seat cushions, trying to find the will to get out and go inside. My phone buzzed. I turned it off without looking.

When the heat inside the car became stifling, I finally opened my eyes. The next-door neighbor sat in her yard, weeding a garden full of BLACK LIVES MATTER and BIDEN HARRIS 2020 signs. She shot me a look when I got out of the car.

It was four o'clock in the afternoon. I hadn't been home before supper since the task force started, and the lawn showed it. It was long and weedy, dandelions going to seed everywhere. Inside, dishes were stacked in the sink and fruit flies buzzed over a bowl of browning bananas.

"Shelley?"

She wasn't in the kitchen, living room, or bedroom. I found Garrett in the basement, playing *GoldenEye 007* on an old Nintendo 64 he'd dug out of a storage closet, leaving a pile of Christmas decorations and gift wrap strewn in front of the door.

"Where's your mom?"

"She went on a walk."

"How come you didn't go with her?"

He shrugged and fired down a corridor at some incoming gunman. "This game is hilarious. Did you ever play this?"

I sat next to him as he evaded incoming fire. "Yeah." The N64 had been a fixture in the first apartment I got with Jonah our sophomore year. I played it at night when there was nothing to do except wait for one of Jonah's dreams, to occupy the endless hours when everyone else shut down so easily.

"Did you play it through?"

"Lots of times."

Garrett's fingers flew over the controller as the TV flashed hollow light on his face. He'd grown tall in the last year. His arms were still as skinny as string beans, but his feet looked like someone else's, swollen boats propped on the coffee table. Practically as big as mine. His hair had gotten shaggy during lockdown, brushing his shoulders. It looked brown like his mom's down here in the basement, but out in the sun there were glints of red.

"You don't want to go through there. See those stairs? There's a better route that way. Watch your six."

"You're such a cop." He giggled and it caught me under the ribs. High-pitched, tinged with sarcasm now, but an echo of the four-year-old who'd chased grasshoppers around the backyard. I wondered how many more times I'd hear it before giggling went the way of grasshopper chases.

I watched him play for a while, coaching him through the last levels until he got to the final boss and was immediately killed.

"How do you beat him?" he asked as it reloaded.

"I don't remember."

Upstairs, the front door opened and footsteps moved above us. I waited for Shelley to come downstairs or at least call down to check on Garrett. She didn't.

"Tell me about this fundraiser on Saturday."

He sighed. "It's a baseball game. People can bring their own chairs and stay apart. Coach got a guy he knows from the state fair to sell hot dogs and pretzels and stuff, and it's all outside, but Mom's freaking out about it."

"You want to do it?"

He shrugged again, but his chin and mouth sagged. "Doesn't matter. We just thought it would be fun and we could raise money. To help."

I sat up. "It was your idea? You came up with this?"

"Me and a couple of the guys from the team," he muttered. "And now I can't even go."

Shelley hadn't mentioned that part. She only said Garrett wanted to be part of the fundraiser, not that he was one of the organizers. We'd helped with community food drives before as a family and Garrett had done charity events through school, but this was different. This was something Garrett and his friends had created on their own. I wanted to ask what charity they were raising funds for, but it felt like the kind of thing I should've already known.

I ran a hand over my head as the ceiling creaked and Garrett began firing again. "You know why your mom has concerns."

He jerked his chin and made a noise I took for acknowledgment.

"She's trying to keep you safe."

"Yeah."

"We're all trying to do the right thing here, but sometimes . . ." I rubbed the back of my neck, fumbling for words. "Especially now, it's hard to know what that is."

I'd thought being on this task force was the right thing—that I could help shut down the last of Belgrave's operations and save countless people from another flood of opioids on to the street. It had given me purpose, a reason to leave the house and ignore the accusing stares of neighbors. I was trying to take down the forces that had killed Jonah's niece, the men who had left people to die in bathtubs and plane crashes. I was protecting and serving.

And it was all a lie.

Kara had been right all along. Morales, the task force, the interagency cooperation—none of it had been about finding drugs or taking down a new cartel. It was about money. I'd been suckered into a DEA fundraiser. And I'd almost left Shelley and Garrett alone in the world because of it. Because I'd needed to feel important. I'd needed something—anything—to fucking do.

"Garrett, listen—"

He shrugged off the hand I tried to lay on his shoulder. "Mom goes to the grocery store all the time. She's around people—inside—and school starts next week and that's inside and on a bus and eating with no masks in the cafeteria, but I can't play a baseball game in a park because I might get the virus and kill grandma. Even though she's, like, a hundred miles away."

My hand lay awkwardly on the couch between us.

"It's not just about your grandma. It's about everyone's grandma and other people who aren't grandmas. It's our responsibility to keep everyone safe."

"I know that."

"Then don't oversimplify."

"Whatever."

He died again in another ambush and threw the controller on the floor. Any other day I would've called him on it, lectured him about breakable electronics or cut off his screen time. But I wanted today to be different. I wanted *us* to be different.

"You want to play together?"

"No. This game's dumb." He got up to switch off the console.

"Garre—"

There were so many conversations we hadn't had, so many things I'd never gotten around to telling him. He'd been too young. I'd been too busy. It was never a good time. I didn't even know what I wanted to say: something about being a man and how fucking lonely it was, the silent weight always on your shoulders, pressing you down. That you could work your whole life to do good and make a difference and find out that it was the wrong thing anyway, that nothing you did would ever get that weight off you. It only got heavier, harder to carry.

He stopped at the bottom of the stairs, his back to me, waiting for me to say why I'd stopped him.

"I'll talk to your mom."

I grilled steaks for dinner and made mashed potatoes and Caesar salad. We ate on the patio, listening to the hum of the neighborhood at home on a hot summer night. One of the neighbors was showing movies on the side of their house with a projector, so after dinner Garrett went over with a blanket and a Gatorade to watch socially distanced *Goonies*. Shelley and I hadn't talked about yesterday's fight, but things seemed easier, lighter tonight, and I didn't want to wreck the mood by bringing up the fundraiser. We cleaned up and sat outside with the mosquito candle between us. Shelley was working on her second glass of wine. I was thinking about a third beer when she interrupted my train of thought.

"I thought about what you said. About what it is we're trying to stay safe for."

"I didn't mean that the way it came out."

"I know, but . . ." She stopped toying with the stem of her wineglass and looked at me dead on. "Sometimes I don't know why we're doing all this, either. I don't know what good any of us can do."

"You're doing a world of good. You're amazing—way better than me. You know that, right?"

"Obviously." Her mouth tipped up, but her eyes flashed with concern. "What happened to you?"

"What do you mean?"

"You came home in the middle of the day. You mowed the lawn. Made dinner."

"Lawn needed mowing."

"You changed the batteries in the smoke detectors."

I pushed the beer bottle away. "It was a bad day."

"How bad?"

"The task force . . ." I shrugged, twinging my shoulder. "It's not what I thought it was."

"So quit. You can quit the DEA thing and go back to your regular job, right?"

"I don't know. I'd have to talk to Larsen, see what kind of obligation ICPD is under for this."

"Okay, then they swap you out for someone else."

But who? I couldn't see Kara taking to anyone else in the precinct. Not that we were friends, but we'd found a rhythm, which was more than anyone else on the task force could say. She barely acknowledged the rest of them existed.

"It's not that easy."

"You can make it that easy."

"Shel—"

She drained her wine and set the glass down on the table, then slid a leg over my lap until she was straddling me. Scooting closer, she wrapped her arms around me. A low, involuntary noise sounded in the back of my throat and all thought of Kara, Morales, and the task force evaporated.

"You know what I think?"

She tossed her hair and it fell around us like a curtain. I'd wondered why she'd taken it down from the messy bun tonight. Her mouth was stained red from the Merlot.

"What?" I ran my hands up her thighs, over her hips, and squeezed her ass. She hummed into my mouth.

"I think *Goonies* is a pretty long movie."

She kissed her way down my neck as she unbuttoned my fly.

"Right here?"

I glanced at the surrounding houses. We had a privacy fence, but the neighbors on both sides had upstairs levels with full views into our backyard. The windows seemed mostly dark or covered, but still. We could hear people out in their yards, which meant they could hear us, too. I was a police officer. I couldn't just—

Shelley hitched her sundress up and that's when I realized she wasn't wearing any underwear.

"Public indecency." She tsk-tsked me in her sexy schoolteacher voice as she settled more firmly on my lap. Evidence suggested I wasn't completely against the idea. "Investigator Summerlin, for shame."

I held her hips close, tight against me, and whispered in her ear, "We both know it's not the badge. It's because I mowed the lawn."

Laughing, she leaned over to blow out the candle.

Kara

The American goldfinch was five inches long. It weighed a half ounce, barely as much as the pencil in my hand. I sketched short, quick lines, puffing out the breast of the female, remembering the mottled green, yellow, and gray covering her body. She'd been molting, getting rid of the old, worn-out feathers to grow ones that were strong and warm and new.

I drew both coats in an exploded view, the old on top of the new, both layers framing the racing heart at the center of her body, a tiny, glistening thing that wouldn't regenerate. That would beat itself to death.

Jillian said they were vegetarians. She'd watched me watch the bird as it hopped from fence to feeder while we ate enchiladas. They ate seeds, weeds, and grasses, she said. Cowbirds who tried passing off their eggs in a goldfinch nest only got dead cowbird chicks out of it, their freeloading babies starved to death on a vegan goldfinch diet.

"What are you smiling about?"

"Nothing." I snapped the sketchbook closed.

"You and your birds." Phyllis hobbled over to the stove to brew her poison tea.

I chewed my lip, then stopped in case I was chewing it off. The goldfinch was the first thing that had taken my mind off Morales's visit yesterday. One hundred million dollars. It all made sense now, Morales's insistence on searching every bunker and property Sam had ever used. Of course they were after the money. It would keep them flush with wiretaps, guns, donuts, and coffee for the next decade.

I hadn't slept much. Part of me was screaming to get out of town, to leave now before the DEA charged me with everything and buried Celina's story in some bureaucratic black hole. I packed and repacked the bug-out bag, and even limped out to the truck to sit in the driver's seat, staring at the wheel, inhaling the dirt and dust that might as well have been Phyllis's perfume. I couldn't make myself turn the key. Because Celina wouldn't have. She wouldn't leave Phyllis to the wolves, and I'd already betrayed her once this week in Jillian's kitchen. I betrayed her every time the thought of Jillian crossed my mind.

So I stayed.

Phyllis took the steaming cup to her chair, the same one she sat in every morning, and surveyed the garden through the patio door. Afterward, I knew she'd rinse the cup and put it upside down in the dish rack, pull on her gardening gloves, and stump outside. You could set a clock by her. Sam always talked about being unpredictable, creating no patterns anyone would notice. Phyllis either didn't care or figured no one would notice her anyway. And it had worked, until now. Until I showed up and brought the DEA with me.

I flipped the sketchbook open again and retraced the heart in the middle of the goldfinch, making it darker, thick with lead.

"We're going into town today."

"Hell if I am."

"We've got work to do."

One hour and eighty-two fights later, I limped along the ped mall, the crutch catching on every rut and crooked cobblestone on the street. Phyllis walked even slower, stopping at each bench and swearing at me whenever I told her to sit down and take a break. We were a pair, the old lady with half a purple face and the broken tattooed chick hobbling through town. People moved out of our way, doubling the social distancing rules, and avoided even looking at us until we passed and they could gape and whisper to each other.

"Where's your place in Florida?"

"You're not invited."

"Like I'd want to go. Alligators and swamps and talking mice." I checked behind us, scanning the mall for Max or any other task force bros. No one stood out. "But you should be there, right? Lizard ladies sunning themselves on the beach. Charging up your wrinkles. Manifesting all that get-off-my-lawn energy. It's your mothership."

The cane I'd found for her in the hall closet whacked me in the good knee, which buckled slightly, but the effort sent her more off balance than me. I laughed. "Do you want me to pretend that hurts?"

"Go to hell." She stumped forward a few uneven steps. Her hunched back swayed from side to side, held up by pure spite. "'Get a walker.' 'Take your medicine.' 'Let's go downtown.' 'Now leave for Florida.'" She swung on me, and the eye that was still bloodred swam with disgust. "It's hurricane season."

"Hurricanes will take one look at you, turn around, and haul ass for Mexico."

Her lip quivered and she swatted at my crutch, trying not to smile. Her face was an objective horror show, swollen like a balloon on one side and spattered purple, gray, and red, with blue veins snaking under a distorted spiderweb of wrinkles and liver spots. I'd buried cuter corpses.

When we got to the thrift store, her mouth puckered but she didn't seem surprised. I picked the lock and let us in. We stood in shafts of sun and shadow, both of us broken and silent among the wreckage of the world we'd built. This was where I'd first met Phyllis Reed.

"Put that fucking bird book away." She'd told me on my second week at the store, after I drank her pepper-spiked coffee and hauled enough boxes of jeans and band T-shirts to pass some invisible test. It was the first time she'd shown any interest in me since Sam had brought me to the store and introduced us. She sat on a ripped vinyl barstool behind the counter every day, sipping tea and barking orders, ignoring the customers as much as they ignored her. I'd finished moving clothes around the store and was sketching on the other side of the counter when she pulled out a notebook from under the register. "This is your diary now."

The handwriting was serial killer cramped, shaky cursive that wedged itself into every margin and corner. I could barely read the column headers.

"Date, description . . ."

"Amount. Hell, they even teach you to read?" She flipped to the middle, where the rows of information ended. "This is where I left off yesterday. You enter all the clothes that come in and how much you paid for them."

We'd had two sellers come into the store yesterday, but from what I could make out in the serial killer log, we'd bought over sixty pieces of clothes and paid out about seven hundred dollars. Phantom purchases, I learned, led to phantom sales, recorded in another notebook.

Little by little, Phyllis showed me the whole system, how she varied her intakes by day and season. Weekends made ten times more than Mondays. For every designer piece she posted on Facebook Marketplace, she "sold" eight more. Sales dried up in the weeks before finals, and summer was slow and steady without undergrads flooding the ped mall.

She kept foot traffic high with a perpetual two-for-one coupon, and the coupons disappeared after being redeemed, showing full-price sales in the notebooks. After the store closed every night, she walked down the street like some invisible hunchback goblin, unnoticed by everyone as she dropped a bag stuffed with cash into the bank's night depository.

I didn't know how much of Sam's money she was running through the store, and I didn't understand how the money was coming in until a girl showed up one day with a box of clothes to sell.

She was cute, with brown beachy waves in her hair, aviator sunglasses, and a curious smile as she watched me smear paint samples over the wall. Black, deep blue, and Prince purple. If I was going to be stuck here six days a week, every hour that I wasn't on campus, I wasn't staring at white walls.

"Finally getting some help around here?" she asked Phyllis.

Phyllis grunted and pointed a knobby finger at each of us in turn. "Kara. Alexis."

"Nice to meet you." Alexis smiled as Phyllis pulled the box of clothes closer and started burrowing through it. "I like the blue."

"Matches your eyes." I leaned on the other side of the counter.

"My eyes are green." But she laughed and tilted her head, sizing me up. Phyllis pulled her head out of the box and snapped.

"Don't bother. She's already sleeping with someone."

"It's good for him to have some competition." She winked at me, a mostly straight wink, which I usually didn't bother with, and took the plastic bag Phyllis shoved across the counter, picked a shirt at random from one of the racks, and left.

"See you next week."

In the back, Phyllis pulled a brick of twenty-dollar bills out of the box and told me to count it. "Should be five thousand." She squeezed it like she could tell just by the weight and density of the cash. "Make sure."

It was, exactly, and that five thousand made up most of our sales for the week, getting deposited at the bank and coming out as clean as faded, designer denim in the account statements at the end of the month. I got a salary, a barely over minimum wage paycheck that made me laugh out loud every time I saw the name Kara Johnson listed next to shit like FICA and Social Security. But it got comfortable over time. Kara Johnson went to classes. Kara Johnson signed a lease on an apartment. Kara Johnson learned to launder hundreds of thousands of dollars through the thrift store and pass ten times as much under the table. She drove cash to Sam's house, bought Bitcoin through crypto ATMs across the state. Things were fine—good, even. And then, like an idiot, she'd gone and met a girl.

The walls were still dark blue but the band posters had all been taken down and probably ripped apart, the clothing racks in pieces on the floor. The speakers I'd mounted in the corners to blast Bikini Kill and the Runaways were long gone. Nothing had changed since the last time I'd been here, when I'd laid Max Summerlin out on the floor and he accused me—like a Boy Scout encountering his first MLM—of not telling him everything.

"What happened to the rest of it? The cash we didn't deposit at the bank?"

Alexis wasn't the only one coming in here. Sam had various collection points and they all turned their takes in to us. A river of money had flowed through the thrift store. We were the accountants, the ones who told Sam whether everyone was playing by his rules. The cash that didn't get laundered through the bank went out in trucks and cars. It got funneled through other channels back to Sam or wherever he wanted it to go. And one of those channels was Phyllis.

"You took a quarter of it every week, truckloads of cash. It was way too much to be your cut. What did you do with the rest?"

Phyllis moved to the counter and leaned against it. Her barstool was long gone. She didn't answer.

"That's what the DEA's after and they've got dirt on both of us now. They probably bugged the house so we can't talk there." Not that she was talking here. "If we don't cooperate, you're going to jail and they'll bury Celina's story."

She still didn't say anything.

"Are you even fucking listening to me?" I kicked one of the disassembled clothing racks with my cast, sending it shooting across the floor.

She finally turned around, all four and a half feet of her, and shook her head, glaring at me with her monster face. "Sam should have killed you when he had the chance."

"You think I don't know that?" I kicked another bar and another. "You think I don't wish he had? I spend every minute of every day wishing he would've taken me and not her. I would've set the world on fire for her." My voice broke as I crashed through the pile of metal on the floor. Something inside the cast popped. "Everything I touch turns to shit. Everything." I spun back toward Phyllis. "And you knew that when you let me stay. You knew that and you fucking invited me in anyway because you spend every minute of every day wanting to trade your life in, too. Don't tell me you don't."

We stared at each other across the mess of metal. Outside the papered-over windows, silhouettes crossed in front of the store, shadows of people living their shadows of lives. After a stony silence, Phyllis picked her way through the dismembered clothes racks and left the store. I followed her.

"Go to Florida."

She kept walking.

"Are you listening to me?"

She ignored me for the entire length of the street until we ran into a weird group of people near the end of the ped mall. They were distanced but banded together by something I couldn't see. They all faced away and most of them had their phones out.

Phyllis stopped, holding on to a bench to catch her breath, as one of the kids pulled on their parent's shirt and jumped up and down, shouting, "Mateo! Mateo!"

Then I saw what had grabbed everyone's attention. A flock of crows perched in the boulevard trees on the other side of the street, calling to each other. The phone people didn't care about them, though. They were recording the white bird in the middle of the cawing black ones.

"It's Mateo," one Gen Z said to another, their hands intertwining, curling into each other.

"Mateo?"

They turned toward us and spent a few seconds trying not to look horrified by Phyllis's face. "Um, the cockatoo. They held a citywide contest to name it and 'Mateo' was the winner, nominated by some kid in Coralville. It's a hashtag now. #MateoWatch."

The crows seemed way less invested in Mateo than the people live streaming him. The cockatoo pecked at a tree branch, ruffling his feathers and preening for the crowd as he hunted for insects and seeds. He hopped to another branch, cocked his head, and looked directly at me. It caught me hard, like his beak had drilled directly into my chest.

"It won't bring her back."

"What?" It took me a second to register Phyllis's voice. I'd already forgotten our conversation. The bird had wiped everything else away.

"Nothing brings them back. Nothing makes it better. They'll always be dead and you'll spend the rest of your life loving a dead thing. Whatever plan you think you have"—she gave me a long, hard look—"it won't work."

Max

Nights were the best and the worst times. They could drive you insane, lying in bed next to your sleeping wife, willing your breathing to slow and match hers, for your mind to follow hers into sweet and simple unconsciousness. I'd played the game long enough to know there was no perfect pillow position, no app, no magic thought or lack of thought that would send me consistently to sleep. Either it was a sleeping night or not. And my shoulder injury hadn't helped. Before I'd been shot, I could sometimes get a six-hour stretch, but after the nerve pain kicked in it was four hours at best, adding up the various bits and snatches.

There were benefits to insomnia, though, too. After Garrett was born, I wore a path from his crib to the living room, making creaky laps at 3:00 a.m. while he reached for my chin and gurgled. When he was old enough to sleep through the night, I watched him, the rise and fall of his tiny back under his Avengers blanket. I replaced the outlets in the kitchen with the USB port ones. I made French toast and bacon on Shelley's birthday every year. I read every Don Winslow book the day they came out. But mostly I researched. I dove into the endless hole that was the internet, looking up information on cases I was working, people Jonah had dreamed about, facts to back up whatever fight I was currently losing to Shelley. The laptop monitor was my night-light, the scrawled half sentences in my notebooks my bedtime stories. The world was dark and undemanding, quiet enough that sometimes I could hear something I hadn't caught before.

"He knew my name."

The thought came out of nowhere as the dawn light crept across our bedroom wall. Shelley made a noise and turned over, wrapping her arm around my chest and snuggling into my side. "What?"

John Doe.

I hadn't thought about it at the time—there was too much else going on with Kara storming out of the hospital—but the words played back now, with that ghost of a smile on John Doe's poisoned face. *You already have the drugs, Investigator Summerlin.*

I hadn't booked him or introduced myself at the top of the interview, and no one else would have been passing out business cards to this guy at the station, yet he knew exactly who I was. He said I had the drugs—me, as if he knew I was the cop who'd made the truck stop bust. Everything in me went stiff and cold.

Shelley groaned, twisting the covers in her reluctant full-body morning stretch. Normally I would enjoy the shift of her pajamas, but today I grabbed my laptop and went to the kitchen, popping in earbuds and replaying the recorded interview at the hospital.

"I wasn't hired to find drugs."

"Then what does Kara know? What were you hired to find?"

"The same thing you were."

He knew I was on the task force and he knew Morales was hunting for Belgrave's money. How? How did a hired killer have that much insider information?

There was only one person who could answer that.

The hospital discharged John Doe back into the custody of the Iowa City police on Friday morning. I didn't know how long they normally treated a patient for a near-fatal poisoning, but this was a pandemic. The hospital staff weren't putting up with the constant influx of police officers through their corridors longer than they absolutely had to. We were essential workers, sure, but not here.

When I arrived, decked out in my PPE, Morales was alone in the room with John Doe while two officers waited outside. He turned when I came in, surprised. "Didn't know you were coming down today."

"I need another interview with him." I nodded at the bed, where John Doe stared hollow-eyed at the ceiling over his mask. He looked sallow as shit, like he could still vomit at any minute. The IVs and machines were gone, but the restraints and handcuffs kept him immobile. His hands lay limp and flat against the bed rails.

Morales stood aside as the hospital staff filed in. "Don't count on any interviews. He hasn't said one word all morning and we're still coming up with fucking crickets on his ID."

The attending physician gave Morales the rundown on John Doe's care while the officers prepped him for his transfer. He asked to use the bathroom at one point, and they both walked him in there, one on each side, as he lurched unsteadily across the room.

We took him out through the freight elevator, still in his hospital gown, wearing leg and arm restraints cuffed to the wheelchair. His eyes glazed, staring at the elevator doors, as if unaware of the crowd of law enforcement surrounding him. I wanted to drill him with questions, to catch him off guard, but it didn't seem like he even noticed when the elevator opened again.

Outside, dumpsters lined the alley and the unmarked tractor trailer of a semitruck sat on one side of the loading dock. In New York during the surge, they'd run out of room in the morgues and were using tractor trailers to house corpses. The surge hadn't visited Iowa. Not yet. I tried not to think about it as we wheeled John Doe toward the waiting squad cars.

It was early, but the sun shone between the crack of two buildings, the air already hot and still, stifling through the mask. At least the alley was empty and windowless, the scene clear for a quiet transfer. Morales climbed into the front seat as the officers uncuffed John Doe from the chair, preparing to move him to the car. When they ordered him to stand, he doubled over in the wheelchair.

"What is it?"

One of the officers grabbed his arm. His back started to shake like he was having a seizure. He buried his face in his lap, twisting his mask up over his eyes. Something glinted in his hands, the glare of sun off his handcuffs.

"Oh, fuck this."

"Get a doctor. Now," Morales barked from the car. "Take him back inside."

The second officer ran back up the loading dock as the first wheeled the chair around. The hair on the back of my neck stood up. Something was wrong. I had an insomniac flash of a 4:00 a.m.

Google search, reading all the symptoms of digitalis poisoning. Seizures weren't one of them. I glanced at Morales a split second before a grunt and the clatter of metal spun me back around.

The wheelchair lay on its side on the asphalt and John Doe was . . . gone. I drew my gun, sweeping the alley until the remaining officer started being dragged backward, a pair of handcuffed hands wrapped around his throat.

"Stop!" I couldn't get a clear shot. Doe was using the officer—a guy twice as big as him—as a human shield. The officer's eyes were wide, desperate, and a line of blood trickled down his neck. Doe had something: a weapon. How had he gotten a weapon?

"I'll slit his throat," came the voice behind him, calm as a weather report, all traces of sickness gone. The officer stumbled back, pleading now as Doe kept him off-balance. They disappeared behind the tractor trailer.

Behind me, Morales called for backup. The second officer appeared on the loading dock with a guy in scrubs and stopped short. I put a finger to my lips and pointed to the trailer. She nodded, pulled her firearm, and darted to the far side. I ran in the direction John Doe had disappeared, my vision contracting to that single point.

Around the corner, a gunshot fired, sending me slamming back into the side of the truck for cover. Either the officer had gotten off a shot or John Doe had taken his gun.

Another shot. Crouching, I went underneath the trailer, creeping up behind the tires until I saw a pair of feet lying on the asphalt and another pair—wearing hospital slippers—disappearing into a row of bushes. I crawled out into a spreading pool of blood. The officer clutched his throat, eyes white and terrified.

The second officer rounded the far corner of the trailer, radio-ing in as she sprinted toward us. "Officer down."

The bushes were a green wall concealing whatever lay behind them. I got up, pulse racing. I'd already run headfirst into a garden, mindlessly racing after this suspect, and my throat had almost been opened for me, too.

The medic sprinted around the corner, jolting me back to real-ity. I pointed at the greenery and the other officer nodded. We went in, weapons drawn, finding nothing except neatly spaced trees and a picnic bench on the other side where a burning cigarette lay in the middle of the table. A guy in hospital scrubs banged on a locked door. I ran toward him.

"Where did he go?"

"He took my badge. I can't get—" The door opened before he could finish, revealing a wary nurse on the other side. The officer pushed past her and the two of us raced back inside the hospital.

This was a different wing, full of long corridors of closed doors and people dressed in scrubs and hospital gowns. Except for the handcuffs, John Doe would blend in completely.

I called Morales. "He's in the hospital, first floor, west side. We need this locked down now. No one gets out."

I swept rooms, making the patients who weren't on ventila-tors gasp or scream. Nurses shouted procedure. Everyone looked the same, goddamnit, a sea of sterile masks. I ran through another corridor as security guards caught up to me and I briefed them on the description.

It wasn't until I got to the end of the ward, in a room with a sleeping man, that I noticed something metallic peeking out from under the bed. I leaned down and looked underneath. Handcuffs. Empty.

A blow to the back of my head sent me to the floor. I rolled and fired at the doorway just as a flash of blue disappeared out of the room. People in the hallway screamed.

I ran, pushing through the still-swinging doors of the ward, a lobby, and another set of doors until I arrived back at the freight area we'd come through minutes before.

On the loading dock, John Doe pounded down the ramp. I fired again and he went down, the gun flying out of his hands. I caught up to him, kicking the stolen Glock away as he dragged himself up, limping out into the alley.

"Hands up. Now!"

He lurched to a stop, his weight on one leg, arms hesitating at his sides.

"I said now."

He lifted hands that were small and stained with blood. He still faced away. It was just the two of us in the alley. I couldn't hear anyone on the other side of the tractor trailer. They must have moved the downed officer into the emergency room, clearing everyone from the dock in the chaos.

Slowly, the killer turned to face me. The leg of the scrubs he'd changed into were dark and wet. My adrenaline sputtered, seizing my shoulder with white-hot shocks. The gun shook in my hands.

"Get on your knees."

He hissed at his leg, sucking in air as he bared small, sharp teeth. "Beautiful."

"I said get down."

He didn't. He watched his foot turn red as if fascinated by the gush of his own blood. I took a step closer, the gun shaking harder.

"Who hired you? Nilsen? Chase? What do they know about me?"

"It subsumes everything, reduces you to nothing." He looked up at me and smiled. "You're so blind, you can't even see what's right next to you."

He took a lurching step toward me, then another. I aimed at his other leg, but before I could fire, an engine roared, echoing off the walls of the alley. I jumped back as a police cruiser slammed into John Doe, throwing his body into the cement foundation like a rag doll. He fell with a dull thud, eyes open and unseeing.

The cruiser door opened and Morales stepped out.

"He was a danger worse than the virus," Larsen told the group of masked reporters outside ICPD. He called on people mechanically, answering their questions about the murder suspect who was killed while trying to escape police custody.

I stood off to the side, apart from both the cops and the journalists. Across the street a few Black Lives Matter protestors watched the proceedings without finding any need to chime in.

"The suspect did not have Covid-19. He was at the hospital for an unrelated condition and was in the process of being transferred back to await his hearing. An altercation occurred, resulting in the critical injury of a six-year veteran of the force." Michaelson. He was a good guy, had a wife and three kids. Someone in the department said he coached soccer in his free time and now he was lying in ICU with a damaged esophagus, getting fed through a tube. I could still see his eyes, wide and white against the pavement, even as Morales appeared next to me.

"Let's walk."

I headed in the direction of the protestors without bothering to see if he followed.

"Why did you do it?" It wasn't until I got back to the station, after getting a physical evaluation and turning my weapon in for a mandatory review—officer discharge in the line of duty—that I heard what happened in the hospital alley. Morales's version of it, anyway. He'd told the entire force that John Doe had me cornered and he'd had no choice except to drive the car into the suspect.

No one questioned it. No one asked me to corroborate, not even Larsen. The assault on Michaelson colored the department in a silent rage that made the hows and whys of John Doe's death matter to exactly zero people.

Morales didn't pretend to misunderstand my question. He didn't pretend to answer it, either. "He attacked an officer. He was lunging for you."

A protestor had left the group and was walking some distance behind us, texting on their phone, but other than that, the sidewalk was empty. A few windows were open in the buildings we passed, so I kept my voice low.

"I had him cornered. I had a clear shot and he was disarmed and injured. He wasn't going anywhere until you ran him over and cracked his head open like a walnut."

"Are you defending a cartel enforcer?"

"There could be security cameras. Witnesses. People who saw a police cruiser slam into an injured man. What do you think that will look like as a video shared a billion times on the internet?"

"The security camera footage is taken care of and there weren't any witnesses except you." Morales stopped at an intersection and turned: not in my face but not backing down, either. "And I know you're not planning to contradict the DEA account of what happened—not when the scumbag almost murdered you twice and we weren't getting a single piece of intel from him."

I remembered the day Morales had confronted Ciseski's racist comments; how he'd gone expressionless, deadly. He'd told me people were only worth what they brought to the table. Maybe he really had thought the suspect was lunging at me, but a larger truth overshadowed it: John Doe hadn't brought anything to Morales's table.

He produced a bag of chips and opened them, crunching on the salt and oil. Heat waves rose from the concrete on the street. A masked couple with a dog darted uneasily around us into the crosswalk.

"You want me to lie."

"I want you to fucking thank me for simplifying the judicial process so we can get back to work."

"Back to your fundraiser, you mean."

He ate another chip. "We still have Kara. She'll talk."

"And what will you do to her if she doesn't?"

"We have leverage."

Kara didn't give a shit about anyone; she didn't care if she lived or died. I didn't know what kind of leverage Morales could have that would make someone like Kara Johnson care enough to—

"Celina." It clicked suddenly, the audible thunk of what Kara had told me in the cornfield. The DEA promised her they would go public with Celina's story.

"Among other things. There's a few pressure points, but, yeah—she'll do what she's told if she wants her girlfriend's heroics officially acknowledged."

Morales poked around the chip bag like there was a prize inside, like he wasn't talking about Jonah's niece like her life and death was his own personal bartering chip. As though he had any right to tell or withhold her story.

"We've got a crypto expert coming in next week and more 3D ground scanners, so we can canvass more sites quicker. We've got people on Nilsen and Chase, tracking both of their movements. This operation is active, with or without John Doe."

The heat beat down on my head, hitting me in waves. All I could hear was the crunch of that chip bag, getting louder, drowning everything else out. I didn't know what I was doing here or who I even was. Faces shifted in and out of focus. Jonah, Celina, Garrett. John Doe flying across the alley, hitting the wall. My gun sliding across Larsen's desk.

"You're on Kara." Morales was still talking, outlining the next phase in the task force's plan. "Find out what she hasn't told us yet. You can—"

"No."

I blinked the street back into focus. Morales still stood on the curb, his Hawaiian shirt clinging to his beer belly, sweat beading on his forehead. He cocked his chin up, measuring me.

"I'm on leave. Officer discharge of a weapon."

Morales waved it off. "Larsen'll have that settled in a few days."

I shook my head, and once I started, it felt like I couldn't stop. "No."

I stepped back, moving away from the DEA agent until I dropped off the curb into the street. A car honked. I didn't care.

"I'm done. I quit."

Kara

The sun glared off the empty grain bins. The surrounding fields of corn stood motionless in the stagnant air. I leaned against Phyllis's truck in the middle of nowhere, while the truck's grille probably branded a pattern across my back. I didn't have to wait long. A sleek black BMW pulled up in the patch of gravel next to me.

A guy got out of the passenger seat, but the driver stayed in the car, letting the engine idle. I couldn't tell if there was anyone in the back.

"Thanks for meeting me."

"Anything for a friend of Sam's." Frederick Nilsen picked his way over the weedy rocks, wearing a Polo shirt and khakis like he was on his way to an all-inclusive vacation. His drinker nose flashed bright red in the sun. "Are you here to—how did you say it? Give me what's mine?"

"Umm, almost."

"I thought you knew where it was." His eyes were hidden behind sunglasses, but the corner of his mouth danced up, mocking. I didn't know if he was talking about drugs or money—if we were even speaking the same language right now—but I had nothing to lose. Morales didn't know I was here. I'd used a new burner to set up this meeting and taken an hour-long detour out of town to make sure I wasn't being followed.

"Did you see the news?"

He made an uninterested noise. "Case counts. Idiots in politics. People screaming at the void."

"The incident in Iowa City."

"Oh, that." He walked away from the cars and into a crescent of shade cast by one of the grain bins. "Is that what happened to your leg?"

I followed him on my crutch. "Was he yours?"

Nilsen scoffed. "I'm a businessman, providing essential services to the consumers of this country. And you—since you haven't been arrested and you're still asking pointless, blind questions—are obviously working for the cops."

"You didn't answer my question."

"Answer mine first."

I hesitated, feeling eyes inside the idling BMW on me. If Nilsen had sent the killer after me, he already knew I was working with the DEA, and whoever was in that car was probably the next guy on the job. If he hadn't, I still wasn't telling him anything he hadn't guessed.

"I'm off the clock. But I can tell you what they want with you. If you tell me what I want to know."

He considered me for an uncomfortable length of time. I waited him out, swatting at a fly that buzzed between our heads.

"Strip."

"What?"

He repeated himself, calmly telling me to take off my shirt and shorts. "I don't want anyone listening to our conversation."

I chucked the clothes off, leaving them in a pile at my feet. He inspected my cast and crutch and must have found them both bug-free, because he walked to the open door of the grain bin and waved his arm, gesturing for me to go first. I limped into the dark, wearing nothing but sandals and Superman-blue briefs. Inside, dust motes floated in the shaft of sunlight from the door and shadows hid the rest.

"Why are the cops sniffing around? I have nothing to hide."

"Save it for your testimony. You're not on the record here. And it's not just local law enforcement you're dealing with. This is an interagency task force." For the first time since I'd been trapped into this, I felt the joy that oozed out of Morales, Max, and the others whenever they barfed that phrase with all their shivering post-coital energy.

It had the opposite effect on Nilsen. He took off his sunglasses and the uncertainty in his voice seemed to double as it bounced off the corrugated metal walls. "Sam said the payments were untraceable."

"Not originally. That's why they sent me after you." I wiped away a trickle of sweat that was seeping between my breasts. "Were you a distributor?"

I hadn't seen Nilsen at the thrift store, but he could have sent anyone. I didn't know all the people behind the faces that showed up with bricks of cash every week.

"Is that what they think?"

"Were you?" I limped closer. For a beat I wondered what would happen if a farmer showed up and saw the two of us—a mostly naked, tattooed, injured woman intimidating a fully dressed old white man in a grain bin. My life had become a series of bizarre memes. Nilsen glanced down my body with an uncomfortable apathy, a guy who'd already seen all the naked bodies he ever wanted to, pausing for a moment on the bullet scar puckering my chest. He shook his head.

"I supplied Sam with certain ingredients, things I could get through my own suppliers easily without raising eyebrows."

"What kind of ingredients?"

"Bulking agents, from what I could tell. I didn't ask any questions I didn't need the answers to." He jerked his head at the floor. "This was the drop site when I had deliveries for him. I left the shipments here and notified him when they were ready. I never saw anything or met anyone beyond Sam and you, that one time at his house. I didn't even know you were part of his business at first. You looked like some stray he'd picked up on the side of the road. A charity project."

"If I was, he picked the wrong project."

Nilsen humphed a little sound that would have made more sense on a librarian. "There's nothing here anymore. They won't find anything that ties me to Sam's operations. He accepted my last shipment over a year ago."

"They're not looking for product or people to prosecute. At least, that's not their end game."

I limped over the auger on the floor to lean against the doorway and made good on my end of the deal, telling Nilsen about the botched final shipment, the would-be buyer who'd sent his rat-face killer after the rest of Belgrave's people, and the ultimate prize: a hundred million dollars hidden—if you believed Morales—somewhere in Iowa. I could practically see Max's face as I talked. He would be furious. That little vein in his forehead would bulge and his bad shoulder would tense up, aching to punch me. *Don't spill the whole operation to one of our main suspects*, he would rage in his quiet, constipated way.

But I knew in my gut Nilsen was telling the truth. If he'd been the buyer, whoever was in that BMW would've already overpowered me. I'd come here alone and I would've died alone. Instead, I was baking like a dried corn kernel with the CEO of a slaughterhouse.

Nilsen was quiet, absorbing the details, staring blindly out the grain bin door at the ocean of green in the distance.

"Sam could have buried money anywhere, literally anywhere."

"How do you know the money's buried?"

"He was a fan of putting things in the ground." I swallowed the clot of emotion that always caught me by surprise. The sweat had turned from drops into rivers down my temples and arms, making the winding ink of vines and birds glisten. "And most of it got shipped out in cash. But I don't know. When the killer had me trapped, he said something about codes. He wanted a code, maybe?"

Nilsen gaze sharpened. "A key."

"You said the payments Sam made to you were untraceable. How?"

Something shifted in Nilsen. He stood up taller, and a reptilian gleam shimmered over his sweaty face. He wasn't a cornered old man anymore but a businessman. The guy who bragged about slaughtering twelve hundred hogs an hour.

"One million."

"Excuse me?"

"You heard me. You want to know how Sam's payments came in, you're going to make it worth my while."

"Do you take checks?"

"Those are my terms." He walked to the entrance of the grain bin, pausing next to me at the edge of the shadows.

"Government work doesn't pay, Fred. The DEA's not going to agree to that."

"I'm not making a deal with the DEA. As far as they or anyone else is concerned, this conversation never happened." He took a step closer until we were eye to eye. "I'm a respected business owner. I employ hundreds of Iowans, providing critical jobs during an economic meltdown. I'm a pillar of the community.

"Sam Olson paid me once for some farm supplies. He was a distant acquaintance, but I was still shocked, completely shocked"—his face rearranged itself into a mask of surprise—"when his murder and illegal dealings came to light. And I will destroy anyone who claims otherwise. Especially a scum-of-the-earth drug dealer who wouldn't be missed by her own mother."

He walked into the sun and climbed into the BMW without a backward glance. I waited until the car pulled away and the trail of dust settled on the horizon before limping back to my clothes.

I pulled the tank top on, dusty and sticking to the sweat coating my torso, and had just finished easing the shorts over my cast when another engine noise jerked me upright. Two cars pulled into the clearing. They screeched to a stop on either side of me, boxing me in. Sunlight bounced off the windshields, hiding whoever was inside. Retreating to the grain bin would only trap me more. My heart kicked up as multiple doors opened. I lifted the crutch in front of me, both hands clenched tight over metal, ready for whatever was coming next.

Max

The banner hung crookedly over the park sign, a hand-drawn advertisement for the Iowa City/Coralville Community Fundraiser. Other yard signs were stuck into the grass along the path:

Iowa Strong

Wear your mask.

#MateoWatch

Corn dogs $5. Ice cream $5.

We got this.

Have a heart. Stay six feet apart.

#MateoMate

I frowned at the last one as Garrett and I hauled a camp chair and his equipment bag toward the ball field.

"Hashtag MateoMate?"

"Yeah, Dad. That's the whole point."

The park was already busy. Two food trucks were stationed at the edge of the parking lot and pop-up tables dotted the path to the field. We passed a table full of hemp jewelry hawked by a masked red-eyed woman. Another table was piled with the kind of plastic toys I found stuffed in the couch cushions and routinely tossed in the garbage. One table had a blue-haired woman setting up matted photographs of animals: birds on fence posts, goats showing their teeth in exaggerated close-ups, and a lot of different shots of a whiskery, sunbathing pig.

Garrett joined the rest of his team, all of them wearing last year's too-small jerseys, while I set up my chair in a patch of shade off third base and a good distance from the other parents. Some were masked. Some weren't. One woman chased a toddler who'd made a dash for the pitcher's mound. I didn't recognize most of them. Garrett rode his bike to practices last year and Shelley drove him to the games across town. I'd come to as many as I could, depending on my caseload, but it was always a weird little world. Half the parents stared at their phones and the ones who paid attention were alarmingly invested, shouting at the players with unsolicited coaching advice, grumbling about the ref—invariably some unfortunate teenager—and losing their goddamn minds if their kid got a decent hit. I'd bought Garrett his first baseball glove and we tossed the ball around at home, but Little League was a whole different animal. One I didn't touch if I could help it.

Where are you? The message from Shelley lit up my phone, sending low-grade panic zinging through my chest.

Last night I was still reeling from my conversation with Morales when I got home. I hadn't known much about Santiago Morales when I accepted the assignment, but I thought we were all playing on the same level. That we shared a common goal. Yesterday he stripped away any illusions I'd had. There was no new drug trafficking ring about to rise in Iowa. He'd killed John Doe in cold blood and not only lied about it but expected me to lie, too. He used me and the ICPD, and he was leveraging Celina's death—her story—in order to use Kara, too.

Jonah had tried calling three times yesterday. I didn't answer. I didn't know what to say. When I got home I told Shelley I'd quit the task force. She didn't ask questions or demand explanations. She took one look at my face and wrapped her arms around me in a long, tight hug. We went to bed together and I slept almost six hours. A 2020 record.

This morning, Shelley was still sleeping when I found Garrett in the backyard, tossing a baseball in the air and catching it. Maybe it was the sleep or maybe it was walking away from this assignment, but I felt like a new man. Like the bindings had fallen off and I could finally breathe again. The ache in my shoulder was a reminder that I was here and things were possible now that hadn't been before.

As I walked over, I realized what day it was. Not in my world but in my son's.

"Fundraiser today, right?"

He nodded, his mouth set in a glum line, and kept tossing the ball. I reached out and snatched it out of the air. "We better get going, then."

Garrett turned and just like that he was a kid again, pure shock and joy knocking all his teenage angst aside. "Seriously?"

I grinned and tousled his hair the way he normally hated. "Get your stuff. I'll grab the masks. Don't wake your mom up."

Now, sitting in the middle of the park with people teeming on all sides, I was rethinking my decisions. I stared at Shelley's message on the phone, trying to figure out how to handle this with the least possible fallout. Where was I?

Out.

Her response came immediately. Out where?

We can pick stuff up for dinner on the way home. What do you want to eat?

A pause. The three dots appeared and disappeared on the screen. Sweat gathered on my spine. I built rational arguments in my head, counted the number of people wearing masks on the team, in the park. We could settle this calmly, like adults.

WHERE ARE YOU?

Leaving the chair, I walked down the line of trees separating the ball field from the soccer field, where a few kids were tossing Frisbees and doing handstands, and called Shelley. I wasn't having this conversation by text.

She picked up before it finished the first ring and said nothing. All I heard on the other end was running water. I waited a beat before trying a soft opening. "How's your—"

"You're there, aren't you?" she cut me off, her voice low and sharp. "You took him to the fundraiser."

I switched to my *I'm just trying to do my job, ma'am* voice, the one I used for hostile and anxious witnesses. "It's not as bad as you thought it was going to be. Almost everyone—"

She disconnected the call.

"Great." I sighed, wiped the sweat off my head, and went to buy a drink from one of the food trucks. An announcer came over a microphone as I reached the front of the line, listing the vendors and the various ways attendees could support Project Mateo's Mate.

"What's Project Mateo's Mate?" I asked the girl who handed me my lemonade. She couldn't hear me though the mask, so I asked

A WORLD OF HURT

again, feeling like I was shouting into a cloth gag. A voice next to me answered.

"It's for that bird."

Larsen—the last person I expected to see at this sort of thing— jerked his chin up in hello.

"The cockatoo running around with the crows." He gave the girl some money for a water, ignoring the line behind us. "They named it and now, since the thing survived the winter, they're rais- ing money to buy it a mate."

"That's what this fundraiser's for?"

I assumed Garrett's event was for the pandemic: raising money for PPE or food shelf donations or toilet paper—any of the million things we'd taken for granted until this March and now hunted and hoarded like animals. But no. I'd gone behind Shelley's back and set a bomb off in my already strained marriage for . . . bird booty.

The thing in my chest that felt fresh and hopeful this morn- ing, that had even survived the exchange with Shelley, deflated.

"Why are you here?"

He jerked his head at the game, where the announcer was running through the lineups like this was a minor-league day at the park. "My youngest is on the blue team."

"Mine's on green."

We headed in that direction, stopping well before the outfield. Still away from the spectators and far enough past the vendors that no one could hear us. He took off his mask and I followed suit, even as I glanced at the team bench to make sure Garrett's was still on.

"How's Michaelson?"

"Still in the hospital. He'll be there for a while yet, but he's stable. Should make a full recovery."

He lingered on the "should." Should *make a full recovery*— implying that I hadn't. I relaxed my shoulder, ignoring the twinge of nerves, and nodded at the news.

"I talked to Morales this morning. He told me you quit the task force."

I nodded again as the players took their positions on the field.

"Were you planning to tell me about that?"

"I'm suspended from duty, sir."

"Cut the bullshit. What happened?"

I hesitated, watching the opening pitch go wide and the batter swing at it anyway. Cheers rose up from both sides of the field. Everyone was eager to play.

"How well do you know Morales?"

I could feel Larsen looking at me, measuring the question. "As well as you, or probably less at this point. He reports to Chicago. I've talked to his sup a few times." He paused, turning back to the field. "He treats the job like a game."

But what kind of game was he playing? He'd killed a man—a known murderer, but still a man with the right to due process— because he wasn't useful. He'd told his team to hunt one thing while secretly using them to look for something else. And he'd made no apologies for any of it.

"Did you read my last report?"

"What there was of it."

I swallowed. The report I'd filed was vague to the point of useless. I hadn't explicitly lied, but I'd lied by omission and that came down to the same thing. The fight with Shelley was still rolling in my gut, and I couldn't handle this on top of it. Kara was right: I was useless at undercover, at hiding what I was, and hell if I was ever going to be Morales's secret keeper.

I laid out the whole story, which took most of the first inning of the game. Larsen listened without expression as I recapped the scene in the alley and what Morales told me at the press conference, finishing just as Garrett stepped up for his first at bat. He dug in and took a few test swings. He looked good. Ready.

"I couldn't be part of it anymore. So I quit. I was planning to notify the department on Monday."

Larsen didn't reply. I waited him out while Garrett took a ball and swung at one above his shoulders. He always liked them too high. It was 2–2 when Larsen finally cleared his throat.

"Summerlin, you need to—"

A disturbance cut him off. At the far edge of the park, two men shouted at each other, their voices getting louder and angrier by the second. We responded instinctually, putting our masks on and jogging across the grass. No one else had joined the confrontation, at least not yet. The man on the outer edge stood on a sidewalk, masked, with a dog that was barking and pulling at its leash. The other guy faced away from us, wearing a T-shirt, shorts, and a red ball cap. I didn't need him to turn around to know what the hat would say.

Larsen got there first, slowing to a purposeful walk with raised *Let's all calm the fuck down* hands.

"You're the problem!" the guy with the dog was shouting over the barks. "You're the reason it's spreading!"

"Keep telling yourself that. This whole thing is Chinese-manufactured, left-wing propaganda."

"That's enough." Larsen moved between them. I followed suit, not sure which side was the bigger threat. Neither seemed to be carrying, but the dog was a loose cannon and red-hat guy—unmasked, obviously—paced back and forth like someone working themselves up.

"I'm Captain Larsen with the Iowa City Police Department."

"Arrest this libtard." Red-hat guy lunged forward. I intercepted, blocking him off. He smelled like hot dogs and UV, even through my mask, and his bloated, sunburnt face pulsed with idiot rage. He pushed away from me, sending shocks through my arm and up the back of my neck.

"I'll arrest you both for disorderly conduct if you don't knock it off," Larsen said.

"How are you letting this happen right now?" The guy with the dog waved in the direction of the food trucks, vendors, and baseball game. "Is this the police's idea of good PR? Having a superspreader event?"

"They have a permit and they're asking people to mask."

Red-hat guy started in about his rights and how he didn't have to wear anything he didn't want to. I backed him further away from the confrontation, counting on distance to deescalate. "You're going to be wearing handcuffs soon if you don't cool off."

I asked him if he had a kid playing, who he was here to support. Behind me, Larsen did the same with the dog guy, explaining the fundraiser and trying to move him along. I got red-hat to head back toward the food trucks as Larsen walked the other guy down the sidewalk that led out of the park. At the edge of the tree line, just before he disappeared from view, the guy yelled over his shoulder, "Go home!"

The game had stopped. All the players stood stock-still, gloves at their sides, silent. Garrett was still at home plate, gripping the bat against his chest. The cap shaded his eyes and the rest of his face was covered by the mask. I nodded at him, trying to convey that everything was all right. He didn't move until the coaches came out, clapping and shouting instructions as though nothing had happened, jump-starting the inning again.

I didn't hear Larsen until he was right next to me.

"Who else was in the alley?"

"It was just the three of us. Me, John Doe, and Morales." The dock was clear and there were no windows looking into the loading area. It was why we'd picked it as the transfer location in the first place. Morales knew that. He knew there'd be no witnesses except me.

The pitcher wound up and threw. Garrett swung for the bleachers, and the crack of the ball against the bat had both benches leaping to their feet. The hit soared over the shortstop and landed in the no-man's-land between left and center field. Garrett sprinted to first while the runner on second base rounded third, the coaches waving him home. The throw to home was late, the run scored, and the green team's side erupted in cheers.

Larsen waited until the next batter was at the plate before he said, "I'm not going to have you refile the report."

"Why not?" I glanced behind us, making sure no one was around. "Morales killed John Doe. That's beyond excessive force. It's murder."

"You did the right thing by telling me. I need to know what I'm dealing with. But a dangerous felon was stopped yesterday. As far as the public knows, we served and protected them."

"So you're just going to ignore—"

"We need a win." Larsen watched the game, his hard gaze roving the field. "This year has been one nightmare after another. Quarantine, protests, the election. Every goddamn citizen is on the verge of exploding. The department needs something to celebrate, something we can point to and be proud of."

More clapping erupted from the field, but it sounded a mile away. Everything in me had gone numb.

"You're pointing to the wrong thing. Tell Morales that I'm going to Internal Affairs."

Kara

"Fancy meeting you here." Morales got out of the first sedan, and three more guys followed suit. I didn't recognize any of them, which set me on edge.

I flipped the crutch casually in front of me. "You followed me?"

"We've had eyes on Nilsen. Watching his movements." Morales pulled off his mask and opened a bag of popcorn, leaning on the side of the car. He nodded the men forward like an afterthought. They fanned out and slowly moved in. "Imagine our surprise when he meets up with you here, at a known drop site."

The two guys who'd circled onto either side of my peripheral reached for their weapons. I took stock of both, deciding simultaneously that the one on the left would be an easier takedown and that Jillian wouldn't be happy if I re-broke my leg. I flipped the crutch again.

"What do you want to know?"

"Get in." Morales gestured to the car. "We'll talk about it on the way."

"I have to return the pickup."

"No problem. Joe?" The guy on the right stepped forward, a

wall of a human whose chest promised additional broken bones. He held out a meaty hand.

"Give Joe the keys. He'll get it back where it belongs."

Knowledge dripped from his voice with smug confidence. He knew exactly who owned this pickup and we both knew what he'd do to her if I didn't cooperate.

I tossed the keys at Joe and limped to Morales's car. It wasn't until I got in the back that I saw the glass partition and the lack of handles on the inside of the doors. Fuck.

Morales climbed into the front passenger seat and smiled, popping another handful of popcorn.

"Get comfy."

The drive back to Iowa City was long and tedious. Morales drilled me with questions about the meeting with Nilsen. I gave him a version of events: I wanted to sniff Nilsen out without the DEA hovering around. That much was true. But I didn't tell him anything I'd learned, how Nilsen had been a supplier of Sam's and how Sam paid him in some way that required a key. I didn't mention Nilsen's finder's fee, either, the one million he wanted in exchange for his help in digging up Sam's fortune.

I told Morales exactly what Nilsen wanted me to feed him. That he'd sold Sam farm supplies once and hadn't done any business with him afterward. That he was shocked to learn what Sam really was.

"He said he didn't want anything to do with me. That he'd take legal action if I kept bothering him." It sounded like something old white men would say. "I tried, okay? I'm out here fucking trying for you people. And this is how you act. No wonder everyone hates cops."

The back of Morales's neck was lined, more red than brown at this point in the summer. He didn't turn around once as I talked. I stretched the cast onto the opposite seat and leaned against the door, waiting him out. I waited a long time.

"What the fuck?" I woke up by hitting the seat in front of me and rolling to the floor of the car. The sedan lurched to a stop and I blinked at red and blue lights flashing through the windows.

I hadn't meant to fall asleep, but I'd gotten ten hours tops in the last few days and all the sunlight and silence might as well have been a lullaby.

The back door opened, sending me half falling to the pavement. "Welcome home."

Morales's upside-down face grinned at me. I resisted the urge to pull his feet out from under him and beat the smile off his face. And got immediately pulled out of the fantasy when I realized where we were.

Phyllis's house.

Cop cars swarmed the driveway and street, lights flashing, masked officers surrounding the property. Neighbors stood on their front steps and stared out their windows with mind-blown emoji faces. A few recorded the show on the phones.

"What are you doing?" I scrambled up and jogged on the crutch and good leg behind Morales toward the house. "I'm cooperating. I'm trying to find your fucking money."

"By making deals behind my back?" Morales swung on me as he reached the front door, his eyes glowing in the flashing lights. "I'm not Sam. You can't pull your double cross routine on me."

He rang the doorbell, which was broken, but it didn't matter. The living room drapes rustled at one edge. *Get out the back, Phyllis. Leave now. Why the hell didn't you book the first ticket to Florida?*

"Where's Max?"

"Summerlin's off the team."

"What? Why?"

Morales ignored me, calling to Meathead Joe, who'd parked Phyllis's pickup halfway down the block. Joe handed over the keys and Morales started trying one after the other until the dead bolt clicked open.

I pushed in first, half convinced Phyllis was standing on the other side of the door with her rifle cocked, but the living room was empty. I shouted for her as the police swarmed in behind me, searching every room.

They found her in the back, sitting in the garden, twirling a small branch between three knobby fingers.

"Phyllis Reed, you're under arrest for conspiracy to launder monetary instruments."

She didn't look up as they read her rights, exercising the one to silence with the terrifying grace of some ancient witch during a full moon.

It wasn't until they hauled her up that she acknowledged any of us were even there. She looked straight at Morales, one normal eye and one bloodred one, and he shrank from her. Then a shudder passed through her body and she wasn't an ancient, powerful witch anymore but a frail old woman who'd been released from the hospital days before. She made a noise that sounded like *Kara*, stumbled against one of the officers, and dropped the branch.

"Phyllis."

I lunged forward to catch her. She felt fragile as a bird, hollow. Her body shook and shifted, her hands grabbing me as she fell, and as the officers tried to pull me off her, I felt something small and hard being shoved between my leg and the cast.

The episode passed as quickly as it came. Phyllis's shudders turned to insults as she straightened up, or as much as a thousand-year-old woman glued together by literal poison could straighten.

"Get the hell off me," she wheezed as two of them tried to steady her. "I'll have your badges."

They led her away in a housedress and handcuffs, and then—with a warrant to search the property—they took her home apart. They cut the lock to her daughter's room, ransacking the shrine until it was a pile of overturned furniture and ripped pillows. Room by room, ripping the pictures of her ugly kids off the hallway wall, emptying her denture cream, searching for what they knew wasn't there.

"There's no money here." I chased Morales through the house and into the backyard again. "You know there isn't."

"I know Phyllis Reed was the oldest and most trusted associate in Belgrave's empire. The name she used at the thrift store was her son's. She stole her own child's identity to launder millions of dollars."

I stood by and watched—knowing that was the point, that Morales wanted me to see this—as cops invaded the backyard like ants with their glorified metal detectors. They took part of the fence down and a backhoe drove in, digging everywhere until Phyllis's garden—the winding jungle of flowers and fruit I'd gotten used to seeing every morning, the smell of things that could feed or kill you—was completely destroyed.

Later—I don't know how much later—Morales sat down next to me on the front step. Guys were drifting back to their cars, stripping off gloves and masks, joking about the house's cabbage print couch and wood-paneled walls. I twirled the branch Phyllis had been holding. Large, glossy leaves whirred around the flowers and thick berries. A blur of purple, black, and green.

Neither of us spoke until most of the squad cars had packed up and drove away.

"Did you find your hundred million under the tomato plants?"

Whir.

Morales chuckled. I wanted to pull his lungs out. "No, unfortunately the place was clean."

Of course it was. She rented the house out to college kids every year. Like she was going to leave bundles of untraceable cash in the attic.

"You're going to talk to her, tell her she could get a reduced sentence. Hell, we might even drop the charges altogether if she has enough good intel."

"Right." *Whir.*

"Cute plant. Is that what she poisoned John Doe with?"

"Take a bite and find out."

He chuckled again and I flexed my leg inside the cast, feeling the hard bump just below my knee. If I had a normal nervous system, maybe I could've guessed what it was, made out the shape of it or the material it was made of. But if I was normal, none of this would be happening. Maybe I still would've met Sam, but I'd have died by now, shriveled under the pain and given up. The two guys who'd jumped me outside St. Louis would've beat the information about Sam out of me before killing me and dumping my body. Even if I'd made it through that, and all the shit afterward—if I was normal—Celina would never have seen anything special in me. I would've been just another customer, another table full of pain, waiting to interrupt her night with my sad, greasy order. I wouldn't be here, trying to live the life she'd wanted for me, trying to be something I knew I never could.

Celina would've played along. She would've tried to get Phyllis out of jail and find the money for the DEA, tried to lessen everyone's pain and do the right thing, even when those two things were impossible together. But I couldn't live Celina's life anymore. I'd tried and this was where it got me. I sucked at being Celina.

I sat on Phyllis's step, pressing my broken leg into the object she'd wedged inside the cast, listening to men and machines behind me, when I realized. Phyllis had trusted me with something. Not Celina. Me. At least she'd trusted me more than the assholes who'd demolished her home.

Morales was still going on about Phyllis, Sam, and the buyer who was out there somewhere, lurking in the shadows. "Tomorrow morning. Eight a.m.," he said. I had no idea what was happening tomorrow morning and I was done caring.

Handing him the branch, I walked into the wrecked house. It felt like I was breathing for the first time in a year.

I wasn't playing by anyone's rules anymore.

Max

When we got home, a sleek blue Lancer sedan was parked in the driveway. Garrett, already beaming from winning his game and raising $1,500 to buy the new cockatoo, perked up even more. "I didn't know Uncle Jonah was coming over."

"I didn't, either."

I'd ignored the last few days of calls from Jonah, having too much to catch him up on and not enough energy to do it. There were probably five to ten missed calls in my phone, and a handful more unanswered texts. But I was glad to see the car, glad to have a buffer or at least a delay in the fight brewing with Shelley.

I pulled two beers out of the fridge and went to the backyard, where Shelley and Jonah sat in the chairs surrounding the firepit.

"Mom, we won!" Garrett dropped his gear in a heap on the patio, starting in on the details of the day, but Shelley cut him off before he could get rolling.

"Go inside."

He looked at me, surprised by his mom's curt tone and angry eyes. She was typically the indulgent parent, the one who allowed the treats and let him stay up the extra fifteen minutes after bedtime. I patted him on the shoulder. "It's okay. We'll start dinner in a little bit. You can fill Mom in then."

The glow from his day instantly evaporated, replaced by teenage sulk. I waited until he closed the patio door before joining Shelley and Jonah at the firepit.

"You didn't say you were stopping by. Everything okay?"

"No, everything's not okay," Shelley answered for Jonah, who waved off the beer I tried to hand him. He was hunched over, elbows to knees, kneading his temples. With Jonah, that was never a good sign.

"What is it? Did you have a dream?" He shook his head. "Is it something with Eve or her father-in-law?"

He spoke to the ground between his feet. "They're both fine. Max—"

"You didn't tell me," Shelley broke in. Her eyes cut daggers into me.

I sighed, trying not to get angry. It was my bed and I needed to lie in it, but she could've waited to bring up the fundraiser for two minutes. At least until I figured out what was bothering Jonah. "It was dumb, I know. I shouldn't have done it."

"How could you, after last year? How could not say anything? Not a single word."

"What are you talking about?" There were no bird fundraisers last year. There was no pandemic last year.

"I'm sorry, Max." Jonah lifted his head, letting black hair fall into his face. "I asked how you were doing afterward. I thought she knew."

"Knew what?"

"That you were almost killed last week." Shelley's voice exploded through the yard, bouncing off the fence and the surrounding houses. Hurt twisted her face. Her whole body shook from the force of it.

I fell back in the chair, looking between my best friend and my wife, both of them reeling with thick, ugly emotions. I opened the beer and took a long drink.

"I didn't get hurt. The suspect was taken into custody."

"The same suspect who tried to escape and injured another cop?"

"He's dead, Shelley. He's not a threat to anyone anymore." For the first time I was unequivocally glad to be able to say that.

"I tell you everything. Everything I'm worried about, everything that keeps me up at night."

"And that's why I didn't tell you. You've got enough to worry about with the school reopening and your job and Garrett. You don't need to worry about me, too."

She pushed out of her seat, too upset to keep sitting, and stood over me. "You don't get it, do you? That's what this is supposed to be." Her finger jabbed between the two of us, vicious swipes in the air. "We're supposed to tell each other things, to share our lives, but all you want to do is keep me out and keep everything locked away like if you stuff it far enough down, you won't have to deal with it."

"I'm trying to protect you."

Jonah's quiet voice cut through our yelling: "No you're not." I whipped around to stare at him. "You're trying to protect everyone. Always wrapped up in the next case and the next one after that—all the people out there who might possibly need you—and you forget about the ones right in front of you."

It felt like I'd been gut punched. I expected this from Shelley, but Jonah? I'd sacrificed more for him than any friend I'd ever had.

I'd stood between him and the world. I'd taken the bullet in my shoulder because of him, for Chrissake.

Normally I could control my emotions around Jonah, but right now I didn't even try. I let everything seethe out and felt a grim satisfaction seeing the reflection of it wash over him. "Don't pull your psychic shit on me."

"He's not." Shelley sidestepped between our chairs, still glaring down at me, but there were tears in her eyes now. "Everyone can see it. Everyone but you. Do you know what your mother told me the night before we got married? She said, 'He'll never leave you, but sometimes it's hard to know if he's there.' Your mother said that, Max. Fifteen years ago." Her voice choked and cut off.

If she wanted to go there, fine. We'd go there. Leaving the chair, I stalked the perimeter of the chair circle. "You know what else happened? After undergrad, when we were talking about marriage? I wanted to join Jonah's agency."

She shook her head. The memory obviously hadn't stuck in her head like it stuck in mine.

It had always been in the back of my mind while I helped Jonah get his business off the ground; it was his PI agency, yes, but it felt like ours. Like we were building something together. We'd been a team since our freshman year of college and I understood Jonah. I knew how to draw his visions out. I could talk to people when he couldn't, go places his porous head would drown in. "I could've been a private investigator and set my own hours, chosen my own cases. But you said no."

Think of the risks, she'd said. I'd been debating between Jonah's agency and applying to the police academy. Shelley pointed out that a government job—like her teacher position—came with reliable paychecks, a pension, benefits. And I knew she was right. We wanted to buy a house and start a family. I might not be able to do any of that with the unsteady business of a novice private investigation firm. Our only income during college had been through tip line calls to the crime stoppers hotline. But I still wanted to, with a deep and unreasonable need. I knew Jonah and I could make it work, that there was a reason some computer randomly spit out our names as roommates when we were barely more than kids.

If I'd talked to my parents—business owners themselves—they would've had the same concerns. But I never told them. They'd always been so proud of the prospect of having a police officer for a son. So I gave up the idea. I applied to the academy, became a cop, got the mortgage, had the kid, all while trying to be a husband and a friend to the two people who pulled me further and further apart.

"I remember you talking about it," Shelley said now, glancing at Jonah. "But I never thought you were serious."

"You wanted me to become a cop." I threw my arms wide, sloshing the beer and ignoring the familiar shock of pain. "This is what it is. This is what you signed up for."

"Max." Jonah pulled himself up and leaned on the chair. He was pale, sweaty, fighting the emotional current zinging in the air between the three of us. "You can be a cop and not be an asshole. It *is* possible."

Seeing the two of them standing next to each other was surreal. They were united for the first time in their entire acquaintance, backing each other up, on the same team. And that team was taking position against me. I almost started laughing. This, after everything that had happened in the last few weeks. This was what my life had become.

"What is this, an intervention?"

"No." Jonah look like he wanted to collapse back in the chair or drag himself away. "I needed to tell you something Eve found out, but you wouldn't pick up your damn phone. So I called Shelley and she asked me to come over."

Of course she did. They probably had a group chat going with Eve and Earl. Larsen, too.

"Fine. I'm the asshole."

"Are you going to stop?" Shelley took a step forward, challenging, shooting her shot. "I'm not asking for the moon. I just want you to talk to me, Max. To be in this with me."

That's what I'd been trying to do today. To step into my family and be there, really be there, to share a moment with Garrett that was important to him. A day he could look back on and remember with his dad, one bright spot in this whole goddamn pandemic.

"No you don't. You don't want to know what I deal with day in and day out." Dead bodies in bathtubs. Blood seeping onto asphalt. The crunch of a skull hitting concrete at high speed. "If I told you, you'd be begging for me to leave the force."

"So leave!"

"And what are we going to live on, then?"

I threw my arms wide and the beer, slick with condensation, slipped out of my hand, flying past Shelley and shattering in the firepit. I saw it all in slow motion. Her mouth falling open, the jerk and stumble of her body away from me and into Jonah, his hand propping her up.

The neighborhood went quiet and I realized we'd been shouting, raising the kind of volume that could've warranted a domestic call. A patrol officer could be on their way here now to calm the situation down. To calm *me* down.

I turned away from Shelley's mute horror and saw Garrett at the kitchen window. His face was pale and so small in the frame of the curtains waving in the breeze. The window was open.

"Garrett."

I hadn't taken a step before his expression hardened and he darted away, disappearing into the house.

Goddamnit.

I walked across the grass, ignoring Shelley and Jonah's calls telling me to stop. My legs felt numb. I still had the car keys on me. They were heavy in my pocket, pulling me back through the garage and into the driveway, where the car bounced heat waves into the suffocating air.

It wasn't until I got in that I realized someone was already sitting in the passenger seat.

Kara smiled. "Bad time?"

Kara

The bar was shitty. That was my only requirement.

The place was on the eastern edge of the state, lousy with leather jackets, farmer's tans, dark roots, and bleached ends. My ink earned me a few second glances from bikers as we found a picnic table at the back of a gravel lot next to a leaking dumpster.

There were no servers. One surly woman poured foamy pints into Solo cups at a bar made of two nail kegs and some two-by-fours. Max got us cans of Bud Light and dropped them on a table stained with bird shit and beer. He acted oblivious to the glances and murmurs, but I knew him enough by now to know he'd already clocked everyone in the lot and putting his back to the dumpster wasn't a random choice.

We hadn't talked much on the way here, at least not after he'd tried to kick me out of his car—which told me that Morales hadn't been lying, at least about that. Max Summerlin had resigned as my deathsitter.

"Nice place." I cracked open my can, aware that this was the kind of bar where they handed you an ice-cold blunt weapon instead of opening the can for you. "You a regular here?"

Max didn't say anything for the space of three long swallows. Then he put the can down and scanned the crowd like he was begging for someone to fight.

"I followed Doyle here the day you busted into his apartment. This was where I spotted Chase."

I glanced around at unwashed, maskless people. No one gave a crap about Covid-19. All we had to do was pull out a bottle of hand sanitizer to get shit started here. I didn't see anyone who looked like the picture of Chase, Morales's NASCAR-loving suspect, but that didn't mean he wasn't here.

"Morales said you quit."

"Morales was right."

"Then why are we here?"

"You said a shitty bar. This was the first place that came to mind and"—he tipped his can at the general fuckery—"I knew it would be open."

We finished the first round in silence and I grabbed the second. A fight broke out at a table as I passed, and I tossed the guy who took the first punch back into the fray without dropping the beers.

"What do you want?" Max finally asked, like he just remembered interrogating was kind of his thing.

I took another swig of the beer, which tasted like cold pee, as the loser of the fight got hauled off by two of the winner's friends. The woman behind the bar didn't blink.

"Morales."

"What about him?"

"He's shady as fuck." I told him about Phyllis's arrest and how Morales had demolished her house and garden.

"Did he find anything?"

"Nothing to find." Not after Phyllis's pretend fainting fit. I couldn't see down the cast well enough to tell what she'd shoved inside it, so after Morales left, I went to a gas station bathroom and spent five minutes doing headstands to dislodge the thing. Finally, it fell out and hit the floor with a ping.

It was a key. A small metal key with a black plastic handle, like they used for bike locks or cabinets. It didn't have any markings on it, no clues to what it unlocked. I stopped back at the house and tried to match it to the smashed lock on her daughter's time machine bedroom, but it didn't fit. Eventually, I tucked it in my sports bra, as safe a place as any until I figured out what the key was and why Phyllis didn't want the cops to have it.

"He's using her as leverage," I told Max. "He thinks I know where his money is."

Something flared in Max's eyes, a spark of interest for the first time since he'd found me in his car. He seemed annoyed by it yet couldn't help asking, "Do you?"

"If I do, I'm not turning a hundred million dollars over to that guy. Fuck him."

"You can't keep it. That's drug money—blood money. People ruined their lives with the shit you and Belgrave were peddling."

"What would you do with it?"

The question caught him off guard.

I nodded past the dripping dumpster and the line of scraggly bushes that divided the gravel from the town and fields beyond it. "If you went out and found a hundred million dollars, what would you do?"

"I'd turn it in."

"Pretend you're not ancient and boring for a second."

He glared at me, but whatever had slammed the life out of him also made him pause and consider.

"I'd give it to rehab facilities, outreach programs. Food shelves across the state."

"Your shield is showing, Cap."

"What would you do? Disappear again? Buy some private island and live large until you finally break the wrong bone or get shot in the wrong place?"

"Yeah, just don't forget about the obit. 'Criminal Bitch Dies, Feels No Pain.' It'll go viral."

For some mysterious Max reason, he kept pushing. "What would you do really? Try to start over?"

I took a drink. "Money doesn't hit the reset button. It doesn't fix what you've done. It just gives you more free time to feel shitty about it."

Another drink and he pushed the empty can aside. His eyes unfocused. "I'd take my wife and son on a trip. After the pandemic is over and the world opens up again."

"Disneyland?" I grinned. "Stark Tower?"

"Iceland. In June, when the sun never sets. Shelley's always wanted to go. We'd climb volcanoes and swim in glowing lagoons. Rent a house at the edge of the ocean and name the puffins. And after we come home"—he paused, eyes running over the dirty table like he was realizing something—"I'd go into business with Jonah."

"You'd quit the police?"

"Never thought I would. But now . . ." He went silent again, swallowing hard. "You think you're part of something, that everyone's on the same team. Then something happens and you realize you never knew the people you've been standing next to. That they're playing by a whole different set of rules."

It was insane how quickly the grief could rise up and swamp me, but I expected it this time. It made sense—not like when I stood in front of the fridge, thinking about juice, and then suffocating because Celina would never drink juice again and I didn't even know which had been her favorite. Or worse, I did know and I'd forgotten. Those moments were sucker punches, but this time I was crouched and ready. It was why I was here.

I backhanded my eyes and took a hard pull of beer. "Morales was never going to make anything public about Celina. Whether I cooperate or not, he's going to keep her buried."

Max didn't even try to deny it. His jaw tightened and he held my gaze, the truth brimming in the silence between us.

"Did you know?"

He shook his head. "There were a lot of things I didn't know."

My gut said he was telling the truth. It was a mistake to ever believe anything my body told me, but this time I did. I trusted it this time because it wasn't leading me into some fantasy of happily ever after; it was screaming for revenge.

I leaned in. "We can make it right. The two of us."

His expression sharpened and he was one hundred percent cop again, instantly wary of the bait I was dangling.

"What are you going to do?"

"Exactly what they want. I'm going to find the money." Another fight rose behind me in shouts and the sounds of tables being shoved over shifting rock. I didn't turn around. "And I need your help."

* * *

We argued about it the whole way back to the car and onto the highway. Well, I argued and he kept trying to shut me down. But things were clear now, crystal clear, like I'd drunk the perfect amount of coffee and everything was laid out in front of me, sharp and bright.

I knew Sam's operation better than anyone who wasn't dead or in jail. I could find the money; I'd dig up the whole state if I had to, and take down whoever stood in my way. But the one thing I couldn't do was tell Celina's story. I needed someone on the other side for that, someone who didn't just play the part but was actually a decent human, someone the world would believe. I needed Max Summerlin.

"He's got a hard copy of the affidavit somewhere, if he didn't burn or shred it. I signed the fucking thing."

"What's on it?" he wanted to know. That was a good sign. If there was one thing Captain America couldn't resist, it was exonerating the innocent.

"Everything."

"Look, even if it's still around somewhere—" Something in the rearview mirror caught his attention and he sat up straighter, gripping the wheel. "What the—"

Before he could finish, the entire car jolted. I twisted around. Headlights flooded the back window like twin suns. Max hit the gas, pulling ahead of the truck that had rammed us from behind.

"Who the fuck is that?"

We'd left the bar maybe five minutes ago, but the town was long gone. No other cars were on this stretch of road.

"I can't see." It was getting dark fast and the headlights blinded me. The truck slammed into us again, making Max's car fishtail. He kept it on the pavement—barely. "Go faster."

There was nowhere to turn or pull off, the two-lane country road walled by corn on all sides. Max pushed it to ninety, but the truck kept up and started drifting into the other lane.

"He's coming in from your side."

Max floored it as the truck cut back over, hard, missing us by feet.

"Where's your gun?" I shouted at the same time that Max ordered, "Put your seat belt on."

"Are you kidding?" I did, though, while searching the front seat. This wasn't his cop car but a family one, some kind of Toyota. I found wadded tissues, food wrappers, and not a single weapon.

"I turned my gun in. Call it in. Call Morales."

"The fuck I will." Another swerve, this time the truck cutting back to the left. "Faster."

The corn became a blur. The Toyota's headlights shook as he pushed the car to its limits. Engines roaring, we shot through the straightaways and left screeching skid marks on the turns.

"Where is he?"

"Coming up on the left again. Your side."

"Hold on to something." Max's profile was grim. He clenched the wheel and waited until the truck had moved fully into the oncoming lane, then—just as the truck started to swerve back at us—slammed on the brakes. The truck shot in front of us. Max rammed the Toyota into their right rear wheel, sending the truck into a tailspin. It looked like slow motion, the wide arc of the headlights, the truck pirouetting like a dancer in a spotlight, wrapping a full one eighty around the front of the Toyota before it flipped and rolled into darkness.

A crash jerked the side of the car, yanking us off the road in the same direction. Corn flashed in front of the headlights and a thousand drums seemed to pummel us from all sides as we flew into the field.

Max

We were surrounded by a forest of corn. Shadowy stalks towered over the car on all sides. My shoulder screamed from hitting the door when we went off the road, cutting through the adrenaline flooding my chest.

"Are you okay?"

"Never better." She leaned over to flip off the headlights, plunging us into almost complete darkness. We turned at the same time. Fractals of light shone through the black stalks, wavering and dim. It was impossible to tell exactly where the truck was. Behind us somewhere, thirty or forty yards. Not far. The night was suddenly quiet.

"Remind me not to hang out with you anymore."

A rustle of her cast as she shifted. "You think it's another hit man?"

"No, I think they wanted to play tag."

"Well, come on. Let's go meet the new kid."

"I'm calling for backup."

"You do you." She went for her door and I grabbed her arm. Immediately, she flipped the hold, twisting my wrist backward until I had to let go.

"Goddamnit." It was my good arm, for Chrissake.

"Whoever that is will be dead or gone by the time your friends get here. Unless they take us out first."

She was right: we were on our own. Taking a deep breath, I flipped open the glove box to grab a tool kit. Inside lay a wrench, a needle-nose pliers, and a screwdriver. Kara flashed a grin. "Just when I thought you were no fun at all."

She took the pliers and bounced them in her hand. I pocketed the screwdriver and grabbed the wrench. In unison, we opened our doors and pushed out into the corn.

The night was hot and still. A quarter moon hung over the fields, glossing the tops of the stalks and leaving everything below in rustling shadows. The truck's headlights still shone in the distance. The driver either couldn't turn them off or didn't want to. There was only one way to find out.

We traced the path of our crash back over cornstalks crushed flat by the force of the Toyota, until we reached the edge of the field. A farmhouse stood a half mile up the road, dark except for a single yard light. Someone must have heard us. Sound traveled out here, but there was no sign of cars or cavalry.

The back end of the truck stuck out of the field fifty feet away, its upside-down taillights glowing red, tires in the sky. There was no sound or movement near it.

Kara was on her crutch right behind me, having no trouble navigating the uneven ground. We stuck to the shadows at the edge of the corn, our steps silent in the ditch, and I gripped the wrench tighter in my good hand. When we reached the truck, I crouched and looked into the cab. An American flag decal covered the back window, hiding whoever might be inside. It smelled like gas and rubber and dirt, the ditch torn open in deep furrows where the truck had slid and flipped.

Kara jabbed me in the arm and pointed: herself to the right and me to the left. I nodded.

We split up and I moved into the corn, tracking the tires on the truck until I was level with the cab. Just as I was about to move in, a gunshot split the night. I dropped, hitting the ground hard as metal crashed against metal and a grunt and cry came from the far side of the truck.

The cry registered again, hollow against the gunshot echo reverberating in my head, and I realized it couldn't be Kara. She wouldn't feel a bullet.

I army-crawled to the back of the truck. A small boot stood on the far side next to the body of a writhing man. I checked the cab and saw the man's feet. No other passengers. No other visible weapons.

"Get a load of this, Max," came Kara's voice from the other side.

I got up and rushed around the front, where Kara stood over a bleeding, coughing body. She held the gun in one hand and the pliers in the other. "I waved the crutch in front of the window and he shot into the field. Grabbed his gun before he realized what happened. Come on." She shoved the guy's shoulder with her cast. "Show Max your pretty face."

He rolled to his back and a bolt of shock ripped through me. I froze, trying to make my head believe what my eyes saw.

It was George Pyle, the state trooper on the task force, the one who'd rubbed my face in his assignment when he'd gotten a suspect to shadow and I was stuck tracking Kara.

"What the fuck?"

He wasn't in uniform and the Chevy clearly wasn't a police-issue vehicle. Blood ran across his forehead, and he opened and closed his mouth silently. His eyes still focused, though, moving between Kara and me in silent appeal.

Appeal. He wanted our help.

"Did Morales send you?"

He said something too low to hear and his hand flailed against the side of the door.

"We should—"

"What? Call 911?" Kara toed him with her bad leg. "He's not going to make it to a hospital."

"The police—"

"He *is* the police. Don't you get it?"

I didn't. Adrenaline and shock careened through my system, and holding down a line of thought felt impossible. "They're trying to take you out?"

"Not me. You."

My head snapped up.

Kara shifted her weight against the crashed truck. "No one followed me to your place and I don't have their phone on me. They couldn't have tracked me. But you . . ."

Me they could find. I still had the DEA phone. It was pinging our location from the Toyota now.

But I still didn't understand. "Why would they be after me?"

Kara reached inside the truck and turned off the headlights before pulling out the needle-nose pliers. "Let's ask."

Later, it would be a kaleidoscope of images and sounds: a piece of flesh twisted, a scream choking off. My brain refused to string the fragments together into a cohesive whole because that would mean I was there, that I stood by and watched a dying man be tortured on the side of a deserted midnight road, and I didn't lift a finger to stop it.

"Who sent you?"

When he didn't answer, Kara's wrist flexed and Pyle's eyes popped wide.

"Morales?"

"No." He screamed and flopped his head from side to side.

"Then who?"

"Can't . . ." His head kept flopping, but slower and less controlled. "Can't . . ." He trailed off until Kara slipped the pliers under his shirt and he gasped like a man trapped underwater finally breaking the surface.

"I've got this theory, Pyle. You want to hear it?"

Her arm twisted and he made a noise between begging and gurgling. I felt nauseous. "Just get the name."

She ignored me. "Pain is our connection to the world. It's how we know we're here, how we know something is real. 'Pinch me,' people say." He grunted and jerked. She must've tightened her grip. "They want the pain. They need it, to know they exist."

"I wasn't really part of this world until Celina came along. I saw pain. I caused pain. But I never understood how it tied you here until I lost her."

She leaned over Pyle. "It's keeping you here now. So you can tell us who the fuck you're working for."

He panted, sucking air in and out, a raspy noise that blended in with the rustling leaves. I crouched down on the other side of him.

"I'll make her stop. Just tell me what you know."

He focused on me, his throat working. I pulled Kara and the pliers off him and waited, but the rasps rose and seized and then they were gone. His eyes went blank. I'd rammed his truck off the road, Kara had tortured him, and we hadn't learned a thing.

Kara pulled me up. "Let's go."

"We can't leave the scene."

"The scene is a cop who just tried to kill you. Who do you think's coming next?"

She was right. Again. I nodded and we grabbed the shattered crutch and the gun. I propped Kara up as we half stumbled, half jogged back to the Toyota. The engine coughed and turned over, illuminating fifteen different dash lights. "I don't know if it'll drive."

"It has to."

A siren sounded in the distance, high and weak. Leaving the headlights off, I reversed out of the field and got onto the road, heading in the opposite direction from Iowa City. There was no going home now.

Kara

The cabin sat off the highway in a clump of trees, like one of those chain saw serial killer movies. Max pulled into the driveway and cut the engine, which died with an ominous rattle and clunk. He'd taken back roads here. We were probably only twenty miles from the crash site, but by mile five white smoke started seeping from under the Toyota's hood.

Now a cloud rose from the dead car into the night. Max let his head fall back against the seat and closed his eyes.

"Where are we?"

"A friend's." He swallowed. "I hope."

Someone appeared at the front door, unarmed from what I could tell, then went back inside. Max didn't move.

The garage door opened and the man stood in the light with moths swarming above his head. Jonah Kendrick, Celina's uncle. The last time I'd seen him was in the wreckage of a collapsed barn, surrounded by bodies. He measured both of us through the windshield before pacing to the driver's-side door.

He didn't ask what happened or press for explanations. Celina always said her uncle's gifts were more developed than hers, so maybe he already knew, could sense the wreckage on us. He waited for Max to put the car into neutral and the three of us pushed it without speaking onto a lift in the garage.

When the door closed, I leaned on a stack of tires against the wall. The garage was dirty and cluttered with tools, boxes, and rags. Jonah went to the fridge, giving me a wide berth, and grabbed a beer without offering us anything. He stayed in the corner, as far from both of us as possible, waiting.

"Someone tried to run Kara and me off the road tonight. I implemented countermeasures and the vehicle flipped. He died at the scene."

Max acted strangely blank as he recited his redacted oral police report. I couldn't figure it out until I saw the quiet concentration on Jonah's face, the way he tilted his head just like Celina used to. It caught me low, but there was something sweet woven into the pain, seeing how this tiny part of her lived on inside her uncle. And then I realized Max's blankness was deliberate—trying to out–Jedi-mind-trick his friend.

"Technically, he died after we threw him a little going-away party." I pushed off the tires and hopped to the still-steaming Toyota. "He was part of the task force. Someone sent him to take out Max."

Jonah's attention snapped back to Max. "Who?"

"I don't know."

"But you have suspicions."

Max heaved out a breath. "Everything points to Morales."

He ran through the evidence and it stacked up. Morales lying about the goal of the task force. Morales killing the hit man and covering it up, which surprised me zero percent. Morales had given

Max the DEA phone and was one of the only people in the world who could've used it to find him tonight.

"Sounds like a regular cop to me."

Max glared as he lifted the hood of the dead Toyota. Jonah brought a light over and the three of us stared at greasy engine parts.

"It tracks, though." Morales arrested Phyllis on a whim, without any reason other than to put pressure on me. He'd been like a dog with a bone with this money, motivated to the point of obsession, like someone who had way more than professional interests on the line.

"Remember what you said to me after we arrested John Doe?" Max asked Jonah. "You said he was connected to me. And right before Morales killed him, John Doe said something about being blind. Not seeing what was right in front of me."

"So Morales is the buyer?" Jonah asked. "And if the buyer was never after drugs . . ."

"He wants the money," Max said.

"And he'll kill to get it," I chimed in.

"But why would he kill me?" Max paced, rolling his shoulder out, teeth gritting. "It doesn't make any sense."

"Unless you know where it is." For a half second I wondered if he did. Max stuck his nose in everything with the ease of entitled white guys everywhere, but they spoke up at the same time—"I don't." "He doesn't."—and for some reason I believed both of them.

"Then what happened?"

"I quit the task force."

"Boo-hoo, what else?"

Max cut me a look, but he was thinking. He kept pacing while Jonah inspected the engine like it was his emotional support animal.

It was quiet in the garage for what felt like endless minutes. Then Max stopped in the middle of his circuit and Jonah shot up at the same time, looking at him intently.

"Internal Affairs. I said I was going to report everything that happened."

"And Morales can't afford the inquiry."

"Goddamnit." Max deflated against a bright blue sedan, shoving the heels of his hands into his eye sockets. "What do I do?"

He looked so alone, so broken. Jonah's hand twitched, like he wanted to help but had no idea how. And how could he? Neither of them could, these men who'd lived inside society's rules and done what was expected of them, what they thought was right. They had no idea what they were dealing with.

But I did. I knew exactly what drew monsters from the shadows.

I hopped away from the car and balanced on the cast, flipping the needle-nose pliers in my hand until both of them looked at me.

"We find the money before they do."

Hours later, we'd written everything we collectively knew about Sam and his operation on a whiteboard Jonah had manifested from the depths of the garage. And by everything, I meant *everything*. I held nothing back, telling them every last detail of the money-laundering operation, the various pickup points and crypto ATMs. I mapped out all the places I'd ever gone while working for Sam, even the site where the men I'd killed from St. Louis were buried.

It felt like an exorcism, throwing my life at the wall, separating what I'd been from what I'd become. Seeing it laid out in front of me made me realize how much of my life I'd lived for other people. I'd spent years doing Sam's bidding, and then I walked into the Village Inn diner and traded one boss for another. I'd turned myself into what I thought Celina would love. And then she was gone. I'd been so lost this last year, and maybe it wasn't just that the one person I loved had died for me; it was that I didn't know how to live on my own terms, for myself, with no one to live for.

Eve Roth joined us sometime after midnight, brushing my shoulder and giving me a warm look as she strode into the garage. Jonah had called her, saying we needed a cool head that doubled as a supercomputer. She brought a coffee traveler and added a map of Iowa to the wall, pinpointing all the new locations I'd given them. The map looked frustratingly patternless, as random and unpredictable as Sam had always been.

I paged through Eve's notebooks and absently sketched a cockatoo on the back cover of one as we pinpointed the most likely locations for buried treasure.

"But are we looking for cash or crypto?" Max pointed to separate areas of the whiteboard where evidence supporting each form of currency was detailed.

"Cryptocurrency is the most likely source, given what we've learned," Eve said. Max looked confused. She turned to Jonah. "Didn't you tell him about Gemini?"

Jonah muttered something about not having the chance, and they both looked awkward for a minute while I finished the tail feathers of the cockatoo. It was alive, for some reason.

"What's the deal with Gemini?"

Eve explained that she'd been going through her husband's emails and texts. "I found some things in the cloud that he probably thought he deleted."

"She always finds things in clouds." Jonah shot her a half smile as she went to the whiteboard and started making bullet points.

"He transferred some of his Binance activity onto Gemini."

"Another crypto platform?" Max asked, making competing notes.

"Yes, but Gemini's different than the others." Most platforms, Eve explained, provided complete transparency for all their transactions. Gemini was the opposite. It provided absolute discretion, shielding the identities of both the users and their transactions.

"How much did Matthew have there?" Max asked.

"I don't know." Eve finished her notes and turned around. "But if Matthew was using it, Sam could have been, too."

Max turned to me and I shrugged. "I bought the Bitcoin under a lot of different accounts. He could've transferred them anywhere after that."

Max stalked to the map. "So what you're saying is that these locations are pointless. We're not looking for a physical place at all."

"Not necessarily," Eve disagreed. "I couldn't get into Matthew's account. I passed the two-factor authentication, but I also needed a key."

"What, like a code?"

"An actual key."

"Like this?" I dug out of my sports bra the one Phyllis had passed me before she'd been arrested, drawing every eye in the room.

"No." Jonah pulled something out of his pocket that looked like a double-sided USB drive. "Hardware security keys. They provide the highest level of account protection. No one can access or hack your account without having a physical key."

"Where'd you get that one?" Max asked me. I shrugged and tucked it away again before hopping over to Jonah. The cast knocked into several tool chests along the way before I got near enough to swipe the key out of his hand. "I've seen these before. Sam gave one to Nilsen while I was at his house. And Nilsen said something later about needing a key to find the money."

It was right here, all of it, the pieces falling into place. No one said anything for a minute, and it was only when I handed the key back to Jonah that I realized how close I was standing to him. I'd spent the entire night keeping my distance, avoiding eye contact, not wanting to see the accusation or pain. But another part of me—the part that couldn't help it—was cataloging him. Ever since I'd noticed that head tilt, I was looking for more pieces of Celina, finding her in the sheen of his hair, in his quiet awareness of everyone around him.

Max and Eve moved to the map and launched into a debate about where the key could be hidden, both of them talking over each other and arguing different locations. They might as well have been on another planet, completely oblivious to the sudden stillness between Jonah and me.

He picked up the notebook I'd been drawing on, hesitated, and ran a hand over the lines of the cockatoo.

"Is it her?"

Funny how the question didn't surprise me. How it seemed like the most normal idea in the world. Celina as a bird would be just as gorgeous and out of place as the cockatoo in Iowa.

I swallowed. "It was *for* her." I turned away from the hum of activity on the other side of the garage. "She had one as a kid."

"I know."

Of course he did. I swallowed again, trying to keep the things in my throat from choking me, but being this close to someone else Celina had loved made it impossible, like the gravity of our grief had fused into something bigger, heavier. I owed him this. I owed him more than all the hidden money in the world.

"I bought her one, a few weeks before . . ."

His eyebrows furrowed. "We didn't find a bird in her apartment."

"She was so happy about it. Said it was exactly like the one she had growing up. She walked around the place with it on her shoulder. Laughed every time it hid in her hair. She refused to clip its wings, said everything in this world should have a fighting chance."

"Afterward, after—" My throat closed off again, and, next to me, Jonah hunched like he'd been shoved in the gut. "I came back to her place. I couldn't look at the bird, couldn't take care of it. So I took it down to the river and let it go." I barely remembered. It was the middle of the night and everything had been a blur, the bird a white blotch in the night, there and gone. I must've gotten rid of the cage and all its stuff, must've gotten home somehow, eventually. Or maybe I never did.

"I figured either someone would find it or it would die."

"Someone did find it. The whole city found it."

The cockatoo and the crows. It didn't make sense. The bird never should have lived through the winter, let alone been adopted by a group of a whole different species. I finally looked at Jonah, really let myself look at him. His eyes were wet. I wiped my own and nodded. "I think she would've loved that. Knowing he found a family. A home."

He glanced at Max and Eve, who were aggressively writing all over the map, turning the state of Iowa into what looked like an unhinged manifesto. Jonah put the notebook down between us.

"She would've wanted you to find one, too."

Max

"Are you sure about this?" Jonah asked.

It was nearly 4:00 a.m. We'd spent most of the night holed up in Jonah's garage, and now the two of us stood in front of the house while Eve and Kara finished loading supplies.

"No. But I don't see another way to finish it."

Jonah nodded. We'd been over this already, looking at it from every angle until it felt like my brain was bleeding. I should've been exhausted after everything that had happened, drained of adrenaline and ready for at least a gray nap, but insomnia was my secret weapon to the end. I was awake, ready. It was time.

"You didn't develop precognition in the last couple hours?"

He shook his head. "I still don't like this. Someone out there wants to kill you."

"That's why I'm going." It was why I couldn't go home to Shelley and Garrett, couldn't bring whatever was stalking me to our front door. I needed to draw them out and beat them at their own game, as far away from my family as possible.

He sighed and kicked at the dirt. "Max. If . . ." He stopped and tried again. "You've been . . ."

"You too."

I clapped him on the shoulder and went to the car before I could think about it. Eve was handing Kara a walker she kept in her trunk for her father-in-law.

"No horn?" Kara grinned and stuffed it in the back seat. We climbed into Jonah's Lancer and backed out of the driveway, leaving Eve and Jonah in front of the garage, hands linked, watching us go. The last time I drove the Lancer, I'd gotten it shot up, got myself shot for the second time, and single-handedly captured the majority of a retiring drug empire. This car was basically my good-luck charm.

I powered up the DEA phone and tossed it into the console. "Let's hit it."

Two hours later the sky was brightening from black to blue, the stars slowly disappearing as Kara and I stood at the bottom of a hole the shape and depth of a shallow grave.

The abandoned farm sat on the border of Iowa and Missouri, a property where Kara had met Belgrave once to dispose of two bodies. It was the only location she'd never given to the task force, the one place we hadn't checked.

We'd scouted the area and decided to dig in a spot behind the barn, a patch where the grass wasn't as long as the places around it, the earth not quite as packed, as though it could've been dug up recently. We used flashlights until we didn't need them anymore. The work was hard, my shoulder aching and cramped, but Kara dug like a machine and I wasn't letting her show me up. Half my size, with arms probably dripping in lactic acid she was completely unaware of, she grinned and taunted me the whole time. Side by side, we bored into the earth, two broken people shooting their last shot, until the predawn light illuminated a dirt-covered case at the bottom of the hole.

"Here we go."

Kara plunked herself down next to it, ass in the dirt, her filthy cast stretched in front of her. She ran a finger over the lock as a movement at the edge of the barn caught my eye. I pivoted, raising the shovel like a shield as two guns were drawn and pointed at me. The people attached to them were all too familiar. Grimes and Olson, the other DEA agents on the task force. They gave no hint that they even recognized us, no sign that we'd been working side by side for weeks.

"All right. Back up slowly; move toward the barn." The voice came from behind me, but I didn't need to turn to see who it was.

"You gonna shoot us, Morales?"

"Drop the shovels."

I looked back. Morales was alone, his weapon drawn but hanging loosely by his side. He didn't even spare us a glance; he had eyes only for the case.

"Only three?" I clocked the crest of the fields, the shadows of the smaller buildings that half stood, half crumpled around us. "Why didn't you bring the whole team?"

"The rest of them are still at the murder scene."

I put myself between Morales and the case. Kara had gotten up again and faced the opposite direction. We were back-to-back in our makeshift grave, the unearthed case between us as all three agents slowly moved in.

"Who died?" I asked, all conversational.

"You know damn well who died," Morales said, eyes still fixed at our feet. "Your phone GPS puts you right at the crash site. We'll match the second set of tire tracks to you, don't worry. Did Pyle figure out you were going after the money for yourself? That you two formed an alliance of your own?"

"That's a good story. Almost as good as you sending him after me when you heard I was going to Internal Affairs."

Morales's gaze snapped to mine and he huffed a half laugh, finally lifting his gun. "Drop the shovels and move to the side of the barn. Slowly."

Heart pounding, I set the shovel down, the only weapon I had, and elbowed Kara until she did the same. Climbing out of the hole, I gave her a hand up and together we shuffled backward until our heels hit the creaking, sun-bleached wood. Rusted nails stuck out of the boards at odd angles, the closest one inches from my head.

"Did he die on impact? Pyle?"

The man's screams echoed in my head, the flash of the pliers glinting as the sun broke over the horizon, washing everything on the farm in oranges and pinks. "How would I know?"

Morales stepped between us and the hole, turning to Kara. "Did he?"

"You seem kinda sweaty over it." She wrinkled her nose. "Afraid your boy might've said something?"

"I need to know if the charge is manslaughter or murder."

I cut in. "I've been wondering the same thing about John Doe's death."

One of the other agents jumped into the hole and went to work on the case. Before he could get it open, though, Morales ordered us to turn around. We complied.

I'd never been arrested before, and maybe I wasn't being arrested now. I didn't know if we were getting cuffed or killed. My heart thudded against the broken slats. Just when it felt like the facade was going to break—that my racing heart would shake the whole barn down on top of us—Kara turned her head, caught my eye, and winked.

A split second later a voice boomed over the fields. "Hands up."

"What the—" Morales swung around.

Larsen crested the ridge of the closest field, his military cut and beige uniform lit orange in the morning light. He had his weapon drawn and locked on us—on Morales—and the wink Kara had thrown me felt like it caught and ballooned through my chest. The cavalry had arrived.

I'd called Larsen on our way here, telling him Kara and I were on our way to get the money and—if we were right—Morales wouldn't be far behind.

I'd heard the familiar growl in my superior's voice. "You're on leave, Summerlin. Wait for backup."

"We need a win, Captain." I gave him the location. "Maybe I'll see you there."

I hadn't expected him in person—not in the first wave, anyway. I figured he'd dispatch some local boys or the state patrol, whoever could arrive on the scene first. But here he was, weapon drawn, striding across the weedy ground toward us with casual confidence, like this entire situation was just another day at the office. No movement came from the other buildings or the open fields behind him. Was he alone?

"What are you doing here, Larsen?"

"I could ask you the same thing." Larsen stopped on the opposite side of the hole, glancing at the agents with the case while keeping Morales in his sights. "Arresting one of my investigators because he's better at his job than you?"

"Pyle's dead."

"I know." The shot came without warning, a crack splitting the morning air. I jerked in front of Kara at the same time she moved to cover me, the gunshot turning us into two halves of the same instinct. We hit each other hard and went down together. Morales ducked. The agent holding the case tipped to one side, and when my ears stopped echoing, a wet, gurgling sound came from the bottom of the hole.

I couldn't place the shot. No one by the barn had discharged their firearm.

"Put your weapons down," Larsen said, as calmly as if he were handing out daily assignments. There was movement in my peripheral vision, a rush of bodies, but I couldn't register anything except Larsen, standing stone-faced in the unfolding chaos. He didn't react to the man choking and writhing in death throes at his feet. An impossible, horrible certainty settled in my gut as his eyes locked on mine.

And I knew.

"You're the buyer."

Larsen smiled.

Kara

It took the guy holding the case a minute to die. Would've been longer, but the shooter stepped out of the shadows of a shed, took out the agent next to him, walked up to the edge of the pit, and shot the one who was still writhing in the head. And like that, Grimes and Olson were gone.

The shooter trained his gun on Max and me, both of us dirty, unarmed, and lying flat out in the dirt. He smirked. I'd seen him in pictures, Morales's second suspect after Nilsen. The guy Doyle had run crying to. It took a second for his name to come but then I remembered: Chase, the race car driver.

"Search them," the burly cop ordered, and Chase jumped into the pit that was filling fast with bodily fluids.

"Why?" Max asked. He stared at the cop like he was having a stroke. They were both big, bouncer-looking ginger guys. They probably knew each other, or at least Max thought they did, until a minute ago.

The cop ignored him. He was busy dismantling everything Chase tossed out of the pit, taking apart the guns, pocketing ammunition, smashing SIM cards under his boot. They frisked us next, taking our DEA phones and checking the walker for hidden shivs.

"Larsen," Morales said to the cop. "We can make a deal."

The cop, Larsen, laughed once as he pulled the case from under the slumped torso of one of the dead guys. It dripped blood as he set it on the ground. Morales kept talking, piss and panic in his voice, offering Larsen everything under the moon. Protection, immunity, the money, anything he wanted. Larsen pulled a knife out of a belt holder and pried open the case.

"How long were you on Belgrave's payroll?" Max asked, interrupting Morales's pleas. Unlike our unhinged task force leader, Max was deadly calm. The two of us had crouched together throughout the gunfire, his bad shoulder pressed tight against mine. Now he drew up slightly, still carefully submissive, but something had hardened in his eyes. He'd crossed over to the place where I lived.

"How long?" Max asked again, low and deliberate.

"As long as the drugs came through my town." The crack of breaking hinges sounded like nothing after the boom of the gunshots. The tiny pops of metal were a joke. Larsen flipped the lid of the case. "I took a cut for looking the other way, supplying dealers to Sam who could fly under the radar." He nodded at Chase, who'd pushed Morales facedown in the dirt and had one boot braced between his shaking shoulder blades.

"Looking the other way?" I echoed. Something started burning under my skin, a rage that licked and caught fire even before my brain caught up. The guy wasn't wearing any badges or patches or whatever these fuckers used to rank themselves. I couldn't tell how much pull he had, but Max immediately picked the thought out of my head.

"You buried the investigation of Celina Kendrick's death."

Larsen looked up from whatever had caught his attention in the depths of the case and flashed something that was more bared teeth than grin. "Who do you think told Sam where the leak was? I traced the number from the tip line and passed it to him so he could take care of the problem."

The words echoed in my head, breaking apart until they were almost meaningless. Take care. Of. The problem. It all rushed back, the memory of Celina coaxing me through my cold feet. *You don't have to tell Morales anything face-to-face if you don't want to,* she'd said, rubbing my back. *You can do it anonymously.* She'd dialed the number to the tip line on her own phone and handed it to me. Held my hand as I talked.

And Larsen passed the number—Celina's number—to Sam. I'd never stopped to think about how Sam got his information, but the answer had slithered into the sun right in front of me. This guy, flexing over his hand in her death. He was the reason Sam had found and killed Celina. Colors faded in and out. I couldn't see. Could barely hear Max firing off follow-up questions. I didn't claw my way back to the surface until Max had already leapfrogged ahead.

"And you were buying him out?"

"Took everything I'd made and invested over the years and then some. I had to re-mortgage my house, liquidate my retirement to buy the last of Sam's inventory. But the payoff would have been worth it. I was going to double my money."

Max tilted his head, his voice a steely monotone now. "You must have been furious at the weigh station. I ruined everything for you."

"You have no idea how many times I wanted to kill you in the last few months. But you never knew enough to make it worthwhile. Just a fumbling Boy Scout to the end. I needed my money back and everything else Sam owed me, so I hired a professional." Larsen sighed. "He turned out to be a disappointment, too. I owe you for taking care of him, Morales." Larsen kicked the DEA agent in the side, making him grunt. "I'll make it quick, how about that?"

Morales said something, his voice muffled in the dirt, but Larsen wasn't paying attention. His focus had dropped back to the open case. Lifting a plastic bag out of it, he shook the thing wrapped inside out onto his palm. It was a security key. The key to Sam's fortune.

"It's not enough." I sat up next to Max, swallowing the bile and hatred that was trying to close my throat. "You need the username and password before you can unlock the account."

"I've got the full task force case file. Everything Summerlin researched and typed up in that interview room was recorded."

"It's not in there," Max said, his shoulder pressing into mine again. "I didn't put his username in the file."

"And I haven't told anyone the password Sam gave me." I cocked my head at Larsen, flicking dirt casually into the pit on top of the two dead bodies even as I returned the pressure against my arm. We were speaking through osmosis, figuring out how to play this, how to gamble our way into thirty more seconds, a minute, as much time as we could get. I could feel the rage in Max, too, the welling, bubbling fury pinging back and forth through both of us at that single point. This wasn't ride or die. It was ride *and* die, and we were both all in.

It took Larsen a minute to decide, but he held all the cards and had all the time in the world. No one else was coming. If we were bluffing, he could always pull the trigger, and he knew it. Pocketing the security key, he kicked one of the shovels over to Morales's prone body.

"This hole's gonna need to be bigger. Dig."

Chase stood guard as Morales got up and started to shovel the bloodstained ground next to his agents' bodies. Tears leaked down his face.

Larsen ordered Max and me across the property to where he'd parked his car on a dirt strip between fields. His laptop was there, and the only way to see if we were lying was to try to log in. He handcuffed Max's wrists but let me keep my hands free to use the walker. I made a production of hobbling over the bumpiest spots in the field, looking weak and scared while Max marched dead-eyed next to me. It took ten minutes to reach the car, ten minutes of clocking the horizon and trying to spot anyone driving or working, but the road was too far away, the corn too ripe to need attention. No one would see what happened next.

I caught Max's eye and it might as well have been a mirror. Everything boiling under my skin was reflected in that look, the furious, fuck-all endgame I'd been waiting for my entire life. Twenty-seven years and finally here it was.

When we reached the car, Larsen made Max sit in the dirt a dozen feet away. Not point-blank range but close enough. He probably knew it was easier getting blood out of a ditch than a trunk or a back seat. Max lowered himself down, arms cuffed behind him, as Larsen kicked the walker away and twisted an arm behind my back, shoving me against the hood of the car.

I wriggled and grunted, gasping when he wrenched my arm tighter, and I heard something pop in my shoulder. That goddamn socket.

"Hurts, doesn't it?"

I let a small whimper escape and shook my head violently from side to side. The gun barrel pressed into my back.

"If you both cooperate, we'll get through this with as little pain as possible."

I fucking hoped not.

Still twisting my arm with his gun hand, Larsen pulled the laptop out of his front seat and booted up the Gemini site before shoving it in front of me. "Type."

Max gave the username. I typed it in slowly, hand shaking over every letter, repeating each character as I keyed it in. Larsen was absorbed, memorizing everything, and behind him Max's face had turned a rich shade of red. Veins stood out on his neck and forehead, and he slowly rose an inch off the ground.

I started entering the password, saying it as I did, but before I could finish typing a shot echoed over the field. Max jerked. I half turned but Larsen slammed me into the car and growled in my ear. "Guess Morales got done digging."

He ordered me to keep typing and I did, finishing the password and hitting "enter."

A welcome screen popped up, asking for the security key.

"Do you have it?" I held out a trembling hand. Larsen shifted to get the key and that's when everything happened.

Max launched himself up, springing off the ground like a fucking rocket. His arms flexed on either side, cuffs flying off one hand and the other dripping red.

Larsen flipped around to put me between him and Max, but my foot was already braced against the side panel and I kicked off, sending us both straight back into the field. The gun fired as we fell, deafening me. When we landed, I was on top of him. I didn't know where his gun went, but I threw my good elbow back into his throat. His chest convulsed as I rolled off him. It felt like slow motion, like everything in my body was shutting down. I didn't check myself, didn't want to know where the shot landed. Larsen's gun gleamed dark in his hand and I attacked it as it went off again, another impact, this time on my cast. It sounded like it was happening underwater. I couldn't hear anything. Couldn't feel if I was staying or going.

I clawed at his hand, bending his pinky finger back until I felt the bone crack through his glove. I moved to the next finger, wishing he had more than five. Someone might've screamed. I couldn't tell. Before I got to the third finger he released his grip and I yanked the gun away, noticing Max for the first time.

He stood over Larsen, legs spread wide, slamming the walker down on Larsen's head. Lifted it, smashed it down. Again and again.

Let him die first. The thought repeated with every crunch of metal against bone. All I wanted was to outlast this bastard, to see the person who set Celina's death in motion take his last fucking breath on this planet. Then I could go.

Larsen's face was a mess by the time I stood up and pointed the gun at his chest. His chest shuddered through the sad, garbled noises he was making. Max lifted the walker up and held it, suspended in midair. Before I could squeeze the trigger, a set of handcuffs flew through the air. We both looked up.

Morales stood at the crest of the field, expressionless, covered in dirt from head to toe.

"Arrest him already. Let's get the fuck out of here."

September
2020

Max

There wasn't any money. No hidden treasure. No crypto fortune. There never was, or if it did exist somewhere, we never found it.

It had been Kara's idea to set the trap. We opened a fake Gemini account in Jonah's garage that night, found a battered suitcase and wrapped up the blank security key inside it. Before we dug the hole and placed the case at the bottom, we taped a phone to the inside of one of the ruined barn slats. I started a voice recording and called Jonah, too, as an extra layer of security, so he could record remotely and save any conversations that might be lost if the phone was discovered.

Larsen, though. That was a blow that kept hitting me in the middle of the night, jarring me out of every gray nap. Despite every red flag at the department, the problems that made me question my decision to be a cop, I'd still trusted Larsen, had actually thought my superior would provide the backup I needed when I called him from the road. I had no idea how right Jonah had been when he said the killer was connected to me, how close I was to him the whole time.

I didn't know the woman they'd brought in to replace him. She was a transfer from Muscatine County and she didn't have much to say when I handed her my resignation.

No one threw a party on my last day at the ICPD. Most of my coworkers avoided even making direct eye contact with me, as if the shit I'd uncovered was contagious, viral. Ciseski, the investigator whose desk had sat next to mine for years, muttered something about being time to clear out and rapped my desk twice as he lumbered away.

Larsen had sustained moderate to severe injuries. A traumatic brain injury I heard, but no one was filing a complaint for police brutality. He was in stable condition and they expected him to make a full recovery in time for his trial. Chase had proven surprisingly useful. When Morales turned on him with the shovel at the barn that day, his shot went wide, which was the gunfire we'd heard by the car. Morales subdued and arrested him, and since then he'd been talking more than any DEA informant in years. Thanks to him, a few other desks in the department sat conspicuously empty as I walked through the place for the last time. It was a familiar walk, and everything about it felt foreign.

Belgrave's empire, and the one that tried to rise in its ashes, were both dead. Some of the smaller dealers and runners had scattered, like vermin do when the lights come on, but Larsen's fall represented the last of the eastern Iowa drug ring. I stuck around long enough to do two things: hand in my full report to the chief of police and give an interview to a prime-time news show in my uniform. The program hadn't aired yet, but they were going to headline it with Celina Kendrick's photograph, talk about her life, and tell the world how her death led directly to the downfall of a drug empire. It wasn't justice, but it was the eulogy she deserved.

I didn't have a severance package or benefits. I had one more check coming for my unused vacation time, a few thousand in savings, a pension I couldn't draw for another twenty years, and some government bonds my grandmother gave me as a high school graduation present. That was it. But I was alive, intact—more or less—and somehow the people I cared about the most were still by my side. It was more than a lot of people could say this year.

By the end of September, the air wasn't as suffocating. The leaves were still green and heavy on the trees. Garrett lit the mosquito candles and Shelley brought out actual plates, not the paper ones she usually used for backyard meals. *It's a celebration*, she said. *A new beginning.*

Jonah and Eve arrived early. Jonah helped with the grill while Eve and Shelley opened wine. The women hadn't met before and I didn't know how they'd get along. They were both teachers, smart, levelheaded, and too good for the men they were with. It seemed like they'd make fast friends, but I'd learned you could never predict female camaraderie. While I flipped burgers, Shelley poured two glasses of pinot noir and dragged Eve to the Adirondack chairs by the fire, where they laughed and talked and tossed glances at us that probably meant we'd be in trouble later. I didn't mind.

After dinner, Garrett packed away at least ten s'mores before retreating to the house to play video games. When he'd shut the patio door, I stood up and raised my beer.

"Oh, god," Jonah groaned.

"Fuck you, this is gonna be great." I cleared my throat without any idea what I was going to say. Jonah, who knew it, just shook his head. Eve sat up straight and pasted a blankly pleasant smile on her face like the professor of undergrads she was. She slipped a hand over Jonah's arm, which made him straighten a little, too. Shelley's face glowed in the firelight, her eyes bright with wine and the first dinner party we'd had in six months.

"When I started on the force, I wanted to make a difference in people's lives. I wanted to find the answers they couldn't, to keep them safe, to bring their loved ones home. Being a police officer seemed like the best way to do that while providing for my family. It wasn't about power or politics or loyalty. It was about answers."

"And money."

"And money." I saluted Jonah. "Pensions are a beautiful thing. But there are other things, more important things."

As of today, I'd officially joined Jonah's PI firm. We filed the paperwork to create a partnership and renamed the business. Celina Investigations didn't have an office, a website, capital, or any active clients, to be honest—Jonah had never been the go-getter of the two of us—but I wasn't worried about any of that today. Today was for celebrating.

"I know it's going to be hard work, and it's probably insane to do this in the middle of a global pandemic. But people are hurting." I looked at Jonah and something passed over his face, a shadow of emotion, a current he was picking up on that no one else could. Maybe from the yard, or beyond. He raised his drink, though, along with everyone else.

"We can help them."

Kara

Serafina the pig lounged in the front pasture of Wild Hearts Sanctuary. She hadn't bothered to get up when I slammed the pickup door or when I went to the fence with a giant handful of sunflower seeds.

"Here, piggy piggy." I made kissy cat noises. Shook the sunflower seeds like I was throwing dice on the craps table. Serafina barely looked over.

"How the fuck do you call a pig?" I muttered.

"With confidence."

The voice scared the shit out of me. I dropped the sunflower seeds and spun around. Jillian stood a dozen feet away, looking the same as she had the last morning I was here. Dirty boots, cowboy hat, a half-amused, half-intense expression on her sunburnt face. My heart wouldn't settle from the scare, and I wondered if I would feel it if the thing pounded straight out of my chest.

"Can I help you?"

That was the question, or maybe it was the other way around. How I could help her, for once. I didn't know. I wasn't sure how any of this would play out.

"I heard you might need solar panels for a goat barn."

She moved forward, dangerously close, an arm's length away, and did a very Jillian scan down my body.

"The cast is new."

I turned a shoulder, flashing the divot that Larsen's first bullet had carved out of my arm. "This too. Sorry, Fluffy didn't have time to make an appointment."

Max hadn't let me out of his sight that day or the next. He personally checked me into a human hospital and insisted they bandage his hand in the same room where they treated the bullet grazes on my arm and leg. I hadn't been near death at all, it turned out. Just at the end of a long, terrible road.

I stuck around Iowa City long enough to make sure Phyllis got released from jail and settled back home, Covid-free. Morales didn't have the evidence he'd claimed when he arrested her, no fucking surprise, and he lost all interest in me when they moved the hunt for Sam's money into the crypto exchanges. Max leaned on him until he released the affidavit about Celina, and that's when I knew it was time to go. To let her go. And let it be done.

I meant to leave the state, to go back to Canada if I could get across the border again, but when Phyllis gave me the truck, with her usual bitching about how I ruined everything I touched and at least the truck would get me the hell out of her life, something insane happened. We were standing in her driveway, shoving the keys back and forth at each other, when a sudden chorus of squeaks and cawing filled the air. A dozen crows landed on her fence and street, strutting across the pavement, and right in the middle of them, like they belonged on a side street in a town set in the Midwestern cornfields, were two bright white cockatoos.

I stopped arguing. Stared, dumb and still, as the birds pecked at the grass, circling each other, every move delicate and precise. They were part of the flock but alone, too, with eyes only for each other. Phyllis dropped the keys on the driveway and left me standing there, cursing as she toddled back into her house and slammed the door. When the birds finally moved on, I picked the truck keys up and drove to the sanctuary.

"There was someone before," I faltered, trying not to lose my nerve as I stood in front of Dr. Jillian Ostrander. "And I lost her, because of who I am. What I was doing—all that—it's done. Finished. But I'm still the same. I'm still a hot mess long past my expiration date. And I'll understand if you want me to go."

I waited, holding my breath. After a moment that seemed to last forever, she stepped into my space until the brim of her cowboy hat shaded my face from the sun. Nerve endings, the ones that refused to transmit messages of pain or warning or anything that would actually be useful, buzzed to life as Jillian's hand slid along my jaw. Her fingers dug into my hair and her sky-blue eyes seared into mine.

"One question."

"Anything."

She tipped my face up and ran a dirty thumb over my lower lip. "What's your name, Fluffy?"

I smiled as it came back, the name I'd had before I met Sam, the one my mother used to shout through the back door after I'd run wild all day, calling me home.

"Jordan."

* * *

There were a few things I knew about Sam for sure. He loved the land, the rolling hills and patchwork fields of Iowa, the place he called home his entire life. He also believed in bug-out bags, in being ready for any situation. Phyllis hadn't just given me the keys to the truck. We'd traded keys. I gave her back the one she'd smuggled to me when she'd been arrested and asked what it was for.

"Contingency plan."

I thought about the bag Sam had given me that day on his porch, the identity, a new, shadow life I'd taken without a second thought. Maybe he'd done the same for Phyllis. Or himself.

"What does it open?"

She'd snorted and tucked it away in her housedress, refusing to answer.

It took me a few months to find the money. I drove from site to site after the cast came off and I didn't use any of the stupid DEA equipment. I took a shovel and memories. I walked the places Sam had walked, looking at things the way he had. And that's how I found Sam's own bug-out bag, inside a zombie-looking garden gnome tangled up in a dying poppy bush in his own front yard. The gnome was big enough to hide the essentials: a passport and driver's license in a different name, a gun, a burner, and a ring of keys. Not the tech kind. Old-school keys, real ones, that I found out opened a dozen safe-deposit boxes across the state. All in all, I pulled a little over two million dollars in cash and debit cards out of those keys. It wasn't the crypto fortune Morales was hunting, not enough to ping any radars, but it bought solar panels for a goat barn. A bunch of recovery centers and food banks got anonymous donations at the end of 2020, just like Max wanted, and Celina Investigations received a FedEx package containing an untraceable two hundred grand.

Maybe he'd go to Iceland, but I doubted it.

Acknowledgments

I didn't know I was going to write a pandemic book until I finished *To Catch a Storm*. In the final scene, the characters are telling themselves the worst is over. That's when I realized it was December 2019, and—like all of us at that time—they had no idea what lay ahead. The Covid pandemic was wild, not just because it affected the entire human planet, but because it affected everyone in different ways and degrees. My pandemic was not your pandemic, and Max's pandemic is nothing like Kara's. I wanted to capture a few of those Covid realities and show how, for a time, even thrillers were changed by an upside-down, reeling world.

I wouldn't have made it through either the pandemic or this book without the help of some truly extraordinary people. Thank you, Stephanie Cabot, for believing in these stories and helping them find their readers. Thank you to Joe Brosnan for your excellent editorial guidance and seeing the things I couldn't. Thank you to Jenny Choi, the most wonderful publicist and champion for the Iowa Mysteries series. Thank you to Morgan, Deb, Zoe, Erica, Judy, Natalie, and the whole Grove Atlantic team for your tireless work and support. You make the book magic happen.

Thank you to Claire Miller, who read most of this story in bits and pieces as it was forming. I'm grateful for my Saturday morning sprint squad and Satish Jayaraj, my new Sunday morning writing partner. Thank you, Mom and Dad, Mya, Sean, and Tara for putting up with me and supporting me book after book. Thank you to Logan and Rory for showing me what resilience and adaptability during a global pandemic really means. A special shout out to the pharmacists and critical medicine ICU team who work with Tara Griffin at M Health Fairview University and all their delightful ideas for how to kill (a fictional) someone via IV.

The Twin Cities is a phenomenal place to be a writer because of people like Pamela Klinger-Horn, Devin Abraham, Mary Ann Grossmann, Rob Jung, Emily Kallas, and the hundreds of booksellers, librarians, and literary stewards who make this place such a vibrant and robust community. I'm forever grateful to be part of it.